HER MAFIA
Bodyguard

USA TODAY BESTSELLING AUTHORS

J.L. BECK &
C. HALLMAN

Copyright © 2022 by Beck & Hallman

Cover design by C. Hallman

All rights reserved.

No part of this book may be reproduced in any form or by any electronic or mechanical means, including information storage and retrieval systems, without written permission from the author, except for the use of brief quotations in a book review.

PROLOGUE

MIA

Everything feels so much quieter now that the party is over.

I don't know how many times I've walked around the grounds of my father's house in the year since I came to live here with him, but it's been enough times that I should be used to how silent it gets around here at night. That will happen when you live on a huge stretch of land with nobody around for what feels like miles. If I want to go visit neighbors, I have to get a ride—not that I go call on neighbors. And if I did, I wouldn't go alone. The only time I'm allowed to be alone is in the bathroom and my bedroom. That's it.

Tonight, it doesn't matter. I'm sure sneaking a few drinks during the party didn't hurt anything. I feel warm, free, happy. High school is over. It's time for my life to begin. Finally.

I know I shouldn't feel that way. Millions of girls would probably love to be in my shoes. I mean, how often does something like this happen? Growing up like a regular person with a single mom who went through men like they were tissue—rather, they went through her, unfortunately. And they would throw her away once they were finished.

But she never learned. Never figured out they were bad news. I grew up living in a home with a revolving door; at least, that was how it felt. I went to school and had a few friends, but my big dream was to get away and make a life for myself. A life where I would never have to rely on a man the way Mom always figured she had to.

Then all of a sudden, everything changed. I lost her, but I gained all of this. My mystery of a father swept in and rescued me. At least, it's obvious that's what he felt he was doing. And I guess, in a way, he did. Otherwise, how would I have survived?

I couldn't have imagined all of this, though. A kid who never met their father will always wonder about them. Where they are, who they are, what they do for a living. And of course, when I was little, I used to dream that my daddy was a big, important man. That he couldn't be with us because of his work taking him all over the world, and one day he would show up at the front door and tell me all my problems were over. That I could live like a princess.

Wouldn't you know it? That's precisely what happened. And since then, I have lived exactly like that.

Nobody tells you that living like a princess can be a real pain in the ass. That princesses need to be watched. Guarded. Princesses aren't allowed to go anywhere by themselves for fear of what might happen to them.

Which is why I'm not even sitting alone by the pool after my graduation party has wound down and everybody has gone home. I can't even be alone now, staring at the water, noticing the way it moves gently with each gust of air that floats over it. I can't admire the strings of lights or the lanterns that sway back and forth in the evening breeze without feeling the penetrating stare of my bodyguard.

I don't know what Zeke's problem is. Most of the time, I'm pretty sure it's me; that he resents having to tag along everywhere I go. I can't even sit in my own backyard without him nearby. As much as it sucks for me, it must be ten times worse for him.

That's not what's on my mind right now, though. It's the fact that we're alone by the pool. Zeke's dressed in his usual black outfit: jeans and a T-shirt. A T-shirt tight enough to highlight every single one of his rippling muscles. My mouth waters at the sight of him. What would he think if he knew about the many nights I'd spent fantasizing about what he'd look like if I pulled that shirt off?

"You never did go for a swim," I remind him, teasing a little now that I'm buzzed, and it doesn't feel so scary and awkward.

He jumps a little, like the sound of my voice startled him after so much silence. "I'm not in the mood for a swim." Coming from him, that's practically an entire novel's worth of words. For a while, I actually thought he was mute, that he didn't have the ability to speak at all.

"The party is over. There's nobody here to guard me from." I take a look around, grinning. "Go ahead. I won't tell on you."

His gray eyes meet mine from the other side of the patio. "Why does it matter? What do you care?"

I wish my body wouldn't get so hot and prickly all over when he looks me in the eye. How can he not see what he does to me? That I went from resenting him to craving his presence? And now, it's not his presence I want more than anything. It's his nearness. He might as well be a million miles away instead of sitting in a deck chair, not thirty feet from where I am.

"I just figured maybe you should have a little fun for once. I mean, it can't be fun for you, always having to follow me around. Right?" I get up, a little unsteady in my platforms. It's easy enough to slip out of them, and now I'm on level ground, I'm a little more sure of myself and make the barefoot walk around the Olympic-sized pool to where he is.

"It's my job. It's not supposed to be fun." His gaze darts away in the direction of rustling in the trees surrounding the property. It's just the warm night breeze, but he's always on guard.

"Don't you ever get time off?"

"You should know better than to ask a question like that." There's something close to humor in his deep voice. A hint at a personality under that stony exterior.

"So come on. Let's go for a swim. I won't tell." I even give him a coy little smile, biting my lip at the end. He's a man, like any other man. And

I'm not blind. I've seen him looking at me, glancing my way when he thinks I'm not paying attention. I know what it means when a man looks at me that way. I'm not a child.

"I'll go first, if you're too chicken." I reach behind my neck, my fingers finding the ties from my cover-up. I tug the ends and let the fabric fall from my body, revealing the skimpy two-piece my father would absolutely die if he knew I was wearing.

And Zeke knows that, too. His head snaps around in the direction of the house before his eyes find me again. "Are you out of your mind? He'd kill you if he saw you in that."

"Yeah?" It must be the vodka cranberry giving me courage, driving me closer to Zeke one step at a time. Of course, he'd kill me, which is why I changed my suit during the party and kept the cover-up on over it. "Then I guess he shouldn't see me in it, should he? What do you think I should do?"

"Mia…" He groans, stretching out his long legs and laughing in a regretful sort of way.

"I mean, I could always get rid of it. Would that do the trick?"

Zeke's tongue darts over his lips like they've suddenly gone dry, and it makes me bolder than ever. It gives me the courage to reach behind me again, this time tugging at the strings holding my top on.

He lets out what sounds like a strangled groan. "Don't do this."

"Come on. I'm a grown woman. Almost nineteen years old and out of high school now. What are you afraid of?" I let the top fall away, my nipples going hard the second the air hits them. Before I can lose my nerve, I tug at the ties on my hips and let the bottom fall off, too.

He can't pretend he's not interested—otherwise, why are his eyes glued to my chest? He might be the most difficult, unreadable man I've ever met, but at the end of the day, he's still a man. He knows a good body when he sees one. Just because I've never been with anybody doesn't mean I don't know what I have working for me.

"Well?" I challenge. "Are you ready to get wet?"

His mouth falls open, eyes wide. This is it; this is happening. He wants me the way I want him. I can feel it. Finally, after all this waiting and wanting, it's going to happen. Everything I've been fantasizing about. I'm close enough to him now that I can almost feel his breath on me. It would take no effort to reach for him, to take his hand and put it on my body.

"Get your clothes on." He stands, his hands tightening into fists. "And have a little respect for yourself."

My insides go icy while a sick feeling washes over me. "What are you talking about?" Only the confidence is gone from my voice now. It's barely a whisper and a shaky one at that.

"You know what I'm talking about. Pull this little slut act with one of those shithead boys who were here earlier. Not with me." He waves a hand, indicating my clothes. "Now, before I tell your father."

Bile rises in my throat as I see the disgust in his eyes. I can't believe it. I want to die. I want to jump in the pool and go straight to the bottom and never surface. How could I have been so wrong? I thought he wanted me. I thought—

It doesn't matter what I thought. Now he's looking at me like I'm a piece of filth—like I disgust him. I barely have time to pull the cover-up over my head before grabbing my bathing suit and running full out for the house with tears in my eyes and a lump in my throat.

How could I have been so stupid?

How am I supposed to face him again?

1
ZEKE

My shoes click on the marble floor of the passage leading from the employee quarters to the main house. It's only minutes after my phone rang, the voice on the other end inviting me to join him in his office. It might be well past midnight, and I might've already been in bed when he called, but I know better than to keep the boss waiting. Besides, I'm used to these last-minute emergencies. I doubt I've slept deeply in years.

Mr. Morelli is in his office, in the east wing of the house. The mansion is bigger than anything I ever imagined living in back in the day. Though it's not mine, and it never will be. I'm a hired hand. My position is still one of the elite ones in the Morelli family, but it's also the most precarious. One false step and I'm out on my ass.

And that would be a best-case scenario kind of thing. Worst case, and probably closer to reality? They'd find me somewhere with half my head blown off, my teeth and fingers missing to make identification more of a challenge. Because if there's one thing the boss values more than anything, it's his daughter—even if he barely gave a damn about her until a year ago. Some guys my age can fuck up at their jobs and get a slap on the wrist, or at worst, they'll have to find a new company to work for.

I fuck up, and I'm dead.

He's pacing in front of the windows, the way he usually is when he has something on his mind. I rap against the heavy wooden doorframe before stepping into the room.

I catch something moving next to his desk, almost reaching for my gun until I realize it's just one of his girls. I call them girls because they are barely old enough to be called women. The half-naked blonde with her tits spilling out of her little schoolgirl uniform glances up at me but quickly lowers her eyes back to the floor, where she is kneeling the way he likes it.

Ignoring her presence, I step deeper into the room. A wave of his hand tells me to close the door. That's something I had to learn to get used to pretty quickly when I first came to work for him. He won't waste time using words when a hand gesture will do.

"What can I do for you, sir?" I stand at ease, hands clasped behind my back, feet shoulder-width apart. Ready for anything.

"You can pack your things."

His words are like a vise around my heart. I conceal my features, keeping them cold and uninterested. "Excuse me, sir?" A hundred different excuses come to mind, though I'm not sure what I'm excusing myself for. What did I do? How did I fuck up? He couldn't know about that night back in June, no way. If he did, I wouldn't be standing here now.

His lips twitch, and I realize he's screwing with me. *Asshole.* "What I mean is, pack your shit because you're moving to Blackthorn."

Blackthorn? Maybe I'm a little slow on the uptake in the middle of the night, but he's not making any sense. "College?"

"Yes, and I managed to secure a position for Mia there."

Now it makes sense. I could offer a bunch of comments here. I could point out the fact that Blackthorn is much farther away than some perfectly fine schools in the area. Since he guards his daughter's life so carefully, I would think he'd want to keep her close by.

But I know the man. After working for him for years, I know how he thinks. From what I understand, Blackthorn Elite is the cream of the crop, a school for kids in Mia's position whose parents have a ton of money. They're a higher class of students over there. He probably figures she'll be safer going to school with a bunch of trust fund babies.

Why wouldn't he want his daughter there?

When he turns to me, there isn't a hint of humor in his dark eyes. Not that I expect there to be. This is not a man who spends his days enjoying the empire he's built. He's too paranoid for that. And when push comes to shove, he's not above going to extreme measures for protection's sake.

This is where I come in—at least, I did before I got assigned babysitting duty over a year ago.

"I don't need to tell you how important this is." His voice is flat, almost hollow. I've heard him sound this way before. The last time was when he ordered me to eliminate another member of the organization who he discovered going behind his back. Flat, no-nonsense. Only a fool would argue with him.

"No, you don't." Even if I have to bite my tongue against dozens of reasons this is a huge mistake. Why he should choose anyone other than me to travel to Blackthorn and guard his daughter. But doing that would end up causing more harm than anything else, and even though that girl puts me through more torture than she's worth, I couldn't do that to her.

Especially when I know he would take it out on me, would find some way to make it my fault that his daughter threw herself at me the night of her graduation party. A night I've replayed more times than I would admit, even to my closest friend if I had one. I'm not proud of myself.

"Does she know yet?"

He shakes his head. "I'd planned on speaking to her tomorrow after I broke the news to you. I know I can trust you with this."

I only incline my head, smiling briefly. The message is clear. *Fuck this up, and you're a dead man.* "She's safe with me. You don't need to worry." Though even as I say it, my hands close into fists behind my back. I have to hold it together until I'm alone. Good thing I have so much practice hiding my true feelings around virtually everyone.

"I need you to take extra care with her safety—and her purity."

I'm used to him firing off random things like that, but it still comes as a surprise. "Pardon?"

"Her purity. Come on, you're a grown man; you know what I'm talking about." When all I do is stare at him, he chuckles. "I know she's untouched. Her doctor confirmed this for me after the first appointment I arranged once she moved in here, and you've kept your eye on her through just about every waking moment since then."

"True."

"No boys. Right?"

"Right, of course."

"Well?" He shrugs with another chuckle. "I mean, it's plain. She's still unspoiled, and that's the way I need her to stay. I can't marry her off to an associate's son if she's already been used."

This is the first I'm hearing of any of this. Sure, keeping her away from boys has always been the top priority, the way I would assume it would be for any father in a position like my boss's. He doesn't want her running around, pissing money away on parties and drugs the way some kids in her position do. Kids who fuck their way through their classmates. He wants better for her than that.

But only so he can get the highest possible price when he sells her in marriage.

"Well, I suppose you'll want to get to bed before packing up your room... unless you want to have some fun with Melissa over here?" Mr. Morelli is all smiles as he waves toward the girl kneeling on the ground.

"She might not be untouched, but she likes to pretend she is, and her pussy is tight enough to believe it." He chuckles.

I glance over to the girl who's grinning at me, her eyes twinkling with excitement. She pushes out her breasts, trying to lure me in, but there is nothing she could do or say that would get me excited. Only one pair of tits has my dick hard, and if her father knew about that, he wouldn't be sending me to Blackthorn.

"Thank you for offering, but like you said, I better get to bed. Long day tomorrow."

"Of course. See, this is why I trust you with Mia. You don't think with your dick like most men."

You have no idea.

He goes back to his desk, where he spends so much of his time. Deals are made and broken behind that desk.

The fates of many men have been decided there, too.

To think, I figured it was a lucky break. A promotion, even, working my way up the ranks. Going from just another one of the boss's hired men to a cushy indoor job involving a teenage daughter none of us knew about until she was practically on the front doorstep. How very wrong I was.

And now, it'll just be the two of us. Nobody looking over our shoulder. No excuse to check myself when the temptation to admire her ass or tits is too much to resist.

RIGHT NOW, I feel worse for myself. I'm not the sort of guy who walks around complaining and blaming others for his own shit. That's never been my way. But if I was in the habit, I'd be just about as depressed and disgusted now as I've ever been.

It's bad enough having her around all the time here at the house, where there's always the promise of being discovered holding me back. Holding us both back. What happens when we're on our own, without the promise of being discovered? How strong am I supposed to be?

I was as strong as I've ever been that night by the pool—because never in all my life have I been tested the way she tested me. It was almost like she knew all the filthy, perverted fantasies I've had about her since her father assigned me to her care. Like she'd reached into my head and plucked a dirty thought out of the file. Dropping her clothes in front of me, offering her body up as a prize.

I deserve a prize for restraint. Only the very clear understanding of what would happen to me kept me from fucking her until we both passed out.

Since then, she's been impossible to deal with. The girl was never quiet and shy to begin with, but now it's like she's determined to drive me out of my skull. Like she wakes up every morning and asks herself how she can test my self-control. Smarting off, rolling her eyes, slamming doors like a spoiled brat.

It's better this way. I know I hurt her when I turned her down. I saw the tears in her eyes, and I'd have to be blind not to notice how she ran away up to the house. Some sick part of me wanted to stop her, too. I knew how humiliated and horrified she had to be. I'm not a monster. I didn't want to hurt her.

But goddammit, I would end up being the one who got hurt if I did what any red-blooded man would have done in my position. She might as well have offered herself up on a silver platter. It was probably the hardest thing I've ever had to do, which is saying a hell of a lot since I've done a lot of things.

She doesn't know. She can't know. How she lives in my dreams, my fantasies. Sick, dark fantasies, most of them. The things I've done to her in my head... if she had the first clue, she wouldn't want to come anywhere near me for fear of what might happen. How I would defile her tight, lush little body. She's never been touched, not like that. What would it mean, being the man to break her?

I can't think that way. It's dangerous. Even if I tell myself I have no intention of following through on any of my fantasies, thinking about it makes the temptation worse. Practically impossible to resist. I can't even let myself get in the habit of thinking this way.

Especially now that we're going to be alone. Nobody watching over my shoulder.

How the hell am I supposed to resist her when the last thin barrier between us is gone?

2
MIA

"I knew you would be happy about this."

Happy? Maybe I would be happy if I had a chance to catch up with what my father is telling me. Right now, I'm too busy trying to understand what he just said. I'm going to Blackthorn Elite. "But I didn't apply there."

"You didn't have to. I took care of everything. Don't I always?" Yes, he does, and right now, that doesn't make me feel happy. As usual, I don't get any say in my life. What a trade-off. I have all the money I could ever want. I never have to worry about anything, but I also don't get to make a choice. Not even where I go to school.

He's looking at me like he expects me to be grateful, so I put on a smile. "This is great." Under the table, though, my nails dig into my palm hard enough to hurt. It's sort of a habit I've developed for when I have to pretend to be happy about something.

I'm not ungrateful. I know how lucky I am. My life could've gone in a very different direction if he hadn't found me. I could be out on the streets or just scraping by while working two jobs. Instead, I practically live in a castle.

Even the most pampered princess wishes for freedom sometimes.

I'm not allowed to drive. I can't go out alone. I don't get the chance to see friends. I miss my best friend, Blair, so much. Sometimes, it's enough to make me cry myself to sleep. Anybody else would feel lucky to be in my shoes. Am I ungrateful for wishing I could go back to when things were simpler?

"Only the best education for my girl," my father says with a satisfied little grin. I know he likes to take care of me, and when I see how glad he is, it makes me feel bad for that first flash of irritation. "Everything is taken care of. I already have your housing sorted, and the furniture will be there in another day or two. You'll be all set once classes start."

He even picked out where I'm going to live and how it should be furnished. "Thank you," I murmur, looking down at my breakfast and wondering where my appetite went all of a sudden.

"I have to say, it will be different, not having you here." There's an almost wistful tone in his voice when his eyes meet mine from across the table. "Isn't that crazy? I haven't had you with me all these years, but I've gotten used to you. Now I wonder how much quieter and emptier this house will feel."

"I'll come back for holidays and breaks. And it's not all that far away—I could even manage some weekends. You'll be tired of me really soon."

"I don't think that would be possible, though you are at an age where a father has to get used to the idea of not having his daughter around anymore." When he looks at me, he must see how confused I am. "Well, usually a girl either goes to college, or she's married off. One or the other."

This isn't the first time he's made a comment like that. I never know whether I should take him seriously or not. Do people really still think that way about girls? Like we're not worth anything other than property to sell off to the highest bidder or forge some kind of business alliance?

At least I don't have to worry about getting married off anymore. If I'm at school, he won't expect me to suddenly pack everything up and get hitched. When I look at it that way, this is the lesser of two evils. "I guess I have a lot of work to do. Getting everything together and all that."

"You know someone around here will do that for you." He waves a hand, sort of vague, the way he usually is when it comes to planning things. He's used to staff tending to his every need. I haven't lived this way long enough to think the way he does. "And once you get there, Zeke can always help arrange things."

There I was, thinking I didn't have much of an appetite. Now, it will be a miracle if I don't throw up all over the table. I have to swallow back the bile that rises in my throat before answering. "Zeke? What's he got to do with anything?"

My father's attention drifted down to his phone, but now it snaps back to me. "Obviously, Zeke will go with you."

"To school?"

"Naturally." He stares at me, unblinking. "What did you think? That I would let you go by yourself? Do you know what happens at these colleges? Even one like Blackthorn? Granted, you'll be around the right sort of people there, but I'm not under any illusions. Boys will be boys, that kind of thing."

I have to bite my tongue over that one. Boys will be boys. When did they come up with that one? When dinosaurs were roaming the earth?

The last thing I want to do is piss him off, which means I have to be careful. "It's just that Zeke… I mean, what's he going to do? Come to classes with me? Follow me around? Sit with me when I eat?"

"If I say he does, yes. That's precisely what he'll do." His eyes narrow, and I know I'm dangerously close to the edge of his patience. He has a short fuse—not that he's ever blown up on me, but I've been in the house when he's blown up at other people. And every time, I found myself glad I wasn't in that person's shoes.

"Is the school going to be okay with that?"

"They will if I tell them to be. Besides, I'm sure you won't be the only girl who's ever required a bodyguard. Some of the wealthiest families in the tristate area send their kids to that school. I'd frankly be surprised if you were the only one with a detail."

Sure, but I'll probably be the only one who threw herself at her bodyguard and ended up crying herself to sleep that night and for a week after. I can barely look at Zeke—now, I'm supposed to let him shadow me everywhere I go at this new school? "He's not going to live with me in the dorm, is he?"

Dad scowls. "You're an intelligent girl, Mia. Where is all this coming from?"

"Is he going to be living with me?"

"Well, I'm not going to have you living alone, am I?" He blurts out a laugh like this is hilarious rather than a nightmare.

"Couldn't I share a place with another girl? Isn't that usually how it's done?"

He scowls, and right away, I know that was a stupid question. "Why would you want to share a home with a stranger? Wouldn't you rather live with someone you know you can trust?" He picks up his knife and fork, shaking his head. "Like I would let my daughter live with just anyone."

There's no point in reminding him how he just got done telling me about the higher quality of people I'll meet at this school. Why is it okay for me to go to class with these people, but God forbid I live with any of them?

Why would he rather have me live with Zeke, a man, than another girl my age? "So it would just be the two of us?"

"Yes, it's a two-bedroom condo not far from campus. There's a security guard in the lobby, and an alarm system is going to be installed shortly." He sounds very pleased with himself. "I'll rest better at night knowing you're safe."

I'm glad he'll sleep easy. Me, on the other hand? Then again, it's pretty obvious I don't have a say in any of this. Why would it matter how I feel about the decisions being made regarding my life?

I have to push food around on my plate for a while to make it look like I'm eating before excusing myself from the table. All I want is to be alone. For him not to see what this is doing to me.

Not so fast, though. "Mia. Are you… that is, has Zeke…?"

My heart threatens to burst out of my chest, and I realize I'm holding my breath. "Yes, Dad?"

"Has he done anything he shouldn't have? Has he been inappropriate with you?"

"No! Of course not." What does he know? How much does he know? I wish I didn't feel so guilty. "He's always professional. I just don't think… he likes me very much."

His smile hardens a little. "He's not supposed to like you. He's supposed to protect you and keep you safe. So far, he's done that job well."

"Yes, he has."

"And that's why he's the only person I would trust with the thing that's most precious to me in the world." Funny, but shouldn't that make me feel good? All warm and fuzzy inside? Instead, I feel the way I always feel when he says things like that: like I'm an object. Hardly even a person. One more of his possessions.

Still, I manage a little smile before leaving the dining room and going up the stairs. Here I was, finally getting used to living here even if I can't shake the feeling of being in a cage, and now I find out I'm being transferred to a new cage.

And my keeper is coming with me.

Of all people.

It doesn't hit me until I'm halfway up the wide staircase that I could have given my father a different answer down there. I could have told him Zeke tried to seduce me or something, and I wouldn't have to worry about any of this anymore. I would never even have to see him again. I wouldn't have to be humiliated every time he looks at me with that little smirk of his. Like he remembers what a fool I made of myself and thinks it's funny. Like my humiliation is worth laughing about.

At least here, at home, I know he'll keep it to himself. He wouldn't want Dad to know we were ever in that kind of situation together. He would end up getting blamed for it even though I was the one who made a move. Sure, I might get grounded for a little while or something, but Zeke would lose his job.

At least. I don't know what my dad does for a living or how he earned all this money in the first place, but there are times when I can't help wondering if everything he does is legal. It's enough to make me wonder what would really happen to somebody who crossed the great Bruno Morelli.

I can't do that. Sure, I wanted to kill Zeke for making me feel the way he did that night, but I wouldn't actually do it. It's not his fault he doesn't want me. It's not his fault I was dumb enough to think he would.

Even now, months later, the pain is so fresh. My whole body cringes from humiliation when I remember the look in his eyes. Cold and disgusted, like I was nothing but trash. Like he hated me, or worse, felt sorry for me. I'm still not sure what would be more humiliating.

And ever since, there's not a day that goes by that I don't know for sure he's thinking about it. The way he sometimes looks at me—or worse, when he won't look at me at all. I know why he won't look at me. And it makes me want to die. If there's one thing I could go back and change, it would be that night at the pool. I'll never be able to live it down.

I hurry down the hall, my footsteps muffled by the thick rug running down the length of the passage. Only a few of the rooms up here are used, including the suite Dad gave me when I first moved in. It's basically an entire apartment to myself, and I have to admit, I'll miss it a little. I've done everything I could to make it mine, to add little bits of myself to it. It sort of intimidated me at first, but now it feels like home.

And I'm going to have to leave it in just a few days. No warning, but then I didn't get any warning about the way my life would change after Mom died, either. I might as well be a leaf that fell from a tree and got carried by the wind, eventually landing on the water. And now, all I can do is float, letting the current take me where it thinks I should be.

"Hey, princess."

My blood turns to ice the instant I hear his voice. There's always a snicker to it now, like he's barely managing not to laugh at me. Even if he did laugh, I know there wouldn't be any humor or kindness in it, more like bitterness and resentment.

I turn to face Zeke, reminding myself for the hundredth time that I can't think of him the way I used to. My eyes are in the habit of finding all his best features, though, and they never got the memo about us hating him now. That's why I can't help but take in his chiseled jaw and slate gray eyes. Right now, they're almost stormy, swirling with dangerous energy. His broad shoulders and firm chest. The way his generous mouth ticks upward at the corner, his lips practically begging to be kissed or at least touched. I wonder how soft they would be.

It takes a second for me to snap out of it. This isn't the sex god of my wildest fantasies—and no matter how much I used to want him, he's not going to be my first. He will never be anything to me but a jailkeeper.

And he hates me. That alone is reason enough for me to fold my arms the way he does. "I don't see any princesses around here, so I don't know who you're talking to."

He only rolls his eyes. "Right. Keep telling yourself that, *princess*."

"What do you want?"

"I guess he told you. We're going to be roommates."

"I wouldn't put it that way."

"So how would you put it?"

"We'll be sharing a condo. Separate rooms."

"If you shared a two-bedroom place with anybody else, wouldn't you call them your roommate?"

It's obvious he thinks he's really clever like he's got me backed into a corner or something like that. If there's one thing he needs to learn about me, it's that I'm never backed into a corner. Not by somebody like him. "You work for my father. You're an employee. The live-in nanny."

His only reaction is a twitch of an eyebrow, the slight tightening of his jaw. "I hope you don't think just because you'll be away from him that security is going to loosen up any."

"What did you have in mind? Shackles?"

"Not a bad idea if you try pulling the sort of shit you've been pulling all summer. Thinking you can sneak out when you have to know, I'll be two steps ahead of you all the time." Now he does lift an eyebrow, his lips curving in a grin. "And if you're half as depressed about having to go away to school as you looked coming down the hall, I could tell him all about it, and your problems would be over. He'd never let you out of the house again."

He would do it, too. All for the sake of getting rid of me. If I was always in the house, he wouldn't have to watch over me anymore. "What are you trying to say? You can't handle your job? Is that what this is about, you being afraid of how much harder I'll make things for you when it's just the two of us at school?"

"I know how your brain works," he warns in a low voice that sends a shiver down my spine. "I can practically read your thoughts."

"You should know better than to talk to me the way you are right now. Or else maybe I'll have to ask my father to assign somebody else to me. Somebody who can actually do the job without whining to me about it."

"That's what you think this is? You think I'm whining?" Before I know what's happening, he backs me up against the open bedroom door. There's so much of him, all at once. His size, the smell of his cologne, the warmth coming from his body. The fine hairs on my arms stand straight up when his hot breath washes over my skin as he leans down. "It's a warning, princess. The first sign of any of your shit, and he's going to hear about it."

My knees threaten to buckle, but I can't let that happen. The one thing I've had on my side all summer is knowing how much Zeke wants to keep this job with my father. Not that I think there's any affectionate feelings on either side or anything like that, but more like he doesn't want to let Dad down. He's not a guy you disappoint. Zeke can pretend all he wants, but we both know he would be blamed for anything my father found out about. I might get a tiny slap on the wrist, but that's it.

Which is why I'm able to lift my chin despite the way my body trembles. "Go ahead and tell him. We'll see how much longer you have a job once you do. I think we both know it'll be better if you keep your mouth shut and let me do what I want. I'm going to college. I should be allowed to have my freedom."

"That's what you think. But the guy who foots the bill has other ideas, and we both know it." His voice drops to something closer to a growl, one so deep it makes me wet. "Behave yourself, princess. Otherwise, I'll have to deal with you myself. And you won't like that very much."

I barely have time to catch my breath before he's gone, disappearing as silently as he appeared in the first place.

And I'm supposed to live with this man with nobody around to keep him in check.

Or to keep me in check.

This can only spell trouble.

3
ZEKE

"Turn on some music."

My response is to stare straight ahead through the windshield. The way I've been for the past hour. I don't even glance up at the rearview mirror, where I know I'd find Mia glaring daggers straight through me.

"Hello? Did you go deaf? Music. It's too quiet in here."

Again, she gets nothing from me. My hands tighten around the wheel, and I can't help but imagine them tightening around her slender neck. It's bad enough I spend most of my waking moments reminding myself how dangerous it would be to give in to my craving for her. Why does she have to make it so much more difficult?

Then again, maybe I should thank her. Hating her is so much easier than wanting her.

Though the level of intensity is about the same.

She mutters something under her breath. "Zeke. I know you can hear me. I'm only asking you to put some music on… please." She whispers the last part.

"Huh? Sorry, I guess I couldn't hear you. It's this funny problem I have. My ears don't pick up when people are being rude little assholes."

"I didn't know it made me an asshole to want music in the car while we're on our way to school."

"You know damn well what I mean." I finally take the chance of looking in the mirror, and I end up wishing I hadn't. She's wearing a skirt just barely long enough that her father didn't tell her to get changed the second he saw her in it.

But it was short enough for him to pull me aside. "Make sure she doesn't wear shit like that around school." Right. Now I'm supposed to dress her in the morning. Why not put me on diaper duty while I'm at it?

Ordinarily, back at the compound, it would have been bad enough trying to function with her looking the way she does.

Now it's so much worse because there's nobody nearby. Nobody looking over my shoulder, nobody to report back to the boss that I spent a little too much time eyeing up his delicious little daughter. Her long legs, so smooth and tempting. I bet she feels like silk, though I wouldn't dare put a finger on her. I haven't even touched her arm or her hand since that night. I don't trust myself.

She crosses one leg over the other, and my mouth goes dry. "Excuse me, Zeke? Would it be too much trouble to turn on the radio? I think the ride would be much more enjoyable with a little music." Her sickeningly sweet voice carries a bitter edge that's almost enough to make me laugh. She's got an attitude on her, but then so do I.

"I think I can arrange that." I touch a button on the wheel, and the radio flips on. "See? You treat somebody with respect, and you get respect."

"Who are you? Mr. Rogers?" She gives me an epic eye roll before returning her attention to her phone, scrolling mindlessly through whatever social media platform she's on at the moment. I only chuckle, focusing back on the road.

I've seen pictures of the condo we're moving into, and I can't pretend it's not impressive. An entire family could live there comfortably—the bedrooms are enormous. I would have killed to have a room that big when I was a little kid, crammed into what was little bigger than a closet with three cousins my grandparents were caring for along with me. Two sets of bunk beds were almost too much for the room to hold. I used to have to turn sideways to get between them.

On the surface, I've come a long way. And my job, while infuriating and harder than just about anything I've ever had to do, is a hell of a lot easier than digging ditches and walking for miles in both directions to get to a factory, both of which my grandfather did when he was my age. It's something my dad always liked to remind me of whenever I would complain the way kids sometimes do. But that was before he started working for the boss—before our lives changed. Before I got pulled out of my grandparents' house and into the Morelli family, too.

I don't dig ditches, but I've dug more than a few holes, which I later filled with what was left of the people I was assigned to eliminate. I can't help but wonder what my granddad would think of that.

"Can you change the station? Something a little less boring?"

I look at her in the mirror. "This is classic shit."

"Classic?" Her nose wrinkles in disgust. "That's just another word for ancient. Music from, like, the eighties."

I know she's doing this to fuck with me. I know she listens to stuff from so-called ancient times, too. She wants to start a fight, is all. "This is the stuff I was brought up on. It's good if you give it a chance."

"I don't feel like giving it a chance today. Just change the damn station." I should know better than to try to talk any kind of sense to her. We could be in a burning building, and she would bitch me out if I so much as offered to help get her to safety. All because it was coming from me.

It's safer this way. I have to remember that. It's better if she hates me because then she won't throw herself at me like she did that night. How many times have I jerked off to the memory of her perfect body so close to mine? Right there for the taking. All I had to do was reach out and grab her, and that would've been the end of it. There would have been no way for me to stop myself once I got a hold of her. Once I knew what she felt like under my hands.

Instead, I've spent my nights obsessing over her. Fantasizing about what might have happened if I wasn't so strong.

"Do you have all your classes scheduled?"

She glances up from the phone. "Why do you care?"

Is this what I have to look forward to for the next few months? "I care because it affects me. If you don't have your shit together, your father will find a way to make that my fault."

"It doesn't have anything to do with you."

"It didn't have anything to do with me the day you decided to get a septum piercing, either." Needless to say, she took the nose ring out and never put it back in.

She flinches at the memory, and I can only imagine she remembers the way her father screamed the walls down. We both heard it from him that day. "I made sure he knew that was my fault. Don't blame me for that."

"I still had to hear about it. I don't think I unclenched my ass for a week after that."

I can tell she doesn't want to giggle, but she does anyway. "Everything is scheduled. Not like I had anything to do with it."

I shouldn't keep talking about this, but I can't help it. Not when I hear a disappointed note in her voice. "You really didn't know he was arranging for you to go to Blackthorn, huh?"

She keeps her eyes on the phone. "It doesn't matter."

"So you really don't care that you didn't get any say in where you go to school?"

Her head snaps up in time for me to catch sight of it in the mirror before focusing my attention back on the road. "What are you trying to do?"

"Huh?"

"You heard me. Are you trying to make me miserable? Save your breath, okay? I know how lucky I am. You don't need to remind me."

"That's not what I was trying to do."

"Right. Because you've never rubbed it in, how lucky I am. How I don't have any room to complain about anything in my life."

She's got a good memory. I'll give her that much. I have given her a lot of shit in the past when she's being a brat and acting like it's so painful and inconvenient having somebody devoted completely to making sure she's safe. "I wasn't trying to rub it in, either. And it does affect me since I'll be following you around all over the place. Sue me for wanting to know if I was going to get to hear anything interesting."

Her lips twitch a little like she's trying not to smile. "It's all pretty basic stuff, intro to this and that."

"So long as you don't expect me to do classwork for you."

She finally sets down her phone. "Are you seriously going to come to my classes with me? Like, isn't it enough to sit outside the room?"

"I don't make the rules. I only follow them."

"But that's embarrassing. Isn't it embarrassing to you?"

I don't know if she's deliberately trying to get under my skin or if she's sincerely asking because she wants to know. "Why would I be embarrassed?" I finally grunt, wishing traffic would clear up so I can get moving faster again. At least then, I might have a reason to ignore her.

"I mean, having to sit through classes with me? All because somebody told you to?"

"It's my job. Would you ask a professor if they were embarrassed because they had to stand in front of the room and teach you things? It's what they get paid to do. Same thing for me."

I glance her way in the mirror. "Besides, there are lots of rich kids who go to this school. I'm sure you won't be the only one—and even if you are, they'll be used to seeing bodyguards around. It only seems weird to you because you're not used to it yet."

"Is that supposed to be an insult?"

"Why are you so hell-bent on taking everything I say as an insult? No, I said it because it's the truth. You didn't grow up the way these kids did, so it only seems strange to you. What's so wrong about that?"

She folds her arms, staring out the window. "You made it sound like an insult. Like you looked down on me."

"Trust me. If I look down on you, it doesn't have anything to do with the way you grew up."

"So you do look down on me."

"Jesus Christ, Mia. Can we not?" I ask through gritted teeth. "You're giving me a fucking headache."

"Whatever." She huffs and turns her head toward the window with the cutest little pout on her lips.

She spends the next twenty minutes grumbling and muttering to herself, and I'm perfectly fine with letting her do that so long as it means not having to have a discussion. Just when I start feeling sorry for her a little, she finds a way to make me hate her.

She spends so much time acting like I don't exist that it surprises me when she raises her voice. "Can we stop here at this gas station?"

"We're only twenty minutes from campus. Can you wait?"

"No. I have to go right now. Please?" It's the please that tips me off. She's never this nice unless there's something she wants. Something more serious than having to piss.

I should probably floor the gas pedal and blow right past the station, but now I'm curious. "Yeah, okay. Just don't take too long."

I pull in in front of the store, past the gas pumps, and park. When I open the door, prepared to follow her inside, Mia clicks her tongue. "Are you going to follow me into the restroom, too?"

"Should I?"

"That's going to look weird to the guy behind the counter." She looks through the window, and I see the kid working the register. He can't be much older than her. "It'll look like you're, like, my pimp or something. Or my trafficker."

I almost blurt out a laugh until I realize she's serious. "Quit stalling and get in there. I thought you were in a hurry."

"I'm not stalling. But I think it would look better if you hang out here." I roll my eyes, which only makes her grunt in frustration. "Fine.

Come in, stand outside the bathroom door with that look you get on your face when you're trying to act all threatening. I'm sure it'll look totally legit."

"Fine, already. Just go." It's not worth arguing—besides, she has a point, not that I would ever admit it to her. I do have my pride.

Is this what the next four years are going to be like? Because if it is, I'm not sure I want any part of it. Fighting for every inch. I guess that's easier than fighting to keep my hands off her. Hating her is easier than wanting what I can never, ever touch.

Since I have a minute to myself, I pull out my phone and call the boss's direct line. "Checking in," I report when he answers. "All's clear. We made a pit stop at a gas station outside town."

"Glad to hear it. Once you're settled, check in with me again, and make sure Mia knows to keep a list of whatever she feels is missing. You have the bank card?"

"In my wallet."

"Good. I double-checked the account this morning. There's more than enough in there for her books and other supplies." Yes, and he won't let her have the card. I have to carry it. That's a fight I'm not in the mood to have, so I haven't broached the topic yet. It's only a matter of time, though.

The call ends, and I turn my attention back to the inside of the station. A familiar head of dark curls is close to the front counter. I know she has cash on her—I watched her accept it from her father before we left, and she has a debit card, which won't be working much longer—but she's taking too long. I should've gone inside.

My hand's on the door when she steps away from the counter with a plastic bag in hand, wearing a huge smile that doesn't slip when she joins me outside.

"See? The world didn't end. I bought you a pack of peanut butter cups. I know you love them." She reaches into the bag and pulls them out, holding them up for my inspection.

Now I know she's up to some shit. "You've gotta get better at lying if you think you have a chance of getting around me." I don't care how it looks. I take her by the arm and pull her to the car. "What else did you buy?"

"Get your hands off me, you asshole." She tries to tug away, but it only results in my hand closing tighter around her bicep.

"If you insist on getting in the way of me doing my job, this is how I'm going to have to treat you." I practically throw her into the back seat before reaching into the oversized purse that slid off her shoulder. The bit of plastic peeking out from inside turns out to be part of the packaging to a prepaid cell phone.

"Give that back. It's mine!" She scrambles for it but is too slow. I snatch it away, drop it on the ground, and stomp on the phone while maintaining eye contact.

"You know damn well you're not supposed to have a secret phone." The remnants are still lying on the ground when I get behind the wheel and peel away. "Keep pulling this shit, and you won't visit a bathroom alone for the rest of the time you're enrolled at this fucking school."

"Fuck you," she spits from the back seat. "I fucking hate you."

I shouldn't laugh. It's the worst, cruelest thing I could do. But I'm in a cruel sort of mood.

Which is why I meet her eyes in the mirror before smirking. "Keep telling yourself that." Her face goes a deeper red a second before she buries her nose into her father-approved phone again. Probably trying to come up with another plot around me. I know why she wants a different phone, to evade her father's peering and have some privacy, but she can't. Her father would kill me, so she can keep trying, but she's not going to win.

All I have to worry about now is how I'm going to keep hating her without her father around to remind me why I need to.

And whether it's really, truly important, she is kept pure for her future husband…

4
MIA

Stupid me, thinking things might be a little different now. Like if Dad wasn't around, I could have a little bit of freedom for once. I mean, in whose world does an employee not slack off at least a little when they're miles away from their boss? I guess in mine.

No, I had the bad luck of getting stuck with the last Boy Scout or whatever the hell Zeke thinks he is. Like he's got to earn brownie points. I'm sure he'll deliver daily reports, too. I wonder if he has to track the times I go to the bathroom and the outcome.

My arm still aches from the way Zeke gripped it as we roll up in front of a building that looks more like a spa or a fancy hotel than an apartment building. "This is it?" I mutter to myself as we pull past a series of meticulously maintained topiaries and a marble fountain shooting water high into the air. It sparkles like diamonds before dropping into the pool surrounding it.

"What? Not nice enough for you?"

"Did I say that? Tell me when I said that." All he does is snicker. "I didn't expect it to be this nice. That's what I meant. It seems like a lot for a college freshman."

"Nothing's too good for the princess."

"Would you stop calling me that? You know damn well I didn't live like this before my mom died." And just the thought of her makes my throat go tight. What would she think of all this? Probably that it's too much. I know she wanted the best for me, but I didn't earn any of it. That would be a different story to her.

"Don't act like your life didn't get better."

It's my turn to snicker. "So did yours. Or were you living in a palace like this before I came along?"

He grunts but doesn't argue with me, which means I'm right. It's not exactly easy to get the last word with him, so I'll take it as a victory after he humiliated me at the gas station.

I can't even have a phone my father doesn't monitor. I know he has access somehow, and I know he'll continue to even though I'm away at college.

It's funny in a sad way. I know my best friend, Blair, thinks I've got it made, like having all this money is a huge win or whatever. And yes, it is in a lot of ways. I don't have to worry about getting a job to support myself, for one thing.

But when she goes to school, she'll have a life of her own. No having a guardian watching her every second. No being spied on or having her phone calls tracked. It would be heaven compared to what I have ahead of me.

Dad was right about everything being moved in and set up by the time we arrived. There's a full set of living room furniture, a big TV, even artwork on the walls. It's all kind of bland, but I'd rather it be bland than tacky or over the top.

The kitchen's amazing, too. I wonder if I'll have enough time to do any cooking because the shiny appliances and gleaming, untouched pots and pans are practically begging to be used. The fridge is fully stocked and looks like something from a high-end supermarket.

What I'm most interested in is the room where I'll probably end up spending most of my time. The bedroom is huge, with an en suite bathroom—thank God for that. I was worried about having to share a bathroom with the asshole whose bedroom is across from mine. From what I can see through the open door, it's practically identical to this one.

Although would it really be so bad if he caught me coming out of the shower? Or vice versa?

Dammit. I need to get him out of my system, or else things will only get worse. It's awkward and painful enough to face him already, especially when he makes little remarks like he did earlier. We both know I don't hate him—who the fuck says that? Oh, right, ignorant dickheads who think they're better than me because… why? Because he gets paid to follow me around like a dog? If I were him, I wouldn't be too full of myself.

"Princess? You okay in there?" He pokes his head into the room and looks around. "Nice. Big bed. Mine, too."

"Good for you." I turn around to where my suitcases were left. The one thing I wouldn't give an inch on was unpacking my own clothes. Sorry, but I don't love the idea of total strangers putting their hands on my underwear.

When I explained it that way to my dad, he got it. Like all he cares about is keeping me pure, making sure no man ever so much as sees my panties. It's almost bizarre.

And pointless. If he wants me to stay a virgin for the rest of my life, he should've sent me to a convent. Or to a cabin on top of a mountain. Instead, I'm at college, and there's how many guys here? Guys my age who want to drink and party and have sex.

I know I'm not ugly. I might be a virgin, but I do know some things. Once everybody's settled into their dorms or apartments or whatever, they'll want to start throwing parties. It'll be like shooting fish in a barrel—I think that's how the saying goes. I could stroll into a party anywhere and hand over my v-card by the end of the night. No problem.

I hit the bed with a thump when reality finally sinks in. I'm never going to be allowed to go to a party, not without Zeke. And I'm not about to walk around with him practically brushing up against my back all the time. Breathing down my neck. Like any guy would want to come near with him standing over me.

There won't be finding a boyfriend or even dating casually. Hell, I won't be able to give a dude a hand job while we're making out in a dark corner.

There has to be a way out of this. Somehow, I have to find a way to make Zeke see he doesn't have to jump through Dad's hoops now that we're miles away. What if he meets somebody he likes and wants alone time with her?

I hate the ache in my chest when the idea hits me. Zeke with some random skank. Kissing and touching her. Doing all the things I've imagined him doing to me. Letting her do all the things I want to do to him.

No. Wanted. Past tense. I grip the bedspread with both fists, squeezing my eyes shut as tight as I can. I need to stop thinking of him that way. I was stupid and had a crush, and that's it. One of those dumb things.

Nothing was ever going to happen between us. All the looks I thought he gave me were in my head. He's never been interested, never seen me as anything more than a spoiled brat. A princess.

And now, after that awful night, he hardly touches me. The dull ache in my arm reminds me of his touch. I'm surprised he didn't wash his hands right after like I'm dirty.

He was too busy destroying the phone I bought, the prick. Money down the drain. I wanted to kill him right there in the parking lot, in front of anybody who passed by. Running him down with the car, crushing him the way he's crushing me, even if he doesn't know it.

"You hungry, princess?" His voice floats in from the other side of the closed door.

I grit my teeth rather than telling him to go fuck himself for calling me that. He knows it gets under my skin, which is the only reason he keeps using the word. If I show him how much I hate it, he's only going to do it more. "Yeah, I was thinking about fixing something in a little bit," I reply as evenly as I can.

He snorts. "Right. Like the princess is going to cook her own food."

I shouldn't do it, but I can't help myself. This snide son of a bitch. I march over to the door and fling it wider. He's standing there, hands in his pockets, smirking like this was exactly the reaction he was looking for. I fucking hate him. "You can go fuck yourself, you know that?"

"Ouch, such language."

"What? Are you going to tell your boss on me? Because that's what you do, isn't it? You scamper back to him like the little lapdog you are and report every fucking thing I do. Apparently, some people call that a job nowadays."

That did it. His eyes aren't twinkling anymore. "Watch it, kid."

"No, you watch it. For one thing, you're not even that much older than me, so cut the bullshit, okay?" When all he does is smirk, I have to dig my nails into my palms to keep myself centered. Otherwise, I might use those nails to claw his eyes out. "For another thing, I know how to cook for myself. I know how to do a hell of a lot of things, and you want to know why? Because until my father found me, it was just my mom and me, and I was home alone most of the time. If I was hungry, I had to cook for myself. If there was a mess, I had to clean it up. In fact, I did most of the chores around the house because my mother was so tired from working two jobs that she never had the energy. I did the laundry, the dishes, scrubbed the bathroom. I made sure something was waiting for her to eat when she got home from a shift." I have to stop. I'm either going to scream or cry if I don't. How dare he? He doesn't know the first thing about what my life used to be like.

His jaw twitches. "Do you want an award?"

I'm pretty sure I'm breaking the skin on my palms. The stinging pain is almost welcome. "No, asshole. I don't want an award. I want a little respect. I wasn't raised with money. There were years when my clothes for school all came from Goodwill, and even then, Mom had to save up while she went to work in shoes with holes in the bottoms. So you can fuck yourself with this princess bullshit."

I can't even believe he needs to think about this. If I were him, I'd be apologizing right now. Maybe even on my hands and knees. But no, he's going to stand there, looking me up and down, with his lips pursed tight like he's actually thinking it over. Like this is up for debate or something.

"Fine. No more princess bullshit."

Wow. I'm almost too surprised to speak. "But the way you talk to me still makes it sound like I'm a big joke to you. Do you think that could change, too?"

I should have known better. "Don't push your luck, kid."

"You and my father can go to hell."

All of a sudden, he's maybe two inches away from me, lowering his head until his face is almost touching mine. "Now that, I'm not going to let slide. You can call me whatever you want; you can curse me out until your face turns blue. Go ahead. But you're not going to disrespect him."

"Are you for real? Do you have a crush on him? He's not here. He's not going to give you a Milk-Bone for being such a good boy."

"How ungrateful can you be?" he snarls. "He did all of this for you. He got you into this school. He got you this place to live in. Do you know how many people your age would kill to be in your shoes?"

"Oh, right. Except they have to be okay with being shadowed everywhere they go, right? Having every single move they make watched and reported on. Yeah, I'm sure they would be totally okay with that."

I wish he wasn't close enough to feel his warmth seeping into my skin. I don't know if I want to kill him or bury my face in his neck and inhale his scent. Jesus, what is he doing to me? Why can't I get him out of my system? I know he doesn't want me. I know he thinks I'm a pathetic joke. Why would I still want him?

For one long, breathless moment, there's nothing but the two of us staring into each other's eyes. Daring each other. Seeing who will make the next move. My nerves are buzzing, my brain is humming. There's nothing in the world but him and me, and the sound of blood rushing in my ears. I can't help but think we're on the edge of something. If only I knew what was going through his head.

His eyes dart away from mine, grazing my lips before darting up again. "You're right. Every move you make is going to be watched and reported. So you should keep that in mind going forward—otherwise, something tells me things could get a lot worse for you."

An icy shiver runs down my spine. It's not so much what he said but how he said it. "What do you know?"

"Know?"

"You made it sound like you know something I don't."

He blinks rapidly, and not for the first time do I notice how unfair it is that his eyelashes are so thick and dark. I'd kill for lashes like his. "You shouldn't read so much into everything." He stands up straighter again, clearing his throat before backing away. "I'm making spaghetti. I've put in enough effort today."

That's fine. He can cook for me if he wants to. If he thinks I'm a spoiled brat, maybe I should really start acting like one. I can make him wish he had never treated me like this.

"Let me know when it's finished. I'll eat in here." I slam the door between us, then finally slump forward with my hands on my knees as I try to catch my breath. My heart's pounding, my head's spinning, and my nipples are tight enough to make me wince. I'm so wet I can feel it spreading past my lips and soaking into my panties.

I have to. I'll die if I don't.

My hand slips under the waistband of my shorts and inside my panties. I find my clit and bite my lip against a groan of relief—but the relief doesn't last long. My fingers move in a familiar, circular motion over the bundle of nerves, my breathing picking up, my body tensing. What if he grabbed me instead of walking away? What if he threw me on the bed and did what we couldn't do back at home? I would be totally at his mercy. And I'd love it.

My body tenses, eyes squeezed tight. My free hand rubs my tits before I pinch my nipples, moving back and forth. But it's not my fingers. It's his lips, pulling and sucking, his tongue lapping at the very tip.

Filthy images flash across my mind. Fantasies. His body pinning me to the bed, his hands all over me. Moving inside me. Taking me. Fucking me until I scream his name—

"Zeke." It's a whisper, barely a breath. My head falls back, and my body goes rigid a heartbeat before the wave crashes, and I lean against the door, spasming until my legs shake. So good.

My eyes open, and the sight of my own reflection is the first thing I see. I'm flushed, trembling with a hand down my shorts and another cupping my tit. I don't know if I should feel embarrassed or sorry for myself.

Is this what the entire year will be like?

Because this is the first day, and already, I don't think I can take it anymore.

And I don't know how much longer getting myself off will be enough to get by.

5
ZEKE

She meant it about eating in her room. She came out just long enough to fix a plate of spaghetti and sauce, then marched down the hall and slammed the door again. I would've pointed out her father won't like having to pay for a new door this soon, but I didn't feel like having my head cut off.

What the fuck am I supposed to do with her? We haven't been here for two hours, and already, the tension is enough to break the walls. She has no idea how close I came to throwing her over my knee and spanking the shit out of her for being such a little brat. Talking to me like she did, making it sound like I'm her father's errand boy. A lapdog? The little tease is lucky I have self-control, or else she wouldn't be able to sit for days by the time I finished with her ass.

She has no idea who she's dealing with. I told myself from the beginning she would never know. The past is the past and all that. I did what I had to do. Looking after her might be boring, but it's a reprieve from all the blood I used to get on my hands.

She's dancing on my last nerve. I'll be lucky if I don't lose it by the end of this first week.

I take my time cleaning up, figuring the simple, repetitive act of rinsing dishes and pots, and putting them in the brand-new dishwasher will soothe my anger, but that's not even close to the case. By the time the last of the dishes are in the dishwasher—aside from hers, still in her room—I'm as pissed off as ever. It's not enough that I know she's wrong. I want her to know it, too. I want to break her, to stare into her eyes and see fear and understanding. I want her to apologize for ever underestimating me. Just the thought of it makes my cock twitch a little bit, the idea of making her regret ever fucking with me.

Right. Like she wouldn't go straight to her father. He'd have my head on a stick before the day was out if he knew I laid a hand on her. He might understand if I managed to get a word in edgewise before he ended me, but I don't think he'd give me the chance.

There's music coming from her room by the time I leave the kitchen and walk over to the closed door. Loud, driving, heavy on the drums and guitar. At least she has decent taste in music. One small reprieve. Instead of bothering her, I'll count my blessings and leave her alone. Maybe she'll be in a better mood by the time she ventures out.

Good or bad mood, I'm stuck here with her. That's one thing she doesn't understand, and I doubt she ever will. She feels like a prisoner? Welcome to the club, kid. Our situation might not be exactly the same, but I'm in a cage, too. She just can't see past her anger.

I go into my bedroom, fucking pissed at her for talking to me the way she did—and more pissed at myself for letting her get away with it. I'm not a pushover, usually.

Still, she set me straight earlier. I can't pretend I didn't feel slightly like a piece of shit when she reminded me where she came from. I already knew most of it. At least, I was aware her life wasn't easy before her father found her. She and her mom both went through a lot in the years my boss lived his life exactly how he wanted to, free and clear of family responsibilities.

What I can't tell her is how it's better for me to hate her. It's easier for me to stay away and make sure there are no complications both of us would end up regretting. Safer.

I can either pace my room like a caged tiger, or I can take a shower and hope it calms me down. The bathroom is way bigger than I need, with a rainfall shower behind glass doors and a deep soaking tub. I guess hers is the same. Why would there need to be two bathrooms like this in the same condo? Knowing the boss, that was one of his must-haves, so we wouldn't share a bathroom. I should thank him for thinking of me, I guess. Most people wouldn't care about the comfort of the hired help.

My teeth grit when I think of myself that way, and it's all thanks to her. It never bothered me that much before. I mean, it's not like I enjoy having to report everything she does back to him, but I'm not some sniveling little ass kisser. Once again, I had to stop myself from screaming that in her face until she understood. I wish I didn't want so much for her to understand.

The water pressure is good. That's a plus. I run the water hot, and by the time I open the glass door to step inside, the shower is full of steam. I almost welcome the scalding water, the way it turns my skin red to match the boiling resentment in my gut.

I close my eyes and tilt my head back, but all I can see is Mia. Those eyes, those lips. So plump, made to be sucked and nibbled. Made to wrap around a cock.

Dammit, I can't think this way, but it's all that goes through my head in the steamy stall. How all I want is the princess on her knees in front of me, naked like she was by the pool. Looking up at me with those big eyes, eyes full of mixed fear and lust. I can't help but imagine the way they would widen in surprise at the sight of my cock swaying in front of her.

My cock which is now standing fully erect and already oozing precum. I know I need to shut this down—nothing good can come of this. Then again, what good can come of me sulking around with blue balls? That would only make things worse.

I squirt body wash in my palm, and wrap my hand around my twitching length. A groan slips out of my mouth before I can stop myself. Good thing her room isn't close to the hall, or else she might hear.

I close my eyes again and begin the slow, torturous slide up and down my shaft. Only, instead of my hand, it's Mia's mouth. Her lips closed tight around me, her tongue running up and down the underside before swirling around the head.

My stroke quickens, and I grit my teeth, my head falling back under the spray of scalding water. In my mind, I take her by the back of the head and control her rhythm, moving my hips until I'm fucking her face. My fist moves up and down faster, and I can almost hear the way she'd gag and groan as I take what I want. What I've always wanted, ever since the first moment I set eyes on her. "That's right," I growl in my fantasy. "Take it down your throat. Choke on my cock. Show me how good you can be. Show me how much you want it."

And she would because she does. She wants me, wants this cock inside her. Wants to feel my cum filling her mouth and rolling over her tongue, coating her throat. Wants to watch me come across those incredible tits, wants to feel my cum splash over her ass after I've fucked her until she's close to passing out.

So many images overlap in my overheated brain until I can't take it anymore, and I come with a growl, soap and jizz mixing together in my hand. I slow my stroke, sighing in relief. I can think again.

I know this isn't going to last long. The relief will be short-lived. Being around her will make me want her more, and I'll be right back here. It looks like my hand is going to be getting a lot of action in the months ahead.

It's not until I'm out of the shower and drying off, wearing a pair of boxer briefs and nothing else, that I realize there's no music coming from her bedroom. I walk through my room and stick my head out the door. Her bedroom door is still closed, and there's light coming from underneath. "Mia?" I call out.

Nothing. Not even a slammed drawer or a muttered insult.

Instantly, my instincts go on overdrive. She wouldn't. She's not that stupid.

Turns out, she would, and she is. When I open her bedroom door, I find the room empty. The bathroom, too. "Goddammit, Mia." The kitchen is empty, the living room, the balcony.

I don't care that I'm only in my underwear. I go out, looking over the railing, gripping it with both hands, and wondering how much it would take to tear the iron from the concrete under my feet. I'll fucking kill her for this. And if anything happens to her, her father will fucking kill me.

There's something she doesn't know. She thinks she's smart, but I'm still at least one step ahead. There's a reason she can't have a burner phone I don't have access to: if that's the only phone she's carrying, I can't track her. As it stands, I can watch her every move.

My phone is on my nightstand. I open the app and wait no more than a few seconds for GPS to locate her. She's crossing campus. Where the hell is she going? While I wait to find out, I throw on jeans and a T-shirt, a pair of heavy-soled shoes. By the time I'm finished, there's no question where she went. "A fucking frat house?" I groan, checking out the house's exterior through Google Maps. "Why don't you paint a target on your ass, Mia?"

I hope she wasn't planning on doing much partying tonight. By the time I'm finished with her, partying will be the furthest thing from her mind.

6
MIA

I can't believe how easy it was to get away. Good thing the alarm won't be installed until tomorrow. I figured he'd have to take a shower sometime—at most, I was ready to wait until he went to bed before sneaking out. It's not like the party will wrap up early. According to the email I got, Kappa Alpha is hosting an all-night event to kick off the semester.

My first college party. I can't believe this is happening. My hands tremble a little as I tuck hair behind my ears, but I put a stop to it fast. I can't let nerves ruin things. I mean, I already got away from Zeke. I have to take advantage, which means not freaking out. It's just a party. I've been to parties before.

Though the stakes feel higher than they ever have. I'm not naïve. These kids are rich, and they've never known anything but privilege. I'm starting to finally loosen up and feel comfortable in their world, but I can't fool myself into thinking we're the same. We never will be because being able to easily get out of trouble is in their DNA. I can't count how many times I heard Mom click her tongue over reports of yet another prep school asshole getting away with heinous acts all because their parents could afford the right lawyers.

What would she think if she saw me walking up the street toward the three-story Victorian that houses one of the largest frats on campus? Would she be proud? Or would she complain my dress is too short and order me back to my room to change?

The house is like one of those bug zappers, drawing people from all directions. I watch them walk up, shiny cars rolling past and groups of kids pouring out. The girls are so pretty. I have to keep from fidgeting as I walk up the brick steps that cut into the sloping lawn.

I wish I wasn't alone. That's one thing I can't talk myself out of wishing. I know my clothes are just as good as anybody's, thanks to my dad. I know I'm pretty, even if I don't feel quite as hot as the other girls who are used to going to parties like this. Dad hardly ever let me out after I moved in, and it's not like I did a ton of partying before then. Sometimes, Blair and I would go to one and hang out on the fringe, huddled together with our beers, laughing at everybody making jerks out of themselves.

The thought of Blair is like a kick to the stomach. She should be here with me. I never saw myself starting this part of my life with her so far away. I force myself to look like I'm not anxious when I reach the porch where a dozen people are waiting to get into the house.

It's so loud I can barely hear myself think, and almost too dark to see. There are people on the stairs, all over the furniture, but the biggest crowd is around the kitchen. Once I manage to elbow my way through the packed rooms, I can see why. It's where all the drinks are. The table and counters are covered in bottles, and out back, there's a line of kegs already being tapped.

"Here." A tall, muscular guy, who looks like he plays football, presses a red cup into my hand before I know what's happening. He has to lean down for me to hear him over the ear-splitting noise. "Drink up. What's your name?"

"Mia!" I have to almost scream it, and still, I can barely hear my voice.

"I'm Dave. Nice to meet you. This your first party?"

"What, am I wearing a sign?"

He laughs, and it's a nice feeling. He doesn't know who I am, and I don't know who he is, and he's not lording his power over me the way certain men do. Men who, I hope, don't know I sneaked out while they were in the shower. "Yeah, it's kinda obvious. But that's okay. We all have to start somewhere." When somebody shoves past him from behind, he presses me against the wall. "Sorry."

"It's okay." It's actually kind of nice. He's cute, and he has a nice smile. I just now realized how much I've missed having causal contact with guys. Being able to flirt a little without somebody breathing down my neck. I'm free.

Even if I can't stop thinking about Zeke.

"What about you?" I ask, grinning up at him before taking a sip of my drink. It's strong as hell with a fruity taste, like punch.

"I'm a junior. Business major." He shrugs. "I like playing ball a lot more. And partying, obviously."

"Obviously."

He comes closer without being shoved this time, one arm above my head, leaning against the wall. "You here with anybody?"

Man. We're not even wasting time getting to know each other. His eyes move over my face and eventually settle on my mouth. When I bite my bottom lip, they narrow. "No. I'm by myself."

I can just about see the JACKPOT sign flashing in his mind. He thinks he's found the perfect mark. "Maybe we could go someplace where it's not so loud."

"Like the other side of campus?" I ask with a laugh. I can't imagine a quiet place anywhere in the house.

He laughs, too. "You're funny. I can tell you're smart. Not a lot of girls around here are."

Oof. Here we go. Now he's going to praise me for being *not like the other girls*. "So you know all the girls around here?"

His smile slips a little. "You know what I mean. Too many girls play dumb or are dumb. It takes a smart girl to be really funny."

"Thanks. I am pretty smart." Which is why I'm not going to drink any more of what's in my cup since I didn't pour it myself. I'm not saying I've watched one too many Lifetime movies, but I'm not not saying that, either.

"So what do you think? I'm tired of yelling. It'll be quieter upstairs." He slides a hand down my arm before taking hold of my fingers.

I wouldn't say yes anyway because it's obvious he's trying to take advantage of somebody he thinks is stupid and naïve. Maybe the frat boys have a bet to see who can get laid first by a freshman tonight. I want to make friends, but not that way. I'm not that desperate. "I don't think so," I say with a little shrug. "I'm just going to kind of mingle for a bit. But I'd like to hang out down here."

It's like magic. A second ago, he was sweet and cute. When he draws his brows together in a scowl, the mask falls off. "Suit yourself." He pushes off the wall with a string of curses I can't hear over the music and quickly disappears into the crowd.

So much for friendly small talk. That was extremely unpleasant. I'm tempted to follow him around and make sure he doesn't take advantage of anybody. Blair would laugh herself to death if she knew that was going through my head at my first party. I go to the sink and empty the cup before tossing it in the trash. Maybe I'd better stick to beer tonight.

I go outside, and it's such a nice break from feeling like a sardine in the house. I'm the only person out here alone—everybody's paired up or in groups of three or four. I can tell some of the girls are new. They have that same wide-eyed look that I know I must have, even if they're trying to play it off. I lock eyes with one of them, and she smiles. "Are you here by yourself?"

I cringe. "Yeah."

"You can hang out with us. We all just got here today. I'm Posey." She gestures to her friends. "This is Erica and Bri. We're all roommates. What about you?"

"I'm Mia. I'm living by myself. I wish I had roommates to go places with," I admit, and the three of them tip their heads to the side like they feel bad. They seem nice, genuine.

"We'll be your roommates for the night," Posey suggests. She's a tall, slender brunette whose contour game is better than mine will ever be. Erica and Bri are pretty with their shiny blond hair and blue eyes, but Posey's the standout.

Erica laughs. "Yeah, because some of these guys are way too obvious."

"They lurk around, trying to pick off the girls who are here by themselves." Bri wrinkles her nose in disgust. "It's sick."

"I just met one of them inside."

"Girls need to have each other's backs." The girls nod in agreement with Posey, and I do, too. Maybe I've found some people I can relate to.

We get our beers and decide to hang out outside, getting to know each other. All three of them come from expensive prep schools, but they seem pretty down-to-earth. By the time I'm finished and almost ready for another drink, I'm feeling a little buzzed and smiley and happy. When was the last time I felt happy? Probably the last time I hung out with Blair.

"Who is that?" Erica's mouth falls open, her eyes wide. She's staring up at the back door leading from the kitchen, and I follow the direction of her gaze.

And the ground drops out from under me. The music goes quiet—no, that's the rush of blood in my ears, deafening me. I should've known this couldn't last long.

Standing there in his leather jacket, he makes the guys all around us look like little boys in comparison. I can see why the girls are practically drooling.

He locks eyes with me before I can react, then stomps his way down the wooden steps. "What are you doing here? You know you're not supposed to—"

"Who is he?" Posey takes me by the arm, pulling me in close like she wants to protect me. I like this girl. Even if her instincts are slightly off. I do need help from this man, but not the kind of help she thinks.

"Let's go." He comes over to me and takes me by my other arm, but Posey is not about to let go.

"Who do you think you are? Get your hand off her."

Zeke lets out a derisive laugh, looking her up and down, clearly not seeing much of a match. "You don't know what you're talking about, so back off. She's not supposed to be here."

"Would you stop?" I hiss through clenched teeth. People are staring. Even a couple of girls who were making out while a bunch of guys watched stop what they are doing so they can watch us instead. The guys have phones and were recording the girls—what happens if they record us? My father will kill me if he sees the video. I don't know how he'd find it, but he would. I know it.

All of this goes through my head in the blink of an eye. I hand my cup over to Posey with an apologetic smile. "Hopefully, I'll see you around campus."

"Here, give me your number."

I call it out to her, and she calls my phone so her contact info will be there.

Meanwhile, Zeke is leading me around the side of the house rather than cutting back through the party. I'm glad since the last thing I want is to be humiliated in front of my newly made friends.

"You know the kind of trouble you could be in right now?" Zeke's Harley is parked in front of the house, which of course, has attracted attention. I wish the people who brought our things left it behind. The second he snarls at the group that's gathered around the bike, they scatter. It would be funny if I wasn't so embarrassed.

"Stop." I pull my arm free once we've reached the bike. "You're making a scene."

"You're the one who put me in this position. What the fuck do you think you're doing, sneaking out like that?"

"Could you stop? I mean it," I mutter, glancing around.

"It's what you deserve. Maybe you'll think twice before you do some dumb shit like this again." He puts a hand on the small of my back and gives me a tiny shove. "Get on the bike."

"In this?" I look down at my dress. It's a little too short for a ride.

"Not my fault you're walking around with half your shit hanging out." He slings a leg over the motorcycle's seat, leaving me plenty of room to get on behind him. I've never been so embarrassed in my entire life, but I know better than to keep fighting. The idea of any of the guys around here thinking they could be my white knight and get in his face nauseates me. There's no way it would end well.

So I have no choice but to swallow my pride and climb on behind Zeke, wrapping my arms around his waist. Posey's watching, and I give her a smile to tell her it's okay. I'll have to text her later, and... what? Explain that my father doesn't trust me to exist without a bodyguard at all times? That just for once, I thought I could have a little fun on my own?

"If you think we're not going to have it out when we get back to the condo, you're out of your mind." I don't have a chance to answer since he guns the engine before peeling away from the curb.

Yes, I'm sure we're going to have it out.

And after the way he just humiliated me, there's nothing I would rather do.

7
ZEKE

"Don't you dare fucking march around like you're the one with a reason to be angry," I warn her on the way back into the building. There's a separate entrance from the garage, leading straight to the elevator without the humiliation of walking through the lobby with her so obviously furious. I don't feel like getting red-flagged by management, especially so soon after we've moved in.

"Would you drop the act already?" She tosses her hair, and I have to pretend the scent doesn't light me on fire. "Daddy isn't here to give you a gold star. And I'm not impressed with you."

"Maybe you should be." We get on the elevator, and I punch the button. "Because all it would take is a quick phone call."

"A quick phone call, huh? Stop, or I'll piss myself." Another hair toss. It's almost enough to make me want to cut it off.

"You think I'm joking?"

"Considering he would have your ass in a sling, not mine, yeah. It's pretty goddamn funny." She folds her arms, tapping her foot on the floor before almost bursting out of the car the second there's enough room between the metal doorway and the door that's sliding open.

The worst part is, she's right. It would mean admitting I let her get away, and she knows it. "I could point out that you knew better, and I've gotta take a shower at some point. Unless I'm supposed to have you in the bathroom with me, there's no way around it until the security system is put in. You know that, and you took advantage of it." She unlocks the door and tries to close it on me, but of course, that's a wasted effort. I shove the door open, then slam it shut.

She whirls around to face me. "You made a fucking fool of me out there. Do you know how embarrassing that was for me?"

"Don't blame me. You had to know I was going to find you." I strip off my leather jacket and toss it onto the couch, but it does nothing to cool me off. "It's my job."

"You mean it's your job to stalk me."

All that gets is a laugh. "Don't turn it into that. It's not stalking when I'm doing a job. My job is to—"

"Your job is to keep me prisoner."

"My job is to keep you safe!"

"Safe from what?" She throws her arms out to the sides and points through the doors leading out to the balcony. "It's just a bunch of people trying to hang out together. Wanting to have fun. What's so dangerous about that?"

I wave a hand, indicating her excuse for a dress. "Right, and you had to go to that party looking like that?"

"What's wrong with this? Other girls were wearing dresses."

Yeah, but I saw those other girls. They were nowhere near her league, and I'm not thinking that because I know what she looks like underneath. Her tits are about to pour out of the top, and if she bends down, her entire ass would be visible.

"You might as well have laid down in the middle of that party so the guys could take turns."

"You don't know what you're talking about." She folds her arms over herself defensively. "And I don't see why you have to be disgusting about it, either."

"News flash: this is the way guys think. We have disgusting, perverted minds. You're a smart girl. Don't tell me you don't know that."

"Girls have dirty minds, too."

"You're missing my point." Her eyes widen, and she backs away when I approach her one slow step at a time. Like a wolf scenting his prey. "Somewhere along the line, some of us figure out it's more fun to make those dirty, perverted little fantasies come true rather than fuck our fists. Now…"

She hits the wall, trapped. I lean in, one hand on either side of her head. "Some of us are disciplined enough to keep those thoughts to ourselves. But others… especially those teenagers, don't have that discipline. They also don't have the imagination to make those fantasies come true in a safe, legal way." My eyes widen when hers do, and I nod slowly. "Then there's your subset of guys without the discipline or the imagination, but what they do have going for them is the money to make problems disappear. And that's what you're going to find here, at this school. Lots of rich boys who would love to be the one to take you for a test drive."

She blinks, silent. Her pulse is fluttering like mad in the side of her neck—even now, with only the light coming in through the glass door, it's visible. It shouldn't get me off the way it does, knowing I have this effect on her, but I'm fighting off a hard-on while staring her down.

Her grin takes me by surprise. "You really think I'm stupid, don't you? I already faced one of those guys before you even got there, and I took care of myself."

"Oh, yeah?"

"Yeah. I also threw out the punch he gave me, which was probably spiked, but even if it wasn't, it wasn't worth the risk." Dammit, she's so triumphant. "Anything else?"

So scaring her is off the table. She's not naïve. "Fine. I'll have to bring out the same threat as always. You know, I'm getting tired of using your fear of your father to keep you in line."

She sucks in a deep breath that pushes her tits closer to me. "Fuck you."

"I thought we already went over that. It's not going to happen, remember?"

Her hand is up in a flash, pulled back like she's about to slap me. If I wasn't half crazy with disgust—and the frustration of not being able to get her in line—I might regret being an asshole. But no, this is her fault. This is what she's made me do.

"Go ahead, princess," I growl, leaning in close enough that I swear I smell her hatred. "Slap me. See if that makes you feel any better."

Instead of using her hand on my face, she makes a chopping motion with her arm. It hits my elbow, bending my arm and knocking me off balance. She uses that to her advantage, getting herself free and scrambling across the room. I'll give her this much: she's quick.

Her brain moves pretty quick, too. "You need to stop projecting onto me, you know that?" She plunges a hand into her tiny purse and pulls out her phone. "Out of the two of us, you're the one who's really afraid of my father. Anything I do, he'll forgive. But you?" She blows out a low whistle, shaking her head like she feels sorry for me.

"Why don't you test that theory? Give him a call and tell him what you've been up to tonight. I know that's what you're about to threaten me with. I'm pretty sure you'll find him taking my side."

"Not if he finds out you made a move on me." She bats her eyes. "Poor, innocent me, all alone with a predator."

For the second time, she's knocked me off balance, but this time, it doesn't show outwardly. At least, I hope not. "You would lie like that? Are you that fucked in the head?"

"Would it be a lie?" The little bitch even pouts. "I mean, you did just get awfully close to me. You described how gross and sick your brain is. And fantasies—you talked about having filthy fantasies. It made me very uncomfortable. I think you behaved extremely unprofessionally."

She holds up her phone, wiggling it around. "Now, whose side do you think he's going to take?"

There are limits to even my patience. "So help me, God. Mia, I will take you over my fucking knee and spank the shit out of you if you ever try something like that."

She thinks I'm bluffing. "Oh, so you want to give me more ammunition. Awesome. Come on, threaten me again. Keep making my job easier."

I lunge for her, and only then does she panic, scrambling for the kitchen. I'm too quick for her—one arm is all it takes to grab her around the waist and haul her in close to me.

And that's a mistake because now her wiggling, overheated body is rubbing against mine in the best and worst way possible. I don't know how much longer I'll be able to fight off the erection that keeps threatening.

"Now you listen to me," I warn in a growl. "You lie to your father about me; you make up stories where I'm the aggressor, and you're the innocent party. He might get to me, but believe me, I'll get to you first. It takes ninety minutes to drive here from the compound. That's an awfully long time for a bad girl to receive her punishment, don't you think?"

"Release me," she grunts, doing her damnedest to break free. While I pull her closer, whirling her body around in the process. I'm not going to make it easy for her this time.

"No way. Not until I know you understand." I take her by the chin, lifting it so we're eye to eye. "I'm the one with the power here. And you are going to behave yourself. Not because I give a shit whether some frat boy uses and discards you like a cum-filled tissue, either. Because it's my job."

Something I don't recognize flashes in her eyes, drawing her brows together in what looks like sadness. Hopelessness.

"Tell me you understand," I mutter, my fingers pressing against her jaw a little tighter with each passing moment she's silent. "Tell me, or else we can stand here like this all night."

She trembles, but something tells me it's not from fear. More like blinding rage. "I hate you."

"Is that a yes?"

"Fuck, yeah. It's a yes, you bastard." My arm loosens, and she shoves herself away from me before running to her room and slamming the door loud enough that the walls shake.

One night down. One night when I was barely able to hold on to myself long enough not to cross the line.

How many nights like this do I have left in me?

Because something tells me I might have won the battle, but the war is far from over.

8
MIA

I'm still so embarrassed after the scene Zeke made Saturday night; I don't know how I'm going to show my face in class.

And he doesn't care. That's the worst part. If anything, he was proud of himself for humiliating me. He wouldn't tell me how he found me, either. I can only guess he tracked me electronically. I have nothing of my own. Not even privacy.

We spent the entire day avoiding each other yesterday, with him in his room most of the time. He set the alarm and of course, didn't bother sharing the code with me, so I don't know how to open the front door without setting off a siren loud enough to make my ears bleed.

And I can't even complain to my father because I know he's behind this. Somebody had to pay for this expensive system. Somebody had to give Zeke instructions since he can't think for himself.

Though I doubt he feels sorry for it. No, I think he's getting off on it a little bit.

One thing I know for sure: I can't hide in my room for the rest of my life. Not only would word get back to my father, but it would mean letting Zeke win. No way am I doing that. Instead, I get dressed in my best new clothes and spend an hour on my hair and makeup. Might as well make a good first impression on anybody who didn't witness the fight.

"How do I look?" I do a little spin for him when I find him waiting for me by the front door. Not that it matters, but he can't pretend he doesn't look at me the way a man looks at a woman. He notices, even if he doesn't want to do anything about it.

"You look like somebody about to start the first day of school. Want me to take a picture to commemorate?" he asks with a nasty little smirk.

"Are you kidding? I'm surprised you haven't already done it to prove to my dad what a good little employee you are." It kills him when I say things like this, so obviously, I'm not going to stop. We ride the elevator down to the lobby in silence, with him brooding and me wondering how I'm supposed to walk around campus with a guard dog at my heels. Why don't I carry around a big neon sign pointed straight at me? I'm like a circus freak.

"This would be a lot better if I could've bought my books yesterday." He's right by my side like a good little lapdog as we cross the campus, a campus I didn't even get the chance to explore yesterday because I was locked up at home. There's nothing like the feeling of sitting there, watching everybody going about their lives while I'm stuck in place.

"You'll live. I don't think they jump right in on the first day."

"And how would you even know that? You didn't go to college."

He lets out a low growl that I guess is supposed to scare me. "No, but I did a little reading yesterday. You're allowed to add classes up to the end of the first week of the semester. Why would they jump into lessons the first week and leave new students behind? You'll get a syllabus or whatever today."

The worst part is, he's probably right. I don't bother answering, trying instead to look around and take everything in. It's a gorgeous place, and I wish I could fully enjoy it. It's exactly what I always imagined college would look like, but that was back in the day when I knew I would never be able to afford it. Not anything as nice as this, anyway. Community college was as high as I could hope to reach when Mom was alive, and it was just the two of us. Now I'm strolling through campus with a bunch of kids who've never had to cook a meal for their parent on a stove where only one of four burners worked—or cooked a meal at all.

If anybody thinks it's weird for me to have Zeke following along, they don't make it seem that way. I have to remind myself these kids grew up with money. Maybe this won't have to be so bad, so long as Zeke keeps his mouth shut and fades into the background the way he's supposed to.

Though how a towering wall of muscle with a face that looks like it belongs on one of those old Renaissance statues can fade into the background is a mystery. He catches the eye of more than one girl on our way to the Science and Behavior building at the far northeast corner of campus. He's wearing his aviators, so I can't tell if he notices—though his lips twitch a little every time I shoot him a look.

My first class is Intro to Psychology, in one of those big lecture halls like a stadium or theater with staggered rows. I sit near the back, with Zeke sitting in the empty row behind me. He was right—all we're getting today is a syllabus and a brief rundown from the professor before being dismissed. I only glance Zeke's way long enough to see his knowing little smirk.

I have an hour break between my first and second class, longer thanks to us getting let out early. It doesn't make sense to go all the way back to the condo, though, just to come back out again. If I was by myself, I would go exploring. With Zeke on my ass, I doubt I would enjoy it. "I guess I should go to the bookstore." I look up at him, smiling wide. "You can carry my books for me. I'm sure Daddy wouldn't want me to lose them."

He arches an eyebrow but settles for snorting. He wants to be a servant? I should start treating him like one.

That's why I don't bother getting a cart or a basket when we enter the store. I pull out my class list and go through the rows one by one, picking up books. Some of the class materials are totally digital, but there are a couple of thick texts required by other instructors. "Here you go." I drop what has to be at least a thousand pages into his waiting arms. There are a couple of girls at the end of the row who, of course, can't help but stare at him. I shoot them a look, and they turn away, whispering to each other.

Once again, the idea of him hooking up with somebody while we're here makes my stomach churn. When I glance his way from the corner of my eye, I can tell he noticed them. Is he trying to fight off a grin? He's so snide, so full of himself. "Here." I drop another book in his arms, then move on to my last class. "Hurry up."

"Drop the act," he mutters, following close behind.

"What act? You're the one who announced yourself to everybody two nights ago. You want to strut around like you own me?" I smirk at him over my shoulder. "Then I'm going to let everybody know why you're really here."

"I'm not your servant."

"No, you're my father's servant. Keep that in mind, or else I might have to tell him you're flirting with girls while you're here."

"You think that was flirting?" His nasty laughter rings out. "You have no idea."

"I do know a few things." I find the last of my textbooks and drop it on the pile he's carrying. "I guess that's it. Let's get out of here. I could use a cup of coffee." There's a coffee shop next to the bookstore, so we head there after I use my student ID to put my textbooks on the account Dad set up for me.

"And can I get you anything?" The girl behind the counter is all smiles when she sets eyes on Zeke, standing next to me with my books in a bag. I have to bite my tongue before the impulse to tell her he doesn't matter becomes too much to fight. I can't help it. He needs to be put in his place. But I know that would only make me look petty and childish, and I don't want to get that reputation around here. It's not a very big school, and I'm sure people talk.

"I'm good." It's barely a grunt, and I have to press my lips together tight to keep from reacting to how surprised the girl is. I guess she expected him to be friendly. Sorry to burst her bubble, but he's the opposite.

I pull out my bank card and hand it over after placing my order, then look around the store. It's cute, with funky music coming from the speakers and a relaxed vibe. I could see myself hanging out here, but only if I didn't have a chaperone. Why does he have to make everything difficult?

The girl clears her throat, and I turn my attention back to her. "Um, it's not working." She tries to smile, but it comes off as more like a grimace.

"My card? It should be okay. It's practically new. The bank just sent it."

"Let me try it again." She swipes it, then frowns at her screen. "Yeah, I'm sorry. It's saying to call the bank."

I know I didn't do anything wrong, and there's plenty of money in my account. But this kind of situation leaves a person feeling like a deer in headlights no matter what. There are people all around us, and I can feel their eyes on me. They know I'm a fake. I'm not one of them. A flush creeps up my neck, and I feel sweaty all of a sudden. "Let me call my dad. Maybe he put a hold on it or something." I step out of line and take my phone from my bag with shaking hands. I don't even know if Zeke follows, and I don't care.

Once I'm outside, I call my father. He picks up on the first ring. "What's wrong?" He always sounds like there's some kind of catastrophe going on.

"Uh, hi, Dad. I just tried to get a coffee with my bank card, and they told me there's a problem. I just used that card to pay for makeup online a few days ago. I swear, there was money in the account. I didn't overdraw on it."

I expect him to get upset or to promise some idiot bank teller will lose their job over it. But all he does is make an understanding sound.

"There's plenty of money in your account, sweetheart. But your card isn't going to work."

"Why not? It's practically new. It doesn't expire for—"

"Zeke will take care of it. If you need to buy something, he'll pay for it."

It's like we're speaking two different languages. "I don't understand. Why? You know I'm not going to waste money."

"I know, and you have all the money you need. But Zeke will take care of it."

"But why?" I hate how whiny my voice sounds, and I try to change its tone. "Dad, please. Can't I at least be trusted to handle my own money?"

He's quiet for a second, and now I know I'm in for it. "Mia, have I ever denied you anything?"

You mean besides your presence in my life for the first seventeen years of it? "No."

"No matter what you want, Zeke will make sure you get it—so long as it's legal," he adds in a stern, fatherly tone. He's got to be talking about alcohol. "But I know how teenage girls can be. You're away from home, you get a little freedom, and that's it."

That's it? He doesn't have the first clue about teenage girls, and especially not about me. I'm practically vibrating with rage and humiliation. My eyes keep trying to fill with tears, but I blink them back because I am not going to break down on the sidewalk. "Please, Dad. At least let me be able to go get a cup of coffee when I want to."

"Zeke will be with you. Zeke will pay for it. End of story. Now, if you don't mind, I'm busy—and you have another class coming up pretty soon." Of course, he's completely aware of every class, of my entire schedule. He's following along from home like my life is some kind of game he can check in on every once in a while.

"Okay." I mean, what else is there to say? There's no use trying to fight because he's always going to win.

I drop onto a bench near the entrance of the coffee shop, feeling just about as helpless as I ever have. When he came into my life, and I found out how rich he was, I actually thought all my problems were over. I wouldn't have to wonder how the bills would be paid. I wouldn't have to worry about being sick, knowing I couldn't afford to go to the doctor. I would have someplace to live and everything I could ever want.

I never figured there would be so many conditions.

"Here. Your coffee." A cup appears in front of my face, Zeke's hand wrapped around it. "I took care of it."

"Of course, you did." I take the cup from him, but now I don't want it. I have to force myself to take a sip, and the icy coffee does help cool me off a little. "You knew about this, didn't you? You must have. He had to tell you when he gave you the debit card."

He jams his hands in his pockets with a sigh. I glance up in time to check out his sharp profile as he looks up and down the street. "I did."

"But you let me stand in there and be humiliated. You knew my card wouldn't work, but you let me try to use it." My voice trembles thanks to the tears determined to spill onto my cheeks. I won't let it happen. I have to go to class soon, and I don't want anybody knowing I was crying. Normally, I'd figure nobody would notice—it's the first day of school, everybody's too busy worrying about themselves—but I have a six-foot-three god attracting attention, so of course, people are going to notice me.

"And you're the one who had me follow you around the store carrying your books. I guess I figured you deserved it." Our eyes meet, and he looks away. "But that was a dick move. I can admit that."

It's like some kind of miracle. All it took was me almost breaking down for him to admit he's being a dick. "You know, there will be times I need to order stuff online."

"And if that time comes, we'll figure something out. I guess your dad figured if you're going to the store, I'll be with you anyway. So what difference does it make?"

I roll my eyes. "You know it makes a difference."

"Yeah." He sighs again. "I know. Come on. You're going to be late for class."

Lucky me, having so many people who care whether I'm punctual. I get up and drag my feet a little, headed for the building where the arts and languages classes are taught. Intro to Writing. I was actually kind of looking forward to this class, but now it's not easy to look forward to anything.

Once again, girls stop and stare like Zeke is swinging his dick around in the open. Do they recognize us from the party, or am I being paranoid? If I'm not careful, I'll lose my mind before the first week is finished.

I wonder if anybody who notices us walking past can guess I'm living in a cage.

I wonder how long it will take before I'm finally free—if that day ever comes.

9
ZEKE

This is so goddamn boring.

I have to keep telling myself how much worse things could be. I could be out there wondering where my next paycheck's coming from. I could be stealing, or worse, in prison, all because I was trying to find a way to put food in my mouth at the end of the day.

When I look at it that way, sitting in this lecture hall, lurking around in the back like I'm not supposed to be here—which I'm not, really—is a pretty cushy gig. It doesn't mean I have to like it.

Especially when I have to sit here behind Mia and watch her every move. Do I technically need to follow the way her fingers fly over her laptop keys? Do I have to notice every time she shifts her weight, every time she twirls a strand of hair around a finger as she's listening to the instructor? Her father didn't order me to trace the curves of her body with my eyes, either, but that's exactly what I'm doing this morning. She's so fucking tempting. Right in front of me, and I'm not allowed to touch. How much self-control is a man supposed to have?

It's been ten days since we got here, ten of the longest days of my life. Only the constant reminder that her father is watching, paying attention to everything she does, keeps me centered. He might not be living with us, but he looms large.

I wish I could tell her how bad I felt about the money situation. I don't think it's fair any more than she does. I even considered taking money out of the ATM so she could have some cash to carry around, but I have no doubt her father would have me on the phone within an hour, demanding to know why she needed to take money out. For a guy with all his wealth, he's pretty fucking stingy.

It's all about control. That's all he knows. Mia doesn't understand him the way I do. He didn't come from some wealthy family any more than she or I did. The Morelli family was low-level back when he was a kid, existing on the fringes of the more powerful players. Morelli's old man had a talent for being in the right place at the right time and knowing how to make himself useful. In our world, being useful is right up there with being faithful. If you know how to contribute and can keep your mouth shut, you have it made.

Bruno followed in his father's footsteps and capitalized on the foundation he put in place. Now he's the big shot, the one controlling all the other families, thanks to his control of harbors up and down the coast. Not to mention his hold on too many shady businesses for me to keep track of. Prostitution, drugs, even trafficking. I know he has a hand in all those things—we don't have to sit down and have a chat about it, but I do have ears. I'm observant.

And he won't even let his daughter use her own bank card.

"It's to keep her safe," he told me when we were finalizing a few details before leaving for good. "This way, nobody can track her activity." I was a split second away from asking if he's really that worried about her. If he honestly thinks somebody would be that determined to get to her as a way of getting to him. It's paranoia; it has to be.

But can I take that chance? She drives me out of my fucking mind, but I'm not a child. I know why she makes me crazy, and it's not because she's a brat or because she stomps around and pouts when she doesn't get what she wants.

It's because I can't have her. Because I want her more than I want oxygen, and I know she wants me, but it can't happen. I hate her because it's easier than hating myself.

The sweet scent of her shampoo and the perfume she spritzed on this morning does things to me no woman has ever done with both hands and her mouth. I'm rock-hard, grateful there's a desk covering my lap. There's nothing for me to do but stare at her, imagining how she tastes. How I would make her come on my tongue while her long, slender fingers tangled in my hair. How she'd moan my name until her voice broke.

And then, I'd take her. I'd break her down with every stroke into her tight little pussy. I'd be her first, and I'd make her remember it always. No man would ever measure up after what I'd do to her. The thought of it makes me smile to myself, even though my straining cock is trapped in an almost brutally uncomfortable way.

A quick check of the time tells me I only have a few minutes before class ends, so I need to get myself together. The memory of my last job before Mia came to live with the boss is enough to defeat me. What a clusterfuck that was. For all I know, it could be the reason I was assigned this bullshit detail in the first place. Payback for dropping the ball and almost getting some of the family's top men killed in the process. Everybody makes mistakes—at least I can say it was one of the very few I've made while working for Bruno Morelli.

Of course, people start getting their shit together before the instructor is even finished talking. One thing I've noticed about Mia: she waits until class is dismissed. She knows how to be polite, unlike these spoiled little shits. Half of them slump down in their seats and fall asleep during the lecture, for fuck's sake. They can't even be bothered to pretend to give a shit. It's enough to make me want to ask them who the hell they think they are and whether they think they could survive five minutes in the world Mia and I come from.

I'd remind them how lucky they are, too, but the truly lucky never appreciate it.

Mia closes her laptop and slides it into her bag before standing. Right away, I notice the way a few of the guys nearby admire her ass. One of them, in particular, sets my teeth on edge. He's always wearing pajamas and the same knit cap, always looking like he just came in from a party or from some girl's bed. I bet if I got close enough to him, I'd smell pussy on his breath. And he thinks he has the right to look at her? To even be in the same room?

"Hey. Can you hear me?" Mia snaps her fingers close to my face, startling me out of staring at the douchebag, who's now slinging a backpack over one shoulder.

"Don't snap your fucking fingers at me," I warn. "I am not in the mood."

"Like you ever are." She rolls her eyes at me. "I said your name, like three times, and you were too busy staring into space. What do you even do, sitting here all this time?"

"I pay attention to the instructor, obviously." I follow her to the door close to my seat.

"Maybe I should send you to class instead of me on the days I don't feel like going."

"Right. Like I would leave you home alone."

"Of course not. What was I thinking?" She's hardly paying attention to what she's saying, though, too busy watching a group of girls getting together outside the lecture hall. They're all on their phones, laughing about something, and she can't hide her sadness.

"Come on." I tuck a hand around her elbow and pull her down the hall. "You know your dad doesn't want you making friends with just anybody."

"He doesn't want me to make friends with anybody, period, and you know it." Her heavy sigh threatens to work its way into my sympathy. "Why am I even here? What's the point?"

"To get an education, obviously. Be glad somebody is looking to foot the bill."

"Do me a favor and never say that again. I don't need you to guilt-trip me." We emerge from the building, stepping out into sunlight bright enough to make me reach for my sunglasses. At least it's a pretty campus, the sort of thing you see in movies about rich, preppy kids. A bunch of guys is playing football on a grassy field in the center of the buildings surrounding it, and a cluster of girls are sitting around watching and laughing and taking video.

And for a second, I do feel sorry for Mia. It's so obvious she wants to be part of it, but there's no way. I have to make sure she hangs out with only the right people. How the fuck am I supposed to know what that even means? Does he want me to run a background check on everybody she meets? I guess a guy with so much on his mind can only think about so many issues at once. He didn't think this part through.

I can't believe I'm about to say this, but the look on her face is going to bug the shit out of me for the rest of the day if I don't. "You wanna go over and watch with them? I can hang out nearby."

She studies me with obvious doubt, and I can't blame her. I'd want to know what was up if I was her. "You're serious?"

"Yeah. What? You think I want to be the only person you talk to on this whole fucking campus? No, thanks. Find some friends or something." I lift my chin in the direction of some girls I kind of recognize from her writing class. "Go ahead. Say hi or whatever people do when they're trying to make friends. I wouldn't know."

"There's a big surprise." But she goes anyway, without giving me another look. I treat myself by watching the way her ass sways back and forth in the tight jeans she's wearing. I'll be thinking about that later when I'm alone in my room. I'm going to chafe like hell with all the jerking off I've been doing. It can't last forever. I'm going to break eventually.

"Hey." I look down to my left and find a petite blonde smiling up at me. She shades her eyes from the sun, squinting still. "I've seen you around campus. No offense, but you look a little older than the other incoming freshmen."

"I'm not a freshman."

"Oh. That must be why. Are you the one with that hot motorcycle? I've seen you riding around school." I've ridden my motorcycle exactly one time since we moved in, and that was when I took Mia home from that party. Otherwise, we've done a lot of walking since campus isn't that far from the condo.

"Yeah, I ride a Harley."

I swear to God, she purrs. "That is so sexy. I've always wanted to ride on a Harley."

"That's cool. Maybe one day you will." I swivel around, looking over at Mia chatting with the other girls. She looks at me, and something passes over her face, something I don't recognize. When she's not stripping down and throwing herself at me, she looks at me like I'm barely a bug she can crush under her shoe. This isn't that.

Especially when she goes from looking at me to looking at the girl next to me.

"I mean, if you were ever free, I'd love to go for a ride." This girl can't take a fucking hint, can she? "You could be my first." Even if she didn't bite down on her glossy lip, I would know exactly what she's talking about. She isn't being subtle.

She also isn't Mia.

Still, I give her the closest I can come to a smile. "I'm usually pretty busy. Are you a freshman here?"

Her head bobs up and down. "So why are you here, anyway? You're not a student. Are you a teacher's assistant?"

"He's here with me." Mia almost knocks the girl over when she reaches us. "We've got stuff to do, so see you later." Next, she does something she's never done before: takes my hand and holds it tight before leading me away. I don't know what part of this is more surprising.

I wait until we're a little farther away before asking, "What was that? I thought you were hanging out with those girls."

"Yeah, I was. I'll see them in class tomorrow." She throws a look over her shoulder before dropping my hand. At least she doesn't rub it on her pants like I'm diseased. "But I have to get home and finish my reading for tomorrow's sociology class."

"You only have that class twice a week. You didn't do the reading yet?"

The look she shoots me could melt steel. "I'm sorry. I didn't know you were here to be my motivational coach, too. In case you missed it, I have other classes to do work for."

"Trust me. I know." I have to hear all about it while I'm sitting behind her.

I can't help but look over my shoulder again. The blonde is gone, probably bitching to her friends about the skank she met who cockblocked her. "It's just that your timing was pretty funny."

"It didn't seem so funny to me." It's amazing how she can talk with her jaw clenched as tight as it is. "You're here for me, not to flirt with the other girls."

"Really? You think your dad would hold it against me if I wanted to get my dick wet?"

She cringes and folds her arms over her midsection. Her shoulders are up around her ears, and her chin is jutted out far enough that if she turned a corner, it would appear first before the rest of her face. "You don't have to be disgusting about it."

"Did I offend your virgin ears?"

"Shut up already."

"Come on. You're not that much of a prude. I know better than that."

"And what is that supposed to mean?" She stops dead in the middle of the sidewalk and glares up at me.

"Come on. Knock off the bullshit. We both know what I'm talking about." Maybe I shouldn't have said that since it would be better for both of us if we forgot that night by the pool. Not that I ever could in a million years, especially considering how many jerk-off sessions have been inspired by that night. If I started describing them now and didn't stop until tomorrow morning, I doubt I would cover the full length and breadth of what I've imagined doing to her. How many positions. How many ways I've made her come in my imagination. "I might be your bodyguard, but I'm not a monk. I do think about fucking every once in a while, and..."

My head swings to the left, to the right. Sure, there are cute girls around. Hot, even. Every ethnicity, every size, and shape, every sense of style. I could take my pick of whatever I'm in the mood for. But I'm not in the mood for any of them. None of them compare to the pain in the ass still glaring up at me like she wouldn't mind me getting struck by lightning.

"And there's plenty of eye candy to get my imagination going," I finish. It's a lie, but she doesn't know it. And she's terrible at hiding what's going on in her head, like the anger simmering under the surface.

"Oh, I see. So it's okay for you to talk about wanting to get laid, but I'm not even allowed to go to a party and meet new people. Yeah, that's totally fair." She stomps off again, her ponytail swinging back and forth like one of those old clock pendulums. It's almost hypnotic.

I lengthen my stride a little to catch up—it's not hard, considering the difference in our heights. "Lighten up, princess."

"For the last time—"

"Sorry. Old habits die hard."

"I do have a name. You can just call me by my actual name, you know."

"I'll keep that in mind." We're headed for the coffee shop, which is where I can only imagine she wants to stop before going back to the condo. I have her bank card in my wallet as always.

I don't know exactly how much is in her account, but the way he made it sound, the sky is the limit. The fact that he knows he can trust me with her account is almost humbling. But I've definitely proven myself, haven't I?

We get to the door, and I reach for the handle, but Mia doesn't follow. "What? You didn't want a drink?"

She glances inside before looking up at me, and the smirk she's wearing doesn't bode well. "You know what? You already know what I like. Go in and get it for me. You're the one paying for it, anyway." With that, she plops down on one of the benches in the front and pulls out her phone, thumbs flying over the screen.

So that's how it's going to be, huh? Putting me in my place whenever she thinks I've stepped out of line. If it wasn't for that girl coming on to me earlier, I doubt she would be this pissy.

And it's only because of that—knowing she's obviously burning with jealousy—that I go into the shop wearing a grin. If it's this easy to push her buttons when I'm not even trying, how much more fun will it be to push them on purpose?

Princess Mia might not know it, but she just made my time at this school a lot more interesting.

10
MIA

"All right, I'll need you to break down into groups of four." The instructor stands at her desk in the front of the room and waits for us to shuffle around and find our study group arrangements.

I can't pretend it doesn't make me feel good when Posey immediately turns around and points at me, eyebrows raised. I nod quickly and try to hide my happiness. How pathetic. Am I that desperate for friendship? The desk next to mine is now empty, so she scoots over and plops down in the chair. "Awesome. I was afraid she would assign us to people we didn't know."

"I know, right? I didn't think we'd have our own choice." I look around the room, letting my gaze drift over Zeke like I don't even notice him. Like I'm not constantly aware of his presence. He's sitting by the door, one ankle crossed over the other knee while he slouches in his plastic chair. He could be asleep with his eyes open for all I know. He's not moving.

I can't help but want to ask Posey if it's weird, him being here, but I also don't want to draw even more attention to him.

Another girl comes over, tucking her bright pink hair behind one ear before pointing at the empty desk in front of me. I wonder how I'd look with hair that color. I've always wanted to try. "Do you have room for another?" she asks, pointing at the nearest empty desk.

"Sure!" Posey reaches over to the desk and pulls it closer while introducing herself. I wish I had her confidence. I guess it comes from growing up privileged and believing the whole world will move out of your way when you want it to. I might have the same resources at my fingertips that she has, but I don't have that deep, ingrained belief. I wonder if I ever will.

"Lucky me." A guy I recognize from class but haven't yet met slides into the desk in front of Posey. "Finding three gorgeous ladies in need of a study partner."

"Who says we're in need of a partner?" I ask. "Maybe we were waiting for the fourth girl to show up."

"If that's true, I'll get up right now." He shrugs and tries to hide a playful grin. "Four girls pulling all-nighters to get their project finished? I think I watched a movie like that once."

"We have room," Posey tells him. "But are you sure you don't want to group up with your bros?" She nods toward a cluster of guys near the back of the room dressed the way he is: jeans, hoodies, ball caps. It's like their uniform. Somebody spent a lot of money so they could look sloppy.

He scoffs, rolling his eyes. "No, thanks. I was thinking maybe I could pull a decent grade in this class if I had study partners who actually want to, you know, study." He flashes me a grin, and I can't help but grin back. He's got that kind of personality that makes people feel easy. "I'm Dean Saunders."

"Mia Casteel." I don't know what gave me the confidence to announce my name like that before he even asked. The girls introduce themselves, too. Zoe obviously thinks he's cute—which he is—and Posey immediately jumps in as the group leader.

"Once we get our assignment, we can break down the work." Without waiting to see if everybody agrees, Posey gets up and goes to the front of the room to get our assignment for the project.

I can't help but sigh and wish I was more like her. "She's going to make a kick-ass CEO someday."

"Or she'll just sit back and live off her trust once she turns twenty-one." Dean lifts a shoulder. "That's what I would do."

"Oh, I didn't know you knew Posey."

"Her dad's some big finance guy in Chicago. You never heard of him?"

Now I want to melt into my chair. Zoe is looking at me with interest, too. "No, I don't pay attention to stuff like that, I guess."

"Trust me, she'll be fine no matter what. Unless she wants to take over the company, but I don't think her brothers would want her to do that." He jerks his chin at me. "What about you?"

"What about me?"

"You're the girl who walks around campus with Frankenstein trailing you all the time." He turns in his chair, looking toward the back of the room. "And there he is."

I don't know whether to laugh or cringe. "Are you serious? Is that what people think? Has word, like, spread or something?"

Zoe at least looks sympathetic. "Not like it's a bad thing. Lots of us know what it's like to have bodyguards or security or whatever."

"Just not here, at school," Dean finishes. "Sorry. I wasn't trying to make you feel bad. I was only making a joke."

"It's okay. Yeah, my dad is super overprotective." I roll my eyes and try to laugh it off, and it's obvious from their expressions they can relate.

"If anything, my family is probably glad to have me out of the house. Out of sight, out of mind, right?" Dean and Zoe exchange a knowing look like they can relate to each other. I wonder if my dad feels the same way. I guess I could understand if he did since he's not used to having a daughter in his life in the first place. I must have mixed things up for him. Now things can go back to the way they were before.

Posey returns wearing a triumphant smile. "We're group number three. We'll be studying the effects of organized crime on society."

Dean sits up a little straighter. "Sweet. I volunteer to watch *Scarface* and take notes."

Posey looks him up and down before scoffing. "Don't even pretend you don't have a *Scarface* poster in your room."

"How the hell did you know that?"

"Lucky guess." She rolls her eyes, making me and Zoe giggle.

"Well, I'll do it. You're welcome." He folds his hands behind his head and wears a shit-eating grin.

"Thanks for your help. I wouldn't want to have to watch it myself." I pretend to gag, and the girls laugh while Dean only shakes his head.

"You don't know what you're missing."

"Oh, I haven't missed anything. I've watched that movie. I just don't wanna watch it again." I offer a shrug. "To each their own."

"I think we are missing the point here." Of course, Posey would be the one to bring us all back around. "We're going to have to research different eras. Prohibition is a big one. Then there were all kinds of turf wars. Money laundering fronts. Trafficking rings. How do those activities affect communities and society as a whole?" I can't help but feel more interested in the project as she goes on. Call me a nerd, but I love learning about stuff like this.

"You know, I did see a TV documentary once that said Prohibition was what brought organized crime to the forefront in the US. If it hadn't been for that, they might have had to find a foothold someplace else, in another industry."

"Then you would be perfect to continue the research on that era. If you're interested."

"Sure. That would be great." I type a quick note on my laptop. I'm actually looking forward to it. God, no wonder it's so hard for me to make friends. Though really, now that we've been sitting around and chatting for a minute or two, it seems dumb that I was ever nervous. This isn't high school. And I'm not the poor girl anymore. I need to remember that.

"Maybe we should all get together and talk about this after class,"

Dean suggests. "Maybe we could all hang out at my place tonight. I was going to the Pi Beta party, but we could always pregame there before heading over."

Zoe bursts out laughing, swatting at him. "Wow, slick."

"Yeah, way to invite three girls over to your place so we can drink." Posey rolls her eyes. "Amateur."

"Have a little more faith in me," he begs, his eyes landing on me. "Well, are you going to bust my balls, too? Come on, I can take it."

"You better be careful, or somebody would say you have a fetish for getting your balls busted." Posey bursts out laughing and high-fives me before the instructor shoots a warning look our way. We're definitely the loudest group in the room.

"I was opening my home to three lovely young ladies," Dean explains in a prim little voice. "And as any good host would, I've offered the contents of my liquor cabinet to my guests."

"That's fine, but let's leave the whole study group pretense out of it, yeah?" We exchange a smile, and it occurs to me he's pretty cute. One of those all-American boy faces with a square jaw and big, blue eyes. The little bit of hair peeking out from under his cap is the color of wheat. And when he smiles, he flashes dimples that threaten to make my heart flutter.

This is getting more interesting by the second.

A sudden, jarring cough from the back of the room makes me jump. That asshole. God for-fucking-bid, I smile at a guy. I won't look at him; I absolutely will not give him the satisfaction of knowing he caught my attention.

If Dean noticed, he doesn't show it. "Does that mean you would come over anyway?"

"Um, we're supposed to be talking about the project," Zoe reminds us. I get the feeling she doesn't like the way Dean is focused on me. Posey, on the other hand, is in her own world, typing notes faster than I've ever been able to type anything on my keyboard. She's not even looking at the keys. If we weren't the same age, I'd say I want to be her when I grow up.

"Of course we are." I know better than to promise things I can't follow through on, and the fact is, I might talk a big game, but I don't know how much I can get away with. Not yet. "I hate to say it, but if we're going to get together to talk about our progress, I might have to ask for, like, Zoom calls or a group chat or something. For now, anyway."

"Right. Frankenstein wouldn't want you out of his sight, would he?" Dean shoots a look toward the back of the room, where I know Zeke is probably glaring straight back at him. I didn't know I had this much self-control, enough to keep me from craning my neck to see Zeke's reaction for myself. I can almost feel the rage coming from him, though, all the way across the room. He doesn't want me for himself, but nobody else can have me, either. It's disgusting.

But what Dean said is right, even if I don't like it. "Yeah, things are a little weird. We're still kind of getting our footing. I don't think my dad really understood what he was asking him to do before he sent us here."

"Parents never understand," Posey agrees, nodding slowly. "Mine think college is the way it used to be back when they went. So what if that was, like, all the way back in the 90s." Dean and Zoe both grunt their agreement.

It occurs to me I don't know if my dad went to college. I don't know much about him at all. Not that I haven't tried to find out what I can, but he's not exactly Mr. Warm and Fuzzy. If he ever sat down with me for a heart-to-heart the way they do on sitcoms, I'd probably faint.

"Fine. Maybe let's do a Zoom call in a few days after we think about our era and what we're researching." The three of us nod at Dean's suggestion. What a relief. I was afraid things would start getting weird if any of them insisted on me going out with them. Not that I don't want to. I'm just not sure I could manage it, and I don't want to make promises I can't keep.

I don't think I've ever resented Zeke the way I do now. Not even at the party when he made a big scene of dragging me out like he owns me. It was one thing when I was actually going against his rules, but now he's dictating my decisions without lifting a finger. He's in my head.

"No, you know what? If you want to get together tonight or sometime this weekend, I'll make it work." I'm not going to be the poor, pitiful girl everybody feels sorry for. And I'm not going to let Zeke rule my decisions.

Dean's eyes light up. "Yeah? What do you think?" He looks at the girls, both of whom shrug.

"I guess so. I could hang out for an hour or two." Posey looks at Zoe, who nods and tries to look disinterested. I can tell she's anything but. She's barely stopped looking at Dean since he sat down.

"Awesome. Ten o'clock? I'll send you all my address." We exchange contact info, and with each passing second, my determination strengthens. I'm not going to spend all my time here talking to people over a computer. I can't live my whole life locked up.

Once class is dismissed, Dean winks at me. "Let me know if you need any help getting out tonight. I could always come over and talk to Frankenstein for you."

"Thanks, but I have it handled." He really is cute, and he's pretty nice, too. I mean, only a real idiot would think all he wants to do is talk about school stuff, but I don't care. That's not all I'm here for. I'm not trying to lose my virginity to this guy or anything, but drinking and flirting is another story.

"What the fuck was that?" Zeke growls over the top of my head when I meet him at the back of the room. I can only imagine he's looking at Dean. "Who's that asshole?"

"He's part of my study group. God, relax."

"I saw the way he was looking at you."

"Good for you. I guess you don't need glasses yet. Your eyes are working just fine." I make it a point to speed walk away from the desks to the end of the hall and down the steps. He has no choice but to follow me, which means he can't hang around and start trouble with Dean.

"You know he doesn't give a shit about sociology, right? That's not what he wants to study."

"Would you get over it? We're doing a group project, the way everybody else is. Jesus, you'd think this was the Middle Ages or some shit. Like I'm not allowed to talk to any males except for you and maybe my professors." He only growls again, muttering under his breath. There's no need to ask him to repeat himself, and honestly, I don't care.

I'm going out tonight. I'm going to live like a normal person.

Now, all I have to do is figure out how to make that happen.

11

ZEKE

She's up to something.

Here's the thing about Mia: she's a smart girl. Very smart. She pulled good grades in high school, even when her life was shit, and she takes her schoolwork seriously now, too. When she's not studying in her room, she brings her stuff out to the living room so she can have the TV on while she's going over her classwork. She's not screwing around online, either—I try to be subtle, but I check on her from time to time, and she's always typing a report or reading her digital textbooks.

The problem with smart people is sometimes they think they're smarter than they are. They might get a little full of themselves and assume they can get away with anything because they're too clever to get caught. If anything, that makes my job easier, the way she practically broadcasts every thought she's having.

And that means I have to play it smart, too. I've never played chess, and I wonder if this is what it's like. Trying to figure out her next move and how I'll counter that move.

When I reach the apartment after finishing my workout at the gym downstairs, it's obvious something's brewing. For one thing, she's in the kitchen, making a ton of noise. I creep through the living room after taking off my trainers, making sure to stay silent. It's like the old days, doing jobs for the boss. Making sure I go unheard as I stalk through the darkness.

Only I never had to sneak up on a girl cooking dinner.

She doesn't notice me at first, too busy listening to whatever's playing through her earbuds. Considering the way her head bobs up and down, it's music, not one of the podcasts she follows. Something with a good beat, too. She's at the stove, stirring something that smells like onions and garlic. My stomach growls. Just call me Pavlov's dog. One of the things I learned about in Mia's psych class.

And when I start salivating, it's not because of the aroma, more the sight of her ass swinging back and forth. I can't take my eyes off it. What I wouldn't give…

She squeals, both feet leaving the floor when she jumps at the sight of me. She rips out her earbuds, and now I can hear the faint strains of classic rock. "What the fuck? Jesus. Are you trying to scare me to death?"

I almost have to shake my head to clear the cobwebs. It's like I forget how to think when I'm around her. "I live here too, remember?"

"Yeah, thanks for the reminder. Maybe you could, I don't know, announce your presence?"

"Maybe you could, I don't know, not listen to music so loud you don't hear me coming in? I could've been anybody."

"Believe me. If the alarm had gone off, I would've heard it." That, I can't argue with. The siren is almost loud enough to make my ears bleed, but that's how the boss wants it. No chance of her sneaking out unnoticed since half the building would probably hear the alarm going off. Especially since she doesn't know the code to disarm it.

I take a bottle of water from the fridge, looking over at the stove. "What's that?"

"It's going to be chicken and rice, eventually." Yes, there are seasoned chicken breasts on a cutting board and a measuring cup full of rice next to them.

"What's the occasion?"

"Could you not make it sound like a big deal that I'm cooking? Somebody has to make sure we both don't die of massive heart attacks after all the shit food we've been eating." I can't even argue with that. After that first night, I told myself I would never cook for her again if she was going to be an ungrateful brat. That leaves the option of her doing the cooking or ordering our meals. It's not like we can't afford it, but the options aren't always healthy. This might be an elite college, but kids are kids. There's only going to be so many options for salad.

She looks me up and down. "So maybe wash off your stink. Dinner should be ready in about half an hour." She pops her earbuds back in, officially signaling I've been dismissed. For somebody who didn't grow up with hired help, she's damn good at being dismissive.

Let her think she's won. I don't know who she thinks she's dealing with, but she is way off-base if she figures I'll cave because she cooked chicken and rice. I take a quick shower and get dressed even quicker. Am I ever going to be able to relax?

Before I'm finished and out of my room, my phone rings. It's the boss. "Shit," I mutter, closing the bedroom door partway. I can still look out into the hall in case she's planning something. Right now, she's in her room, and I can smell the food in the oven. So far, so good.

I answer the call on the third ring. "Hello, sir."

"How's it going over there? I thought I'd check in for a status update at the end of the week."

"Everything's status quo at the moment."

"My girl behaving herself?" I hear voices in the background, vaguely recognizable. He must be in the middle of something. I can see him sitting behind his desk, with his minions doing his bidding. Of course, I know better than to ask since he would never tell me. He only thinks I didn't pay attention to everything he's tried so hard to hide.

"She's doing great. In fact, she's making dinner tonight."

"Is she? I can't tell you how happy that makes me." He sounds like it, too. He sounds practically overjoyed.

"Yes, she's doing fine. Settling in, all that."

"You keep on her about things like that while you're there. That would be a big help."

"Things like what?"

He makes a vague sort of noise. "You know, domestic stuff. Cooking, housework."

"But you have the housekeeper coming in twice a week already. There's not much for her to do when it comes to that." Damn, now the image of Mia on her knees with a scrub brush is burned in my brain. If the boss wants it, I'd have no choice but to make her do my bidding. Poor me.

"I know, but she should be the one to oversee them. Nobody would expect her to do her own house cleaning when it comes time for her to get married, but she will have to know how to run a big household. As for cooking, I'm sure she'll be expected to do that, so it would be for the best that she stay sharp." He barks out a laugh like something just occurred to him. "Do they have cooking classes at that school? I should have looked it up. Look into that for me, would you?"

This is too bizarre. "She's pretty busy with her current roster. She's doing great, too, with A's on her first two exams."

"Sure, sure." He couldn't sound more bored if he tried. "But that's not what's going to make her husband happy one day, is it? Sitting down at the dinner table in front of a plate of burnt food. I doubt he'll think to himself, well, at least my wife got straight A's in college."

It's not until I look down that I realize my free hand is clenched in a fist. "I'll do what I can."

"Excellent. I knew I could count on you. Everything looks fine as far as her bank statements go, so I see you haven't been letting me down in that aspect, either. I knew I could trust you with this. You have no idea how much it means to know she's safe."

"Thank you, sir."

Someone speaks up in the background, and he mutters in response. "I'll have to let you go now, Zeke. I'll check in soon." He doesn't wait for me to respond before ending the call.

I would ask myself what that was all about, but I already know. Sending her to school is just a temporary solution to his problem—I realize that now. He had to do something with her. He couldn't let her sit around the house all day, bored and ready to get into trouble. And he definitely can't have her around him while he conducts business or using one of his playthings. Aside from her safety, his top priority is making sure she has no idea where his money comes from, what he does to earn it. She has to be completely unaware.

So he sent her away. Not to just any school, but one whose students are from the same economic bracket she now lives in. He might as well have put her in a safe deposit box for the time being until he can sell her off in marriage. That's the endgame. He's going to use her to strengthen his own position, the way he's used her to make himself seem more sympathetic and relatable. Sure, he's ordered the murders of countless men and sold I don't know how many girls no older than his daughter, but now that he's got a kid, he's the big family man.

It never disgusted me the way it does now, though. I've always known how he operates, and I'm the one who's pulled the trigger more times than I can count. I know he uses her, and I always have.

But I also know she wants more than that from life. We don't have to sit down and talk about it for me to know. She's taking this school thing seriously, and it would crush her for him to pull her out of school to marry her off to a stranger.

A stranger who would touch her and claim her body for himself. How the hell am I supposed to let that happen?

* * *

Yeah, she's definitely up to something. Dinner was good, even if I couldn't help but remember the boss's idea about her learning how to be a good wife every time I took a bite. That's another thing she'd be expected to do, cook the meals her husband likes, and make sure his life runs smoothly. Everything to make him happy.

She then cleaned up without complaining. That would be suspicious on its own if it wasn't for what she did next: changing into pajamas and setting up shop on the living room sofa. She painted her toenails and did one of those face mask things while some mindless show played on Netflix. I didn't pay attention—I was too busy wondering what she would do next.

Now it's quarter to ten. I'm nowhere near sleepy, but I make the pretense of being ready to turn in. "Don't forget, the alarm's set," I warn her on my way to my room. She rolls her eyes but says nothing.

How long is it going to take her to try to get out? Even with the bedroom door closed, I hear her moving around across the hall. *Mia, why do you have to make this so hard for yourself? Why do you have to make me do things that will only make you unhappy?* And why the hell do I even care? Maybe I feel sorry for her, but big deal. Nobody ever felt sorry for me, and I still turned out fine.

At just around ten o'clock, my phone pings with an alert from the alarm system. *Front Door Open.*

Son of a bitch. She must have been watching when I put the code in.

At first, as I jump off the bed, it occurs to me that I should let her think she got away with it. Maybe wait until she makes it downstairs or until she's crossing campus. Or maybe I'll track her like I did before, embarrass her again. That might be the only way she'll learn that she needs to behave herself.

But no. Because she didn't learn after the first time, did she? So obviously, that method isn't going to get me anywhere. The fact that she keeps putting me in this position sets my blood to boiling as I start out from my room, almost running for the door. She's already closed it, and the alarm is set again. I punch in the code and fling the door open. The elevator doors are sliding shut.

So I take the stairs. By the time I reach the lobby, her elevator is arriving. I position myself near the doors and lean against the wall, arms folded.

She strides out of the car, and for a second, I feel sorry for her. She's proud of herself. She thinks she got away with something.

Until she catches a glimpse of me. Falling back a step, she lets out a little whimper. It has the strangest effect on me. On one hand, I hate to see the disappointment written on her face.

On the other hand? The fact that she's more than a little afraid makes my cock jump. What kind of person does that make me, getting off on her fear?

I seize on that, taking her by the waist and pulling her back into the elevator car. "You're determined to piss me off, aren't you? What? Did you think I didn't know you had something up your sleeve? Like I couldn't tell you were scheming all day?"

"It's just to study!"

"Bullshit. If you wanted to study with people, you could have said something. But no, you're going out to party."

"I am not! I was meeting up with—" Her mouth snaps shut, her eyes lowering to the floor of the elevator car.

"Meeting up with who?" I loom over her, my chest almost brushing up against her shoulder. That's how close we are, and I can't pretend the proximity isn't doing something to me. I can feel her apprehension like it's soaking into me, and all it does is make me want to punish her. Like I'm feeding on her disappointment. Her fear of me.

Let her be afraid. Maybe that will get it through to her. "Answer me. Who were you meeting up with?"

"None of your fucking business." But there's a tremble in her voice, and she doesn't sound nearly as strong as she did before. She's trying her hardest to stay strong, but she's failing.

"Don't bother." The doors open, and I take her bicep in a vise grip, hauling her over to the apartment door. "I know who you were meeting. That asshole from earlier today, right? What? Did he tell you he wanted to talk about your group project?"

"So what if he did?" The second we're inside, she yanks herself free—then, because she's clearly lost her mind, she puts both hands against my chest and shoves as hard as she can. Not that it does much, but it's the first time she's ever tried something like that.

"Oh? Do you want to play it rough?" Fear blooms in her eyes when I take her by both wrists, hauling her in close. "That's how you like it? Maybe that's what will get through to you. If I push you around a little bit. Maybe that's what will get you to behave yourself."

"Release me," she mutters through clenched teeth. "Now."

"Or what? What are you going to do, princess?" I have to remind myself not to get off on this, but being this close to her, feeling the way she squirms against me as I pull her across the living room to the sofa, has me hard as a rock by the time I sit down, pulling her with me.

"What are you doing?" she asks after she flops down across my thighs.

"I'm making sure you remember next time some douchebag asks you over to his apartment. There are rules you're expected to follow." She can struggle all she wants, but she's no match for me. I hardly have to try to get her over my knee, ass in the air.

"Stop it! You can't be serious!" She kicks her feet and slaps at my legs with both hands, but it's no use. There I was, thinking I'd eventually explode and have to fuck her senseless. I didn't imagine spanking her would be my outlet instead.

"This is the only way you're going to learn." But I'm not going to give her any of that bullshit about it hurting me worse than it hurts her. This isn't hurting me at all. In fact, the first slap against her firm little ass is almost enough to release some of the tension I've been carrying around all these months.

She yelps and tries to claw at my other leg. "Stop it! Right now. I'm serious, Zeke!" She almost has to twist her head all the way around to look up at me. There are tears in her eyes, and my God, it only makes me want more. I deliver another blow—not nearly as hard as I could manage, but hard enough that the crack of my hand against her flesh echoes through the room.

"You will not disobey me again." Another slap, and now I wish I'd gotten her jeans down around her thighs before I started this. My mouth waters at the idea of watching her ass turn darker red with every blow. "Say it."

"No!"

All that earns her is another smack, so hard her entire body tenses. "It's just going to get worse, Mia. I'm going to do this until you get the message. Follow the rules, and this doesn't have to happen again. Got it?" When all she does is fight harder, she gets another slap. My palm is stinging now, but I ignore the sensation in favor of enjoying the position I'm in. She's at my mercy, completely, no matter how she fights. All she's doing is tiring herself out, her kicks weaker, her cries softer.

And if this goes on much longer, I'm going to break the zipper on my jeans. It's painful, my erect cock squashed awkwardly. And every time she squirms, brushing against it, it takes everything I have to keep from groaning.

"Tell me you're going to be a good girl from now on." When she hesitates, I make contact again. She sucks in a breath through clenched teeth but doesn't cry out. "Well? Are you going to say anything? Or do you like this? Is that why you can't help testing me? Did you always secretly hope I would do this?"

She looks at me again, her face dark red, her eyes watering, and I could almost believe I'm right. "Go to hell."

"That's not an answer." I lift my hand menacingly. "I've been holding back so far. Do you want to see what I'm really capable of?"

She's not a stupid girl. Good sense wins out in the end. "Fine. Damn you. Fine. Now let me up."

"Maybe I shouldn't. Maybe I should hold you like this for a while." I bring my hand down, but it's not to spank her. This time, I'm almost gentle as I graze the curves of her cheeks. How many times have I imagined doing this? Even with a layer of denim in the way, it's almost more than I can handle without losing control and tearing her pants off.

And when she shivers—a single spasm almost violent enough to knock her off my lap—I let her go before this can go too far. Hell, I'm thinking it already has.

She doesn't look at me. Doesn't say a word. She goes straight to her room and closes the door. Not even a slam. She only closes it, leaving me alone.

And I do what I know I shouldn't but can't help. I lean back and unzip my jeans, sighing in relief as I free my cock from its prison. I take it in my fist and pump hard, the image of Mia's perfect ass burned into my brain.

She shivered. She wanted it. And dammit, so did I. So much that I couldn't even make it to my room before stroking myself like this, like some depraved fucking lunatic sitting out in the open. "Mia," I grunt under my breath, teeth gritted, remembering how firm her ass is, how easy it was to make her submit.

The first spurt shoots from the tip before I can catch it against my other hand. It splashes over my jeans. Again, and again. My balls empty, the tension slowly easing as I loosen my grip and let my softening dick fall against my waistband.

Tonight, I went farther than I ever should have, and I only want more.

What is she doing to me?

And how much longer until jerking off won't be enough?

12
MIA

What the hell just happened?

I haven't even turned the light on in my room. I can't move. I've been leaning against my door for... I have no idea how long. I can't wrap my head around this. How I'm supposed to feel. What I'm supposed to do next.

It was wrong, wasn't it? What he did was wrong. Spanking me like I'm a child. I don't even think my mom ever spanked me when I was little. But now here I am. My ass stings, and it took all I had not to burst out crying.

At first. When he first threw me over his knee.

After that...

I don't think I've ever been so inexplicably wet. My panties are sticking to my skin. I'm so turned on it hurts. It only got worse every time his hand made contact. Am I one of those people who gets off on being spanked? What the hell am I supposed to do with this new knowledge?

Was it only because the spanking was coming from him? Maybe I wouldn't have gotten off on it if it was anybody else. But I'm not going to go out and experiment with somebody else, either.

My head is spinning. My heart is still racing. How can I face him again?

At first, the idea of calling my dad is appealing. He would never pull anything like this again once Dad found out about it. But at the same time, it would mean getting him in trouble and also getting myself into deep shit. I can't forget that part. That's something he's always going to be able to use against me. Everything he does results from me going against his orders, meaning Dad's orders. I'm always going to be stuck. And it's not like I can make up a reason for him to spank me, either.

If Dad found out Zeke ever so much as laid a hand on me, he could say goodbye to his dick. I have no doubt about that. The one thing Dad wants more than anything else is for me to be pure, untouched. It's gross and intrusive, but I guess he's old-fashioned like that.

When my phone buzzes, it snaps me back into reality. Shit, everybody is waiting for me at Dean's. The text is from Posey. *Where are you? Do you need campus police?*

It's almost enough to make me smile. My dad should take a hint from her: she cares about people she likes, but she doesn't have to be up their ass every second of the day. Though that doesn't mean she won't offer to call for help when somebody is twenty minutes late, which is where I am right now according to the time on my phone.

Sorry, can't make it out. But I'm okay. Have fun, and I'll talk to you later. That will have to be enough for now. I leave the phone on my dresser, dragging my feet across the room. I can't even be all that disappointed about not getting to go out. Not when I don't know how I'm ever going to face Zeke after this.

He had to know. When I shivered, he had to have felt it. It wasn't a shiver of disgust or revulsion or anything like that. I wish it was; that would make everything so much easier. No, that was definitely me shivering with pleasure.

I almost wanted more. I wanted to feel his hand on my bare skin, no pants in the way.

I'm never going to get him out of my system, am I? He's always going to be there, tormenting me. Reminding me of that awful night and how embarrassing it was when he didn't want me. Reminding me he still doesn't want me but making me want him more all the time—God, I do, and I hate myself for it. Why couldn't it be anybody but him?

I undress slowly, taking my time to remove my jeans. I can't help but turn on the lamp on my dresser before turning around to see what he did. There aren't any handprints—I don't know if I'm disappointed or not—but my entire ass is red, and it stings to the touch. But in a good way. Just when I thought I understood my body and the way my brain works, something like this had to happen. What does it even mean? Is it supposed to feel good?

A knock on my door scares me enough that I jump and fumble for my jeans like I got caught doing something bad. "What?" I manage.

"I want to talk to you."

"I think you've said enough already."

"I want to talk for real. Seriously." He sounds serious, too. He also hasn't apologized. I don't know if I'd be wasting my time hoping for an apology, though. Something tells me I would be. Even if he's sorry, he's never going to admit it. That much, I already understand about him.

"Give me a second. I'm getting changed." I hurry through pulling on a T-shirt and sweats before unlocking the bedroom door. I don't open it for him, though, sitting on the foot of my bed instead. It still hurts a little, but not too much. If anything, the ache is nice. I hope he never finds out because I would die of embarrassment.

He opens the door slowly, hanging his head a little. "Hey." I notice he's wearing different clothes now—he was still dressed when he caught up with me, and it occurs to me he never got ready for bed. He was waiting for me to sneak out. I have to take a deep breath and calm myself down enough not to start a fight. If I'm easy to read, that's nobody's fault but my own.

"Hey."

"That might have gotten out of hand." He looks at the floor, the wall, the dresser, my desk. Not at me, though. Running a hand over the back of his neck—the hand he used on me—he grunts softly. "I lost control."

"I know."

Then he does something that takes me by surprise. Instead of growling or acting all macho or whatever, he lets out a soft sigh. The kind of sigh that makes his shoulders slump and his body sort of sag. "We can't keep going on like this." He sounds like himself, but different. Like his whole big, badass image is just that. An image. Something he puts on like he'd put on his leather jacket.

"I agree." I'm not going to give him too much. I want to see where he's going with this.

"So you know. I could yell at you a little more and call you spoiled and stubborn and all that shit, and I partly believe that, but at the end of the day, I think you need to remember you're not the only one who's a little lost in all this."

"You? Lost?"

"Yeah." That's enough to make him look me in the eye, and now I wish I hadn't said anything. There's outright disgust in his eyes, in the way his lip curls. "Lost. Congratulations, you got me to admit it."

"But how? I don't get it."

"Obviously." He hooks his thumbs into his pockets—seriously, even their pajama pants get pockets when I can't get pockets on a simple dress—and lowers his brow. "You think this is fun for me? There's nothing in the world your father cares about more than you, and I'm the person who's supposed to be keeping you out of trouble."

"I wasn't—"

"Let me finish. You might not have gotten into trouble tonight, but that's not the point. I'm supposed to be with you. You know, he calls me at all random times of the day and night. Did you have any idea?"

"No," I admit.

"I'm just waiting for the time he tells me to put you on the phone. He's going to test me, and he's going to test you, too." He sighs again, looking away from me, toward the window. "Do you have any idea the kind of man he is? I mean, really?"

"He's rich, and he has a lot of bodyguards and stuff like that."

"Yeah. He needs bodyguards. Do you think…" He closes his eyes for a second before opening them again. "Do you think he does that because he's paranoid or because there's a reason for it?"

My heart sinks. "What are you trying to tell me?"

"You know what? I don't have the first idea." He chuckles ruefully before looking my way again. God, he's so fucking sexy, it's ridiculous. Now I wish more than ever he had taken things further. I wouldn't have stopped him. "But if he was unhappy with me, rest assured, he'd find a way to let me know. And I wouldn't like it very much."

"I know that."

He throws his hands into the air. "Then why do you keep doing this? This is my ass here. I'm trying to do the right thing by him, and you're making it impossible. I don't like this any more than you do, believe me. You think I want to watch over you twenty-four-seven? You think I wouldn't like to, I don't know, make friends of my own? Have a life? I'm not allowed to leave your side. What do you think that does to me?"

I hate to admit it, even to myself.

I never thought of it that way.

What is wrong with me? I've always thought of myself as a decent person. I mean, I don't go around abusing small animals or anything like that. I always try to be kind when I can. I once kicked the shit out of a bully back in ninth grade when they were picking on another kid.

But I never put myself in his shoes. I've only ever scorned him for doing his job. "That must suck. And it's a lot of pressure."

"No shit." He barks out a laugh that trails off quickly. "So you see the position this is putting me in? I know you don't like it, but this is how it has to be. So we'd better figure out a way to make this work."

"Are you willing to compromise?"

He lifts an eyebrow. "Your father's daughter. Yeah, I'd be willing to talk about a compromise."

Great. Now I have to come up with something. "I can hang out with my friends when I want, where I want, and I understand you'll come with me."

His eyes narrow to slits. I can practically see the wheels turning. "Your friends come here. I know who they are in advance in case I have to do any research into them."

"What? Are you going to run their credit reports?"

"Are you trying to shut down talks here?"

"No, fine. What if I want to go shopping?"

"I'd have to go with you, anyway. Remember? Your card. And no," he adds when I open my mouth, "you're not getting that. Those are the rules."

And he wants me to act friendly when he pulls a stunt like that? "Fine. But we agree I can go shopping if I want to. Or out to get something to eat after class, that kind of thing?"

Again, he narrows his eyes. "I drive the car. You can have people in it with you, but you're not getting into anybody else's car."

I can live with that. "Okay. Agreed. But if I go out to eat, you've got to sit away from us. Like at another table or a booth or something."

"You think I want to hang out with your friends? Give me a break."

"I just wanted to make sure you understood." What else, what else?

He beats me to it. "Going out at night. If you want to go out, I'm coming with you. No, you will not go to any guy's apartment or dorm room or anything like that. That is completely off the table. And if there's going to be guys hanging around, I need to know in advance."

I don't like that at all. But if I shut him down, that's it. I might as well give up. "No guys' rooms or apartments. Okay. But I can't promise there won't be guys anywhere I go. Like, if a friend invites me to her apartment, what if her roommates have guys over? I don't have any control over that."

He folds his arms, pursing his lips as he thinks it over. "Fine. Then I come up with you, and I take a look around. I meet everybody or at least get a look at them. Then I wait somewhere nearby. Balcony, outside the front door, whatever. Close enough that I can get to you fast if you need help."

Now I'm starting to wonder what kind of danger he thinks I'm in. "I doubt I ever will."

"But never say never, right?"

It's like he's waiting for me to get assaulted. "What about parties?"

This, he doesn't have to think about it. "What if we settle for keeping a liquor stash here at the condo, and if you want to hang out with your friends and drink, you can do it here. While I'm here, on the premises at all times."

"How many friends are we talking about here?"

"No more than six at a time."

"You've already thought about this one."

"Hell, yeah, I have. Any more than that, and it gets out of hand."

Only six people at a time—well, considering I've only met a small handful of people so far, that doesn't seem totally undoable. "What about sports events? Football and stuff like that?"

"We can go to those. We, you and I, together. And I will sit next to you, and I'm not going to get any arguments about that. You can talk until you're blue in the face, but you're not going to change my mind."

"Okay."

"You accepted way too fast."

"Because I'm not a total idiot, maybe? I know how to compromise."

"And you will not try to sneak out again."

"Only if you promise not to change the code on the alarm." His head tips to the side. "Come on. Don't pretend you weren't going to do it, now that you know I saw you put it in."

"How do I know you're not going to use it again?"

"That's the point. I want to be able to use it. What if I can't sleep, and I want to go downstairs to work out? What if I get up earlier than you and want to go for a run or a walk or something? I can't sit around and wait for you to get out of bed."

"You're not going for a run or a walk by yourself, remember?"

I roll my eyes, even though I know how immature it makes me look. "You get my point. God."

"You could always wake me up."

"And you could always just trust me to remember a four-digit code and not share it with anybody else. And I won't use it to sneak out, I promise."

"You promise? As in, you swear you're not going to try to sneak out ever again?"

"Could you not make such a big deal about it?" When he only grunts, I sigh in exasperation. "Fine. I promise. I'm not going to try to sneak out again."

"If there's something you want to do, you tell me about it."

"But you're just going to say no."

"Why would I, so long as you're following the ground rules we just set down? I'm going to trust you, but you need to trust me, too. Otherwise, your dad's going to kill us both."

I wish he didn't sound so serious when he said that. Like he means it. Dad wouldn't kill him. No way. He's being dramatic. But I'm not in the mood to argue when he's finally loosening up a little bit. I might be able to have some kind of a life, finally. "Sure. I'll follow the ground rules, but I'm going to trust that you'll do it, too. But no backtracking."

"How would I do that?"

"By pretending this never happened. I'm going to hold you to it."

"That's fine. And I'll do the same." He gives me a short nod. "Now, I'm going to go to bed for real. Just remember, I get an alert on my phone whenever that door opens or closes."

Dammit, I never thought of that. He has an app on his phone connected to the system. "Fair enough," I mutter, even though it's not quite fair. He still has all the power in this dynamic.

At least, that's what I tell myself until he reaches the door, and I think of one more thing. "What about guys? What if I meet somebody? What happens then?"

He freezes, and his hand tightens around the doorknob until his knuckles stand out bone-white against his olive skin. If it wasn't for that, I would think he didn't hear me at all—he doesn't say a word.

"I mean, let's be real. We're both legally adults, so I think we can talk that way." Or so I want to tell myself. My mouth is awfully dry all of a sudden, and my heart reminds me of the hummingbirds that visit the feeder back home. It's fluttering like crazy. "Realistically, there's a chance I could meet somebody and want to date them. What happens then? Are you going to get in the way?"

His exhale sounds a lot like a growl, and it makes the hair on my arms stand straight up. "Maybe we'll deal with that if the time ever comes, huh? I don't think I can stand much more of this tonight." With that, he leaves, closing the door harder than he needs to.

I should've known. At least he didn't forbid me or something medieval like that.

I fall back onto the bed, staring at the ceiling. At least I'll be able to have a little bit of freedom from now on. I can live with that, and maybe, if I prove myself, I can earn a little more. I can get around him. I'll have to be smarter about it than I was tonight, but I can do it. The more time I spend with him, one on one, the easier he is to read. And tonight, I learned two things.

Number one, he's not going to apologize for anything, ever. I notice he didn't apologize for spanking me. He technically didn't even mention it.

Number two? The idea of me dating anybody makes him almost feral with anger.

What if he didn't reject me because he didn't want me, but because he knew he couldn't have me?

And what if I make it clear that he can? At the very least, it'll be fun to drive him nuts. Fair payback for the misery he's put me through with his little comments and remarks. Not to mention for how terrible he made me feel about myself when he rejected me.

I smile slowly as a plan starts to form in my head.

He has no idea what's coming.

13
ZEKE

"Zeke? Can you come help me with something?" Her bedroom door is partly open, but her voice sounds strange. Almost muffled. I hurry out of my own room, where I just finished getting dressed. Monday morning. I guess it could be worse. I could be putting on a suit and tie and wishing I could hang myself with it instead of wearing it to a soulless job working at a soulless company.

Instead, I have the pleasure of stepping into Mia's bedroom and finding her ass in the air. She's wearing a skirt that is short enough and loose enough that it rides up and gives me an almost perfect view of her ass.

And her pussy, covered by a strip of baby-pink lace.

Maintain. You can do this. I take a deep breath and think back on one of the last jobs I pulled before Mia came into the boss's life. Blowing some guy's brains out while he sat behind the wheel of his car. Blood and brains splattered the windshield.

That's enough to make my burgeoning erection go back down real quick. Unlike some of the men I crossed paths with in that line of work, I never got off on killing. It was just another job to be done.

But even dozens of kills never quite hardened me against the aftermath.

"What are you doing?" I ask in a choked voice. She's half under the bed, and her soft grunts only bring to mind the sound she'd make if I was giving it to her from behind. I could step up behind her right now, pull those panties aside, and sink in deep. She'd be so fucking tight. And by the time I finished, she would be begging me to never stop.

"One of my shoes slid under the bed, and I can't reach it. My arm just isn't long enough. I'm going to end up dislocating my shoulder. Can you help?"

"Maybe if you get out of the way, I could." I don't want her to. She could stay that way all day. I could stand here, stroking my cock while her ass sways from side to side, and her pussy plays peek-a-boo.

She backs up, bringing her ass closer, and it's all I can do not to reach out and take her. "I accidentally kicked it under there when I was walking by." She snickers, adjusting her tank top as she stands. "If there was a broom around here, I could use that, but we don't have one."

"Right. I guess your dad assumed we wouldn't need one since the housekeepers come by. We'll have to pick one up." I never thought of it either, and I'm still barely thinking about it right now. I can't take my eyes off her tits in that shirt. "Are you wearing that today?"

"I'm wearing it right this very second." She steps back, shaking her head. "Can you try to get my shoe?"

Am I supposed to let her leave the house in something like this? It's still warm outside, hardly more than halfway through September, but it's not like I'm asking her to wear a full-length gown. "You should cover up a little. Maybe put on a sweater over the top."

"Seriously?" She looks down at herself, frowning. "Does it look bad?"

This is so fucking unfair. "You know you don't look bad. That's the point. What were we just talking about a couple of nights ago?"

"I'm sorry." She folds her arms, the little tease. She has to know it pushes those gorgeous tits together, lifting them like she's offering them to me. How much can a man take? "I didn't know I needed to cover myself from head to toe, too. We never talked about that."

"How am I supposed to keep you out of trouble if you walk around like that?"

"What kind of trouble are you talking about?" She bats her eyelashes, pretending to be shocked. "What? Would a man look at me? Oh, my gosh! What would I do?"

"Quit it," I warn.

"No, you quit it." She drops her arms, which I guess is good even though I'm disappointed. I'm only human. "You might be able to tell me where I can go and who I can hang out with, but you're not going to tell me what to wear. This is my body, and I dress the way I want to. I'm not exposing anything, am I?" She drops her hands to her hips before doing a slow turn. She's mouthwatering, top to bottom.

I drop to my knees next to the bed before she can catch sight of my expression, which by now has to spell out how much I want her. Here and now. "Fine. But don't come crying to me when some asshole thinks he can put his hands on you just because you're walking around looking like that."

"News flash, caveman. We live in the twenty-first century. And I'm wearing the same kind of clothes girls are wearing all over campus." Now's not the time to remind her of the sexual assault stats from college campuses, because yes, I looked them up. I wanted to have one of those facts in my back pocket to throw her way when I wanted to win an argument. Instead of throwing numbers at her, I reach for the sandal and bat it her way, sliding it across the bare floor.

"Thanks." I watch as she slides her foot into it. Even that's sexy. *Focus. Get your shit together.*

It's been like this since Friday night. Saturday morning, she strolled into the kitchen in nothing but a nightshirt, when she always wears sweats or at least shorts to bed. She sat cross-legged on the couch, eating a bowl of cereal and watching TV while I did everything in my power not to stare at her legs and hope she'd shift just the right way to give me a glimpse of something more.

Yesterday morning, she convinced me to take her out for a few new outfits. It was boring as hell, and of course, she made me hold things for her as she picked them off the racks, but that wasn't the worst part. The worst part was coming home and knowing she was trying on her new clothes with the bedroom door partly open. I walked past on the way to my room and found her pulling off a new shirt—and she wasn't wearing a bra. I caught a glimpse of side boob before forcing myself to walk away before she could see me.

Is she doing this on purpose? I don't want to accuse her outright. It will only give her more ammunition against me if she knows I'm dying for her. But if she's doing it on purpose to tease me, I have to stop her. She's just a kid; she has no idea what she's fucking around with.

Yet it would mean admitting she's getting to me. Admitting I notice what she's doing. I don't want that, either. What am I supposed to do here?

I swallow hard to dislodge the lump in my throat before trying again. "Just wear a cardigan. Please. Don't make me tell your father."

"Oh, we're on that shit again?" I have to leave the room. I can't even answer. It's more important to get out of her bedroom, where it would be too easy to throw her on the bed and drape her legs over my shoulders.

* * *

SOMETHING STARTLES ME AWAKE.

My eyes snap open, but I stay perfectly still. Listening. What was it? Did somebody get in? A glance at my phone on the nightstand tells me that's not the case. No new alerts from the alarm system. It's also one thirty in the morning. Mia will be asleep by now.

It must have been something in a dream. Or maybe a bat hit the window—I've seen them flying around at night while sitting out on the balcony. Mia was out there with me tonight, typing something on her laptop, and it was almost nice.

Except for the way she stretched her legs out with her heels on the railing. She was still wearing that skirt, too. I couldn't help but wonder if she was doing it on purpose to get under my skin. It's one thing to fight off cravings for her when all she's doing is existing. When she throws herself in front of me like that, it's another situation. Superhuman levels of self-control.

It's exhausting. I'm so tired that I can't believe anything woke me up.

Then again, men like me rarely sleep deeply. Not when we're always on duty, and I always am. It doesn't matter the time of day or night, whether I know she's sleeping soundly and not a threat to herself. I always have one ear open.

Which is probably why I woke up. It's not that difficult to wake up a light sleeper. Now what? I swing my legs over the side of the bed and rub my eyes before looking around the bedroom. No matter how nice it is, it will never feel like home. It would never be mine, anyway. I'm a guest here. The funny part is, I've saved enough money over the past ten years that I could buy a place like this if I wanted. There's something to be said for disciplined saving, and I have been disciplined. That's one part of my personality that's never changed. I know how to behave myself when I need to. Besides, what did I need? I went from living under my father's roof to living under the boss's. Most of my expenses were taken care of.

It's a catch-22. Something else I learned about in one of Mia's classes —I'd heard the term used before plenty of times but never really understood it. Now, I see that's what my entire life is. One big catch-22. I have all the money I need but no freedom to use it. Why would I buy myself a condo when I'm stuck looking after a little girl? And once the boss marries her off, he'll give me another detail. A good one, I hope, an easy one. I think I've earned it.

But the fact is, no matter what job he gives me, my life will never be my own. That didn't use to matter. I mean, what good is my life, anyway? I never had hopes or aspirations for myself. No plans, no dreams. Survival was always the thing. Pulling the trigger before the other guy had a chance to.

What's so different now?

I get up with a groan since trying to get back to sleep would be useless right now. The idea of going down to the gym and taking a run on one of the treadmills occurs to me, and I even eye up my closet with the thought of pulling on sweats and heading down. First, I want to make sure everything is okay around here, just in case.

There's an almost eerie silence. Only the faint humming from the refrigerator is a sign the world hasn't come to an end. That's how eerily quiet it is as I walk barefoot over the cold, bare floors. Who the hell thought it was a good idea to tile the entry in marble? It's icy under my feet as I punch in the alarm code, then open the door to take a look out in the hall. Everything's status quo. I do the same out on the balcony, making sure it's empty and everything outside looks normal before locking the door, then arming the alarm. It must have been something in a dream that woke me up.

Before heading back to my room, I pause at Mia's door. It's closed, but the walls around this place aren't exactly thick. They put marble on the floors, but the walls are paper-thin. I'm sure if I sat around and thought about it long enough, I'd be able to create one of those metaphor things they talk about in Mia's writing class. Everything looks beautiful and elegant on the surface, but it's thin and cheap underneath.

I turn away, but a soft moan freezes me on the spot. I hold my breath, waiting to see if I hear it again. Was it my imagination?

No. There it is again, a little louder now. I open my mouth, prepared to call her name, but before I can, I hear something else.

"Zeke…"

That, I didn't imagine. She moaned my name. Holy shit.

Now, there's nothing in the world that could get me away from this door. I lean in, pressing my ear to the wood. There's a faint buzzing noise in the room, too. A vibrator? How the hell did she get her hands on a vibrator? I would have known about that. Then again, she could've easily ordered one online over the summer or even before then, for all I know. They sell those things all over the place now, and she could have mixed it in with a bunch of other things she needed. The boss looks at the bank statement but stops short of going through her packages. One little bit of privacy he gives her.

He's probably afraid he'd find her ordering tampons or something else that would embarrass him. He'd be worse than embarrassed if he knew she had a sex toy.

I close my eyes, concentrating on the sound of her soft moans. What would she look like in there? Legs spread, eyes closed, mouth hanging open while her head turns from side to side on the pillow. Her hair would be splayed out in a fan all around her.

Is she dressed? No, I don't think so. I think she would strip down and use her free hand to tease her other sensitive places. Starting with her tits, those perfect tits, her pretty, pink nipples standing out in tight peaks. In my depraved mind, she lifts one of them to her lips and swipes her tongue over the tip. Fuck.

The buzzing gets a little louder. My cock is straining, precum soaking into my boxer briefs. That's all I'm wearing, so there's nothing to hide the erection sticking out in front of me. I run my palm over it and groan softly, lost in the mental image of a goddess splayed out on her bed, getting off while thinking of me. Moaning my name. It's me she's imagining with her, my fingers and tongue against her pussy instead of a vibrator. She's probably soaking wet, lips coated in her juices. I'm not going to be able to handle this much longer before I have to release.

"Oh, yes… yes…" I grit my teeth, fighting the urge to open the door and go in, to take her the way I know she's dying for me to. The way I've been dying to since the day the boss brought her home. This is insane. This can't happen. He'd kill me.

But he's not here. And holy fuck, I'm going to die anyway if I don't do something about this. I've been a fucking saint up to this point.

Nobody would hold out as long as I have. And I don't have to fuck her—she can stay whole or pure or whatever. But dear God, I have to touch her. I need to.

My hand closes around the doorknob, and I test it. I have a key for her room—she doesn't know that, it's one of my many secrets—but I don't need it. She left it unlocked.

There's no going back from this, but that doesn't stop me. Nothing could.

"Mia?" I murmur, opening the door and pretending to be concerned.

It's pitch black in here, but my eyes have already adjusted to the darkness elsewhere. She's frantic, hiding the toy under the bedspread, then pulling it up around her shoulders. "What the fuck? What are you doing?"

"I heard you moan. I thought maybe you were sick." If she can see my stiff cock preceding me, she'll know that's a total lie. She's probably too busy freaking out to notice.

"I'm fine. Since when do you just walk into my room? Please, get out."

"But you were moaning. You said my name. I thought maybe you wanted me." It's evil, what I'm doing, but it's also too much fun to stop. Watching her practically implode with embarrassment. There's a cord running from the outlet closest to her bed. It disappears under the blanket, where she's concealed her toy.

"You're imagining things."

"Are you sure about that?" I walk over to the outlet, bending down to touch the cord. She's breathing fast, in short, little gasps. "What do you have under there? You know it's dangerous to have electric things in bed with you. It could start a fire if you fall asleep."

"What the fuck? It's the middle of the night, and you're going to lecture me?" When I try to pull back the blanket, she only grips it tighter. "What game are you playing?"

"No games." Because I'm sick to death of games. I'm sick of pretending not to want what my soul needs. I stand straight, turning to her, and now there's no missing my erection. Her eyes go wide when she sees it. "We both know what you were doing in here. And you were moaning my name while you did it."

"You're crazy," she whispers, shaking. "This is wrong."

"Is it? Was it wrong for you to parade around here for days wearing practically nothing, hoping to turn me on? Were you trying to drive me crazy? Because if I am now, it's your fault." I lean down, inhaling as much of her scent as I can. "Little princesses need to learn how dangerous it can be to play games with somebody bigger and stronger."

I ease the blanket back, noting how she doesn't try to stop me. Her breathing quickens, and I see I was partly wrong—she's wearing a tank top, but her thong is down around her ankles.

"Spread your legs," I order, staring at the place where her thighs meet. When she hesitates, I look away long enough to meet her wide, untrusting eyes. "Do it."

Her thighs part, and oh, my God, even in the darkness, I can see how her lips shine. Shaved smooth, soft, and slick. "Is this how wet you get when you think about me?" I ask in a whisper before placing a hand on her knee and slowly sliding it over her soft skin. Just as soft as it looks.

"Don't make fun of me," she whispers. "Please."

"I'm not making fun. I only want to know." She closes her eyes and whimpers while my fingers play along the insides of her thighs. I could play with her like this all night if it wasn't for the severe ache from my dripping cock. I'm going to need to do something about that, and soon, but right now, I'm under the spell of the moment. Finally, I put my hands on her the way I've always wanted to after all this time.

She nods quickly, her eyes still closed, tension tightening her muscles. "Oh, God…"

"Nobody's ever touched you like this, have they?" I'm close to her pussy, so close, teasing both of us now.

"No, not ever." Her back arches, thrusting her tits into the air.

Right, because she was meant for me. This body was meant for me. I can't help it anymore. I allow my fingers to graze her slit, picking up her juices, and her moan makes me harder than ever. I stroke her lips, watching her writhe, her tiny little squeals music to my ears.

"No toy could ever do what I can do to you," I murmur, dipping my other hand into my shorts and stroking myself in time with my strokes against her pussy. "Nothing would ever be as good as this. And the next time you touch yourself and think about me, this is what you'll remember. Now you know what it feels like for me to have my hands on you."

"It's so good…" She's trying so hard to hold on, but her body has other ideas. "Please, more…"

"I want to watch you come. I want you to come all over my fingers. I want you to coat them. Can you do that for me, princess?" For once, she doesn't argue with the name. She only grips the pillow, one hand on either side of her head, hips now jerking wildly. I don't know if it's my words, my touch, or both, but she's on the verge of something huge. And I'm right there with her, so close, my balls tightening and rising, ready to explode.

All it takes is the slightest brush against the tip of her clit, and she loses it, hips shooting up from the bed, her legs clamping hard around my wrist. "That's right," I pant, fisting my cock furiously and raising my voice so she'll hear me over her hoarse cries. "Give it to me. Give me everything. Come for me, Mia."

"Zeke!" She goes tense once more, back arching off the bed, her body frozen in a moment of total ecstasy before she collapses against the mattress with a broken sob.

And I'm gone. I can't hold it back anymore. I stand, aiming a split second before splashing cum across her thigh. I empty myself, almost roaring in relief. In triumph. I can't get over the idea of marking her like she's mine now.

And when I'm finished, and I can hear myself think again, I find her staring up at me. She's not disgusted or repulsed at the cum running down her leg. I don't even think she feels guilty.

Especially not when she bites her lip like she's hiding a smile. If I didn't know better, I would think she made this happen, but then she couldn't have known I would be awake. I was silent.

"Wait there." I go to her bathroom and wet a washcloth under a warm tap before bringing it back and cleaning her up. Neither of us says a word, and nothing needs to be said. Anything either of us came up with would ruin what just happened anyway.

"Thank you," she finally whispers, and I'm not sure if she's thanking me for cleaning her up or for making her come. Either way, I nod my acceptance before leaving the room without another word.

Son of a bitch. Talk about the point of no return.

And of course, instead of quenching my thirst, all I want now is more. To taste her. To feel the pressure from her thighs around my head while she rides out one orgasm after another delivered by my tongue. To feel her from the inside, to know what it's like for those tight muscles of hers to grip me and milk me dry.

No matter how many times I have her, I don't think it will ever be enough.

And one time would be too many.

How much harder did I just make my life?

14
MIA

*I*t's been days since Zeke got me off in my room. My fantasy came true, a fantasy I've had more times than I can count. Now I know what it's really like to have him walk into my room and take control. I don't have to pretend anymore. I don't have to ask myself how it would feel for him to catch me touching myself. I didn't plan it to go that way—I couldn't sleep. I tried everything I could until finally, the idea of coming seemed like the only other option. I always sleep well after an orgasm.

I would've slept well after that one, too, if it hadn't been delivered by him. If it hadn't opened a whole vault full of questions and worries.

The way he's been acting since then hasn't exactly helped things, either. We're right back where we started, with any ground we made up over these past several weeks vanishing. He barely looks at me and doesn't do much more than grunt when I ask questions. When we're back at the condo, he's either working out downstairs at the gym or sitting out on the balcony. What he's doing out there, I don't know. I can't help but wonder if it's all a way to stay away from me.

And I don't understand why. It was good. He enjoyed it, and there was no question whether I did or not. It's not like I broke down and cried or, even worse, threw myself into his arms and told him I loved him or anything like that. Is that what's worrying him? That I'll read more into this than there actually is?

If I knew that was true, I would tell him he has nothing to be worried about. I don't want anything from him. And I'm not going to get him in trouble—that's the last thing I want to do. And not only because I would be in trouble, too, even though I know I'd be forgiven. I'm sure Dad would blame it all on him, like he tricked me or seduced me.

Nothing could be further from the truth, but he wouldn't believe that. He wouldn't want to. It would be easier to make it into a cut-and-dried situation.

It would mean never seeing Zeke again, and I don't want that, either.

He's sitting directly behind me. I feel his eyes staring holes into the back of my head through those sunglasses he insists on wearing everywhere. I'm starting to wonder if they help him keep watch over the people around me without them being able to tell—they can't see the direction his eyes are moving in, and he's very good at keeping his expression neutral. Almost scary good. I'm starting to understand better why Dad picked him for this job. To call him intimidating would be a massive understatement.

Why the hell won't he tell me what he's thinking? Why won't he give me the slightest clue?

And why can't I shake the sense of everybody knowing what happened between us? There's no way they could know. I don't know what they do at night in their rooms, do I? It's my guilt. I've never gone that far with any guy all this time, not ever. And I've wanted it to be him since the day we met. So why do I feel so bad about it?

Because I don't know how he feels. As simple as that. If he would only tell me it was no big deal, I could get over it.

Well, if he's going to go back to the way things were and leave me hanging, maybe I can get a reaction out of him some other way.

I lean over the empty seat between me and a guy who looks like he might be napping behind his open laptop. "Did you hear him say which chapters will be covered on the exam? I missed it."

He sits up a little straighter and tries to make it look like he's been awake this whole time. "Uh, no. I missed it, too." *Right, because you were sleeping, dumbass.* Then again, it's the first class of the day, and most of the other students look sleepy. Not everyone is as much of a nerd for school as I am.

"Maybe it's on the syllabus? Do you have it with you?" I lean in a little more, and his eyes immediately go straight to my cleavage. Because, of course, they do. It really is too easy.

Is it my imagination, or did something hit the back of my chair? Like a foot, maybe? Zeke didn't exactly kick it, but he definitely jostled it. I ignore him, instead smiling wide at the stranger to my right.

A stranger who is extremely flustered now. "Um, maybe. I'm not sure…"

"Don't worry about it. I'll figure it out." I give him another little smile and look him up and down like I approve. He's wearing clothes he probably slept in, but I'll pretend that's hot for the sake of driving Zeke out of his mind. He deserves it for what he's putting me through.

I settle back in, staring straight ahead, and I'm glad he can't see me grinning.

He doesn't say anything about it after class, which only sets my teeth on edge. What do I have to do? Flash an entire classroom? Maybe then he'd say something. And I bet it would have something to do with my father, too. How Daddy dearest wouldn't like it. I swear, it's almost enough to make me wonder if I imagined that whole experience in my room.

But there's no way. Because even in my wildest fantasies, I never imagined him coming on me.

And I sure as hell never imagined liking it. Between that and the spanking thing, he's teaching me a lot about myself. I'm not sure how to feel about it, and there's nobody I can talk to.

Not even with my new friends in sociology, which is the class immediately after world history. I haven't seen any of them since last week, though Posey and I have been texting. I know she's not going to grill me when we see each other.

Dean is another story. "There you are. I was starting to think something happened to you."

It's sweet, especially in the absence of any kindness from Zeke. I can't believe how starved I am for the slightest bit of kindness. "I'm sorry for freaking you out. You know, you have my cell number. You could text me if you wanted."

"Are you kidding? I was afraid Frankenstein would come after me." He's not even subtle about turning around to look at the back of the room, where Zeke took his customary seat by the door as soon as we walked in.

"Don't start anything, okay? Please." I roll my eyes while setting up my laptop. "And you can text me anytime. Things just didn't work out on Friday." I'm glad the instructor starts her lecture because I don't feel like getting into it. It's one thing for Posey or Zoe to care, but guys are a different story. They get all up in their egos. Like I'm a damsel needing to be saved.

After a half-hour lecture, we break up into our groups to discuss our project. I did a lot of research over the weekend and can't wait to share it. It's better than obsessing over Zeke, too. "I just sent the three of you the link to the Trello board I put together with my research: articles, photos, videos. I plan on adding more to it after class."

Posey lets out a whistle. "Damn, girl. And I thought I was type A about stuff like this."

"You're type A about everything," Zoe reminds her with a laugh. "And you both make me feel like a loser. Though I did find lots of materials about how the different families in New York divided territories. There are so many gross pictures out there of, like, murder scenes."

"I know, right? It's like, research at your own risk." We share a knowing grin before I turn to Dean. "What about you? You're covering the drug trafficking explosion in the eighties, right?"

My question startles him like he wasn't paying attention. "What? Yeah. Drugs. Bad shit."

The three of us look at each other before turning back to him. "Wow. Insightful," Posey murmurs.

"We're going to get an A for sure," Zoe agrees, nodding solemnly.

I don't join in with the joking. Something's obviously bothering him. "What's up?"

He shifts his weight in his chair like he's uncomfortable before scrubbing a hand over his blond curls. "It's just, you know, if we make plans to get together and talk about our project, we need to actually be able to get together and talk about it. Outside of class. The way everybody else is doing."

"No offense, but how do you know what everybody else is doing? Did you take a survey of the rest of the class?" Posey gives me a look that says *I've got this*. "Don't get a hair up your ass about Mia not being able to go to your place. You know damn well we didn't talk about school."

"We were there for, like, ten minutes before we went over to the party," Zoe confirms. I already knew that because Posey told me, but I'm glad they're calling him out. I don't love the feeling of getting blamed for something I had no control over.

He grumbles, glancing toward Zeke one more time before shrugging like he knows he's outnumbered. He'd better not look back there again because something tells me Zeke will only take so much antagonizing. And Dean might think he's tough, but I doubt he's any match for Zeke. I know better than to ask whether he's ever hurt somebody because I'm sure he has. "Believe me," my father said, back in those first days when I was learning how to live in my new world, "there's nobody I trust more than him. He's done a lot of work for me, and if anybody so much as lays a hand on you, they will lose that hand. And that's if they're lucky."

I didn't ask him exactly what that meant or how he could be so sure. I didn't need to.

I didn't want to, either.

Posey takes over as usual, and I'm happy to let her do it. "I've been pulling up articles about the current state of organized crime and how money laundering schemes affect even regular, everyday people. Like there was that one chain of stores that exploded in a million different locations and had all these employees and everything, but it turned out they were laundering money the whole time. Once it collapsed, all those people lost their jobs, and they had nothing to do with anything illegal. They thought they were just working at a store."

"What about all those casinos that shut down?" Dean asks, and I'm glad he's finally over his little hissy fit. "Out in Jersey. Weren't there rumors about that being a front for laundering?"

"Well, I guess if you're going to launder a bunch of money, a casino would be the place to do it." Posey types a note on her computer. "I'm going to look at that, too. Speaking of shore towns, there's a lot of information on trafficking as well. Kids from Europe come over here to spend the summer working in a shore town, and they never end up going home. We don't hear a lot about that sort of stuff because it all gets swept under the rug."

"A lot of shit gets swept under the rug," Dean agrees. "The more digging I've done, the more obvious it is that we don't have a single clue how widespread this shit is. It can go on right under your nose, and you'd have no idea."

Then he grins, resting his chin on his palm. "Speaking of money laundering, what about your dad, Posey?"

I can almost hear her hackles going up, even if she tries to play it off. "What about him?"

"Does he know about any of that kind of stuff? I found an old article about his firm from, like, ten years ago. There were all kinds of accusations."

"You are so full of shit." Meanwhile, I exchange a worried look with Zoe. It never occurred to me we could find something like this while working on the project.

"Am I? I'll send you my research." He winks at me, trying to hide a grin. "I'm just fucking with you."

"You dick." She kicks him, though something tells me she'd like to do worse.

"Hey, I was just being a good boy and doing my homework." Homework on Posey's family, though? Come to think of it, he did seem to know a lot about her financial situation in advance. I assumed it was because rich people go around in the same circles. Now I'm wondering if he didn't do a little digging.

And if he did, maybe he could find out something about my father.

It's wrong to think that way, but the man is a mystery. I've told myself a million times that I should be grateful and stop wondering. If he wasn't so secretive, I wouldn't even care. The question would never cross my mind. And he goes out of his way to avoid ever talking about his business, his plans, any of it. I walk into a room, and he's all smiles, patting me on the head like I'm some possession of his. Who wouldn't be curious over why the conversation in his office stops dead when I so much as walk past the door?

Granted, I could just as easily google his name myself, but that would feel like an invasion. Besides, I'm not totally convinced he's not monitoring my online activity. I wouldn't put it past him, even if I'm unsure how he would do it with me so many miles away. And just like with sneaking out, I don't feel like finding out after the fact that the odds were against me the entire time, like with Zeke's notifications about the alarm system and the way he tracks my phone's location. I don't think Dad would be very forgiving if there was something to hide, and I found it.

Out of nowhere, a message box pops up on my screen. It's from Dean's Facebook account. *Hey, sorry, I didn't mean to make it seem like I was blaming you about Friday night. I know how things are for you right now.*

I glance away from my screen, but nothing about his expression or posture would give away the fact that he just sent me that message. *It's fine. And I'll try to show up next time, I promise. Don't be pissed at me?*

You're not the one I'm pissed at. So he's not going to let it go. *I know there's stuff you don't want to say, and that's okay. I get it. You want to keep things private. But if somebody is hurting you, you can tell me. You know that, right?*

No, I don't know that. We hardly know each other at all. It's nice that he wants to be friends, and I could see us even dating if the planets aligned and I could actually have a private life. I get the feeling he kind of likes me, and it's nice. It feels good. But I'm not trying to lead him on, either, when I have no idea how I would even begin to navigate that situation.

Nobody is hurting me. That's the truth. I hit enter before looking over at him from across the tops of our screens. His eyes move back and forth, and he nods slightly before glancing up at me.

So you're safe? You're not afraid or anything?

Not even a little bit, I reply, then I add a smiley emoji to make sure he understands. *My dad is really strict. Zeke is only trying to do his job and make sure I'm safe. We're trying to work things out and kind of compromise. But it's a little shaky.*

That's good. So your dad trusts that guy?

Posey and Zoe are talking about something, and I know I should be paying attention, but for some reason, it seems important to convince Dean he has nothing to worry about. *A hundred percent, and I do, too. As I said, we're working it out. Things should be easier from now on.*

I hope so, he replies. *I don't want to have to kick that guy's ass for you. But I'll do it.*

It's almost cute that he thinks he could. Dean isn't scrawny—not even close. He has a muscular build, but it's more athletic, whereas Zeke has been working in security in one way or another for years. He's been training with that in mind all this time. His body isn't built for sprinting down a field or swimming faster than everybody else. He's built to bruise, to break. To eliminate, maybe, but I can't imagine a situation like that ever coming up.

He's built for a lot of other things. Heat creeps up my neck and threatens to spread over my face. There's new warmth in my pussy, too, and I'm starting to get wet right here in the middle of class. Not now. I can't think about this right now. I'll have to wait until later when I'm alone.

Thanks. I don't think it will come to that, but I appreciate it. Believe me, none of this is worth fighting over.

Says you, he replies. *Remember. I'm always here, anytime. Day or night. And if you need help, say the word.* I look up to find him watching me, wearing a tiny smile. I smile back. It's nice knowing somebody cares that much. It's been a long time since I've felt like somebody actually cares about me for me. Not because it's their job or because they feel obligated the way Dad does. And not because Dean wants to own me, either. It's just because he likes me.

"What the fuck are you smiling about?" Zeke mutters after class when I reach him in the back of the room. It's the first actual sentence he's uttered since that night. I should've known it would have something to do with Dean.

"Why does it have to be any of your business? And hi, I'm glad to know your voice still works."

He stares around me in Dean's direction. I nudge him. "Could you stop? Please. This is ridiculous."

"I don't like that guy."

"Yes, I know. You've made that clear. But I don't remember asking for your opinion, either. Come on." I give him another nudge, this time trying to direct him toward the door. The rest of the class is moving around us, oblivious. Zeke has kind of blended in now. Everybody expects to see us together.

He won't stop staring across the room—and what's worse, when I look over my shoulder, I see Dean staring right back. For a second, I can't help but think he would be dangerous in the right—or wrong—situation. When he realizes I'm looking, though, that feeling goes away along with the cold look in his eyes. Like I imagined it in the first place.

Maybe I'm getting off on this a little bit. I can admit it. A guy out there wants to fight for me, and not because somebody is paying him to. How refreshing.

"I'm sorry you don't like him," I say to Zeke, "but he is my partner on this project. And eventually, we're going to have to get together to go over our presentation. You're going to have to live with that."

"Just keep him away from me," he growls, sliding on his aviators. "Because I can't promise I'll behave myself if he pisses me off."

Great. Here I am, stuck between these two, and both of them have the wrong idea about the other one.

"I'm going to wipe that smirk off his face one of these days," he vows. "Just wait and see."

I wish he didn't sound deadly serious when he says it. How am I supposed to keep playing both sides? Eventually, I'll have to choose one.

"Would you fight him?" I have to ask. "I mean, for real. Would you risk getting yourself into trouble over that?"

He doesn't answer. He doesn't need to.

His silence is answer enough.

And the thing is… if they do fight, I'm not sure which one I'd want to win.

15

ZEKE

"You said I could have friends over. I've even had friends over before now."

No matter where I go in this fucking condo, she has to follow me. She's not going to let this go. Even if I lock myself in my room, her screeching will drive me out of my skull.

"You didn't care when Blair came to stay," she reminds me. "You didn't care when I had Posey and her roommates over last weekend."

"You're right; I didn't care. Because that was them. That wasn't... him." I know I should at least try not to be so obvious in hating the guy, but I can't help it. Every time I set eyes on him, my blood boils. He has the most punchable face I've ever seen.

"Would you let it go already? Jesus Christ!" She slams the drawer she opened in the kitchen. "What is with your obsession with him!"

"Obsession? I fucking hate the guy. How about that?"

"Why? Because he looks at me? Because he's nice to me?" She holds her arms out to the sides. "Well? Is that it? Does it offend you that much that a member of the male species would actually be kind toward me without anybody paying him to do it?"

It's been like this for weeks. Things will be decent between us—still awkward, but not where we're screaming at each other the way we are now—but little things like this keep popping up. Somebody looks at her, or she insists on wearing something too tight or too short or too low-cut or all of the above. And instantly, it's like an explosion.

Letting her have friends over isn't helping chill her out, either. I still feel like I'm walking through a minefield every goddamn day. At least there's the Thanksgiving break to look forward to in a few weeks. I can take a breather and put a little space between us in that big house.

"Are you going to answer me or not?" she demands with an actual, literal pout.

"You know, every time I think you've grown up a little, you go back to being this bratty little bitch. How's that for an answer?"

Her face goes beet red an instant before she lashes out. "A bratty little bitch? You're lucky I don't have time to rip your balls off right now, but I have to get ready for my guests."

"I fucking told you, he's not stepping foot in here."

"Listen to me." She marches up to me, our toes practically touching, and thrusts a finger at my chest. "I know I've threatened you with this before, but I mean at this time. I will call my father, and I will win. Dean has done literally nothing to hurt me. He's been nothing but nice. And we have a presentation coming up immediately after Thanksgiving, and it's most of my grade. This is for school. And you're not in any position to decide who comes into this condo. You don't pay for it."

She's wrong. I don't even have the heart to tell her how wrong she is. If she called her father and complained I was standing in the way of her schoolwork, he would side with me because he places no value on her work. This is a layover, like at an airport. She doesn't know it, but all she's doing is waiting for the next step.

And if I can't handle that piece of shit Dean setting eyes on her, what am I supposed to do when she's married off? How am I going to handle that? As much as I hate the idea of ever letting her out of my sight, it would be better than being hired as her bodyguard once she's somebody's wife. I'd rather move to the middle of nowhere and change my name than ever subject myself to that.

She's still standing in front of me, glaring up at me with every ounce of passion she owns. That's saying something. I feel sorry for her, the way I seriously shouldn't. All it does is complicate things. But I can't let her call her father. I can't let him break her heart, and that's exactly what he would do. The whole situation with her bank card was bad enough, and it would pale compared to this.

"Fine. No need to call him. I know my place." I incline my head a little, giving her a sarcastic bow. "But so help me God, if he puts a hand on you, I'm throwing him over the railing outside. And if you think I'm joking, just try me."

"Fine. He won't touch me." She turns away, but not fast enough to hide her triumphant little grin.

A part of me still hates knowing she thinks she's won. Like I'm giving in because I'm scared of my boss. When did everything shift? It wasn't the night I made her come—I felt sorry for her even before then. Ever since the boss told me about his plans for her and how she should take a cooking class.

She finishes putting a fancy-ass charcuterie board together. Cheese, nuts, dried fruit, olives, crackers… it goes on and on. She keeps going back to a video on her phone like she's comparing it to what the girl in the video did. I give it a pointed look on my way to the fridge for something to drink. "How many people do you expect anyway? That's a lot for the four of you."

She won't look at me, which tells me there's something she's trying to hide. "Dean said something about maybe bringing his roommates, but there's only another two of them."

"Motherfucker! This is a party."

"So what if we hang out while we rehearse how we're going to make our presentation? Is that a crime?" She doesn't put down the knife she's holding before turning to me, and something tells me that's not by accident. "Remember how you said I could have people over? That's something we agreed on. And it's going to be six people or fewer, so you can spare me that argument, too." She turns back to her work, slicing a green apple as if it insulted her.

"I'm supposed to be checking people out before they come over here, remember?"

"I thought that was if I was going to his place, which I am not. You will be here the whole time." She barks out a bitter laugh. "Believe me, screwing around is the last thing anybody has on their mind when you're—"

I know why she cut herself off. I understand the point she was trying to make, and damn straight, it's what I get paid to do, making sure nobody gets the wrong idea in their head when they're around her.

But she walked into a trap. There's one person in this condo at the present moment who most definitely thinks about screwing around when they're in my presence.

"You should learn to quit while you're ahead," I suggest before uncapping my water.

"Fuck off." She picks up the tray and carries it out to the living room, placing it in the center of the coffee table. It's almost cute how fancy she's trying to be for a bunch of kids who would probably be happier with a couple of pizzas. She wants to be the perfect little hostess.

And I get to sit back and watch. Lucky me.

I also get to sit back and watch her parading around the condo in a pair of leggings so tight they might as well be painted on. "You're not wearing that, are you?" I ask with a tired sigh. Not that I mind for myself. Any opportunity to catch a glimpse of her ass is worth taking. But this isn't just me.

"I'll wear what I want." She pushes her way past me on her way to her room. "But I was going to wear a big sweater anyway, and it covers my ass. Not everybody is as perverted as you."

"Don't you wish they were, though?" I don't always say what she brings to mind, but right now feels like an exception. She breaks stride just enough for me to know I got through to her but continues to her room anyway while muttering a few choice words.

It's only another ten minutes or so before the intercom buzzes. It's the front desk. "I have a couple of girls down here saying they're visiting. Posey and Zoe."

"Send them up." I know better than to hope the guys don't show, but I still can't help wishing they would stay away. I can't come up with any reason to hate this Dean guy except for how he looks at her. He's had it bad since that first day they were assigned their projects.

And because he likes her, he resents me. I've wished so many times he would start shit, just to have the excuse to shut him down, but he hasn't. Yet. There's a sense of inevitability when it comes to him, just like it was inevitable that I would eventually have to give in and put my hands on Mia.

It's cool outside, not exactly uncomfortable. I wait until the girls arrive, then put on my leather jacket and make myself comfortable out on the balcony. It's better for me to be out here. The fresh air will help me think. Besides, this is the perfect vantage point. I'll know when the rest of the party shows up since they'll be passing a few floors beneath where I'm sitting now.

There's a lot of giggling inside, and after a minute or two, the door slides partly open. Zoe, the one who dyes her hair Kool-Aid red, sticks her head out. "You okay out here? Posey and I brought food, too. There's so much."

She doesn't seem like a bad person, and she's not one of those girls who throws herself at a guy. I don't have to fight the impulse to roll my eyes every time she opens her mouth. "I'll come in in a little bit. What did you bring?"

"All kinds of stuff. Posey insisted on a big salad, and I ordered a couple of kinds of calzones."

If she wasn't such a nice girl, I would put on the charm and tell her calzones are my favorite. I'd thank her for thinking of me and give her a smile that would melt her panties. It would be fun watching Mia seethe while I flirt with one of her friends. Maybe she would start to understand a little of what I go through every time I have to watch Dean wink at her or touch her arm or stare at her tits when she's not looking.

I'm an asshole, but I'm not that bad. "Sounds good. Save me some, okay?" She only hesitates for a beat before nodding and disappearing back inside. At least Mia managed to find a few nice people.

Here they come. Dean's out in front with a pair of guys behind him. It's like they were cut out of the same douchebag cookie cutter. I can practically smell their obnoxious body spray all the way up here. And damned if one of them isn't carrying a six-pack in both hands. Yeah, I'm sure there will be a lot of talk about sociology tonight. What a goddamn joke.

Mia's on the intercom when I step inside, and she enthusiastically confirms the guys can come up. Her gaze sweeps over me as she turns away from the device, but neither of us says a word. I guess part of being the perfect hostess means not arguing with the hired help in front of guests.

Rather than get up in their space, I settle for sitting on a stool and the kitchen island. The open floor plan means I'm visible, but there's still room between us. She can't accuse me of interfering.

"Hey! I'm glad you're here." Mia steps back after opening the door—and I glance up in time to find her staring at the six-packs. "What's that? A study aid?" I have to cough to stifle a laugh.

"Come on. Brad and Pete aren't in class with us, so they have to do something." Brad and Pete. Of course, that's their names. Just as generic as they are.

"I'm just busting your balls. Come on in, make yourself comfortable. There's plenty of food, and you can leave the rest of the beer in the fridge." I glance up again and find both of them eyeing me up. I'm not naïve. I have no doubt their roommate bitched about me before they came over. He doesn't exactly try to hide the dirty looks he shoots me during class.

Silly little boy. He doesn't have the first idea of what I'm capable of when Mia isn't involved. Add her to the mix, and they'll never be able to identify his body.

He's very deliberate in the way he avoids looking at me in favor of chatting with the girls. Good. He needs to keep it that way. I can share space with him, but only if he doesn't start any shit. I go back to scrolling through random shit on my phone that I don't care about. It's not like I'm paying attention to any of it anyway.

"Hey. You sure you don't want something to eat?" Zoe flashes an apologetic smile. I didn't even realize she came over to me.

"I'll wait until everybody else has what they want. But thanks again. Seriously, go on over there and hang out. I'm fine." The last thing I want is anybody feeling sorry for me. She goes back and sits on the floor, facing the sofa from the other side of the coffee table. As always, Posey is the group leader and already has her laptop open. Those boys should have known better than to think she would let the whole night pass without at least talking about schoolwork for a little while.

"Mind if we put the TV on?" Brad—or is it Pete? I didn't learn the difference—picks up the remote before Mia can answer. The firm set of her jaw tells them she doesn't like them making themselves at home so soon, but she lets it go. They find a sports channel and settle in front of a football game, both their plates piled with food. I wonder what they would do if I walked over and took their plates away. Fucking freeloaders.

At least I know I don't have to worry about them tonight.

Dean, on the other hand? He's sitting next to Mia, angled in her direction. "So I was thinking we should go in order of our eras, right? Mia would go first, Zoe second, then me, then Posey."

"That makes sense," Zoe agrees. I'm not sure who she likes more, Dean or me. Sadly, she's not going to have much luck either way. We both have our eyes on the same girl, and it's not her.

"Of course, that's how we would do it." Posey snickers, looking away from her screen long enough to roll her eyes at Dean. "Way to make it seem like you're contributing, though."

One of the other two guys bursts out laughing. "Damn, she got you!" Dean only narrows his eyes at his friend, which strikes me as interesting. He gave me the same kind of look that day in the classroom, the week after I stopped Mia from going to his place. It didn't last long, that look, but now I know I wasn't imagining things. Is that why he bothers me so much? He's like the stereotypical so-called good guy who has a nasty streak underneath that he tries to hide.

Now, I don't know that for sure, and I could be making shit up to have more reason to hate him. But I'm starting to wonder. Either way, I can't afford to trust anybody.

Pretty soon, their chatter fades into the background while I play a game on my phone. Maybe I'm the problem here. I'm too protective of her. Jealous of anybody who looks at her in a way I don't like. I would never in a million years admit I'm second-guessing myself since I don't want her getting the wrong idea. But I can't shake the feeling.

To my surprise, a plate of food slides in front of me after a while. "The calzone's cold," Mia informs me in a low voice, "but it's still good." I don't have the chance to thank her before she continues to the fridge. Is this a peace offering? I'll accept it, at least for now.

"She got him food, did you see? I told Dean. She's not into him."

I pretend I can't hear what Brad and Pete are muttering back and forth, munching on an apple slice with my eyes on my phone. Really, I'm focused on them. I can't even taste what's in my mouth.

"Seriously, he needs to move on. If it hasn't happened yet..."

The other one snorts. "Redhead would drop her panties for him here and now. I keep telling him. Stick to what's easy." Can Zoe hear them? I don't think so—she's talking about her part in their project, totally oblivious. I swing my head slowly in their direction, staring at them with a blank expression I've perfected over time. Eventually, one of them notices and starts choking on whatever he's eating. The other one hits him on the back until the choking stops. Fucking assholes.

This confirms what I already knew: he's into her, so much so that he's told his friends about her. That doesn't bode well.

What bodes even worse, I realize as I swing my attention in her direction, is the way she leans against him while she laughs at a joke I didn't hear. The way she touches a hand to his shoulder and the way he smiles when she does it.

Mine. She's mine. Nobody else's.

But how can I keep her for myself? She was never meant for me.

But she is meant for me. Just for me. Nobody else comes close.

That's when it happens.

When Dean goes from smiling at Mia to looking my way—and when he finds me watching, his smile widens. We don't need to exchange a word for me to know what's on his mind. *See this? I've got her. She's mine.*

"Hey, Mia?" I stand fast enough to almost knock the stool over. I don't say another word, heading for her room. If she knows what's good for her, she'll follow me without making a big deal about it.

She murmurs something but joins me a moment later. "What now?" she whispers, arms folded. "I thought things were going well."

I open my mouth but realize I don't know what I want to say. I didn't plan anything to say. I only wanted to get her away from him. How am I supposed to explain that?

I can't. At least, not in words.

This is why I explain the only way I know how to.

By taking her by the back of the head and pulling her in for a hard, deep kiss.

16
MIA

Oh, my God.

At first, my instinct tells me to push him away. Maybe kick him in the balls before I do. He has no right. He shouldn't.

And oh, I want him too. Forever. Right here, in this spot, he could kiss me on and on until we both die of dehydration or starvation or whatever comes first. I don't care. Because the second his hand cupped the back of my head, I knew this was right. This is what was always going to happen. We fought as hard as we could, but it was no use.

So when he forces his tongue between my lips and plunges into my mouth, I meet it with mine. He groans, the rumbling low in his chest, and I'm lost. Completely gone. My hands find his shoulders and press into his unyielding muscles, my need for him strong enough to make my knees shake.

With his free hand, he slides down my back and finally cups my ass, hauling me in closer until our bodies are flush, and I can feel what's growing in his pants. I've never wanted anything more than to reach between us and rub him there, to get him off like he did for me.

But I can't. Not now, not ever. It takes all the self-control I have to break the kiss, and even then, he nips my bottom lip before letting me go. It tingles in the best way. "What are you doing?" I whisper between gasps of air.

"You couldn't tell? Am I that out of practice?" He squeezes my ass again, harder this time, and I moan before I can help myself.

I know that will only encourage him, so I take a deep breath and try to come up with a reason he shouldn't take me here and now. "There are people out there. You can't do this."

"Is that all that's stopping you?" He traces the line of my jaw before stroking my throat. Fire races over my skin, following the path of his fingers like the tail behind a comet. All I want is to lean into his touch and forget everything else. "Send them home."

"You can't do this. You can't screw with me like this."

"Who said I was screwing around?" With both hands, he takes me by the hips and pulls me tight against the rod in his pants. "I need you. I want you. I'm so fucking tired of pretending I don't."

This can't be happening. Is it a dream? No, I can still hear everybody talking out in the living room. Eventually, somebody will come back here, wondering if I'm okay. I can't let them see us like this.

"Zeke. Please. Be fair." I don't know what makes me reach out and cup his cheek in one hand. Maybe it's the way I've always wondered what his scruff feels like. It's soft but rough at the same time. I can't help but wonder what it would feel like against my inner thighs.

I've had way too much to drink tonight. I had no idea I was this drunk. *You're not drunk. You're horny. Stop lying to yourself.*

"There's nothing fair about life, princess." He looks almost sad when he backs away, turning to check himself out in the mirror above my dresser. Once he adjusts what's still jutting out from his pants, he leaves the room. Rather than return to the kitchen, he goes to his room and quietly closes the door.

Dear God. I go to the dresser, too, but at first, all I can do is lean against it and finish catching my breath. Holy fuck. What did he mean by having to pretend he didn't want me? Has he always—

"Hey, you alive in here?" Posey is nice enough to reach around and knock on the open door before peering around the doorframe.

I'm glad Zeke's gone, at least. "Yeah, I'm fine."

"Because the guys out there are getting ready to fight him unless you come out of here looking the way you did before you went in." She looks me up and down, screwing her lips up in what looks like uncertainty. "What happened? You look all flushed."

"Nothing. Really."

"Are you sure?" She tips her head back, looking toward the living room before turning my way again. "What's going on with you two? You can tell me."

"Nothing. Seriously!" I hiss when she smirks.

"Right. The first time I ever saw him, he was about ready to throw you over his shoulder and carry you out of that party. It was almost hot."

"No, it wasn't."

"It was from where I was standing. And every time I've seen him since, he's been watching you."

"Watching everybody around me, you mean."

"No. That's not what I mean. He watches you." She uses two fingers to point at her eyes, then to me. "Constantly. All the way. And from where I'm standing, it looks like he's in love with you."

"That is not true. Trust me."

"Well, he wants you. And it's driving him fucking crazy having Dean here. That's a big risk. You know how Dean feels about him."

"Apparently, everybody does, huh?" I roll my eyes. "Nobody quite gets the way it is between us, but believe me, it's not what you think."

"You make it sound like there's more going on, but then turn around and say he doesn't love you and that nothing is going on between you guys. You're starting to sound like somebody that's making excuses for an abuser."

"Okay, you can stop right there; he's not abusing me." I wave my hands around, frustrated because I can't quite tell her everything. There isn't enough time. "I had a crush on him for a long time. I made a move, he turned me down. Now we're here. So yeah, it's tense and weird."

"And don't forget your father would probably kill him if he touched you."

"I mean, maybe? I don't know. He trusts Zeke."

"So long as Zeke doesn't think of you as a woman." She winks. "Face it, girl. You've got to either tell him nothing is ever going to happen, or you need to fuck his brains out. You can't keep floating around in limbo, or it's only going to get more awkward." Zoe bursts out laughing over something in the living room. "I'm going to go back. Don't be much longer, or shit will go down."

Why is it not enough for me to tell Dean he has nothing to worry about, that Zeke isn't hurting me or holding me prisoner? Hard-headed. Is that the way all men are? Maybe it's just the men in my life.

I look at myself in the mirror, staring into my own eyes. I need to make a decision one way or another. Posey's right. Either I shut down the whole thing right now and tell him it's never going to happen, and he can never kiss me—or anything else—again, or I can fuck his brains out.

Obviously, my body knows what it wants. I'm wet enough that I'm practically dripping, like my body is preparing itself to have what it's wanted for such a long time.

My brain's another story.

"Yo, Mia! You coming back or what?" Dean. Another complication. I stand straight, smoothing out my sweater and hair before hurrying out into the hallway.

"I'm coming, jeez. Can't a girl go to the bathroom?" I roll my eyes, laughing. "Anybody else want a drink? There's plenty in the cabinet."

* * *

POSEY BETTER BE CAREFUL, or she's going to find herself with a new best friend, whether she wants one or not. She played it cool, never hinting at anything I told her in my room. She also managed to wrap things up within an hour and got everybody out of the condo. Dean looked disappointed, but that's no big surprise. I'm not sure what he thought was going to happen. I like him, he's nice, but I've never given him any idea that I see him that way. Have I?

Besides, Zoe's obviously got a huge crush on him. I like her, I want to be friends with her, and it would make me a bitch if I went after him.

Right. Whatever you need to tell yourself. I'm not loving the voice in my head right now, but it won't shut up. I go through the motions of putting everything away, saving what's left of some pretty expensive cheese. I'm sure anybody raised the way I'm living now would laugh at me for doing it, but certain things I don't think I'll ever be able to let go of. I don't want to waste anything, even if I know I could easily buy more tomorrow.

I open the refrigerator door and bend down to make room for the leftovers. Once I have everything put away, I stand and close the door to the fridge.

And I gasp when I find Zeke standing there. "Are you trying to kill me? Because one of these days, my heart's going to stop when you surprise me like that."

He doesn't apologize. He doesn't say a word, in fact.

He doesn't have to. He has that same look in his eye that he did earlier before he kissed me.

I can't get over the thought that this is it. This is where I make a decision. I can either tell him to get this out of his mind, that nothing will ever happen, so he should stop thinking about it…

Or I can give in and take what I've wanted all this time.

Right now, with every part of my body responding to the way he's looking at me, it doesn't feel like I have much of a choice.

We crash together, his hands sinking into my hair and holding my head in place while his tongue does unspeakable things to the inside of my mouth. Nobody's ever kissed me like their entire life depends on it. Slow, sensual, making my toes curl and my pussy throb. He drives me back against the island, and I'm glad for it since it gives me something to lean on before my legs give out.

This is what I've been fighting against? This almost painful pleasure? It's more than that. It's being close to him, smelling him, hearing the way he grunts, the way his breath picks up. His fingertips massaging my scalp. It all blends together until my body is on fire, my nerves tingling, my skin sizzling.

And I'm so hungry for more. So tired of pretending I want anything other than this, always.

He finally lets me up for air, trailing kisses over my jaw, my chin, my throat. I hold on to the back of his head with one hand, running my fingers through his hair. I hardly recognize the sounds coming from me—high-pitched, desperate, pleading. Much more of this, and I'll come when he's barely put a hand on me.

And then he does. He wedges a thigh between mine, parting my legs, before rubbing it against my pussy. I scrape my nails over his scalp before I can help myself, but all he does is grind harder against me. Like he likes it.

"This is what you want, isn't it? Don't pretend." He lifts his head, taking my jaw in one hand. Stopping just short of squeezing my throat. "Isn't it?"

"Yes!" I gasp, and now I'm rocking my hips frantically, chasing the orgasm just out of reach. "Yes, more, please!"

"You want me to use this body, don't you?"

"Yes!"

"You want me to show you what you're capable of?"

"Yes, yes!" I would say anything, so long as he never stops. But I mean it, too. I want more. I've always wanted more. I want him to show me everything, all of it, how to please him, how I can be pleased. I want it to be him who shows me. I've never wanted anything else.

"Good girl." Before I know it, his hands are at my waist, and he's lifting me, putting me up on the counter. I don't have time to be disappointed—I was so close—before he unbuttons my jeans. "Lean back."

I do as he tells me, stretching out on my back, staring up at the ceiling. This is happening, it's really happening, and I want it. More than anything, I do. I want his hands on me, easing my jeans down, running over the length of my legs. I want his face between my thighs. I want to hear him groan like an animal when he runs his lips over my pussy, still covered by my panties. I know I'm wet, I can feel it, and he groans before pressing his tongue against the cotton.

I gasp in surprise, lifting my head to look down at him. He can't honestly like that, can he? But one look at his face tells me he does—his eyes are closed, his expression one of extreme pleasure as he licks up what's soaked through. His groans confirm how much he likes it. Loves it.

And that sparks something in me. I want to give him more of what he loves. I want to give him all of me. I lift my hips without protest when he claws at the waistband of my panties, then spread my legs wide when they're off.

He looks into my eyes, his brows lifted. "Look at you. Showing yourself off to me. Spreading your legs so I can look at this pussy." His gaze drops to that spot, his lids lowering, lips parted so he can take short, ragged breaths. "Teasing me. Almost like you want me to lick you clean."

It's almost painful, the arousal. If this doesn't end soon, I'll die. "Please?" I whimper. "Please, lick me?"

"Only if you promise to come on my tongue like a good girl." My head bobs up and down, eyes wide, heart pounding so hard I'm afraid it'll kill me. I wouldn't even care right now, so long as I know what it feels like to have his tongue on me.

He doesn't take his time about it, plunging down, parting my lips with his probing tongue.

"Oh, fuck!" My voice echoes around the room, then again, and again, with each lap of his eager tongue. He knows just what to do, just how to use it. How to use me. This is what I've been missing out on all this time?

"So good," he rasps before dipping inside again, dragging the length of his tongue along my slit before finally pressing it against my clit. My hips shoot up, unintelligible cries pouring out of me. It's too good, too much—his tongue, the scruff on his cheeks scraping my inner thighs, his grunts of pleasure barely muffled against my dripping pussy.

I can't help but lose myself to it. "Zeke!" That's the only word I can get out before the wave crashes, my body trembling. And he keeps going, licking me clean like he promised until there's nothing to do but sigh in ecstatic relief. I close my eyes, floating in darkness. So that's what it feels like to get eaten out. No wonder girls like it so much.

I pull myself out of it, forcing myself to come to. "Thank you," I whisper. Is it lame? I don't know. What do people say in a situation like this?

As it turns out, it doesn't matter. When I lift my head, searching for him, he's gone. I'm alone, spread-eagled on the counter.

Did I just make a huge mistake?

17
ZEKE

Of all things to wake me up in the morning, the one I expected the least was the smell of bacon. She's making breakfast.

Which means she's probably going to want to talk.

Fuck. I drop back onto the bed, my head hitting the pillow hard. I guess it's too much to ask, hoping she would forget what happened last night. I lost my grip on myself. It should never have happened. I had no right to do that to her.

And something tells me I only made it worse by leaving her there while she was still dazed. It was all I could think to do. I didn't know if I could handle looking her in the eye.

I'm not even sure why I reacted the way I did. She wanted it. God knows I did. So why did I feel so guilty?

That guilt hasn't eased in the slightest. It doesn't get any better once I'm up and moving around, getting dressed, brushing my teeth. As long as I live, I'll never forget the exhilaration of knowing I was the first man to ever taste her indescribable sweetness.

And I'm kidding myself, thinking I won't taste her again. Just like I was kidding myself when I decided that night in her bedroom was a one-off. That we could never do that again. Eventually, my needs are going to catch up with me.

And so will hers.

I can't stay in my room all day, that's for sure. I need to face this like a man. "You've got this!" I tell myself before flinging my bedroom door open. The aroma of bacon and coffee is stronger now, and my stomach growls in anticipation. Man cannot live on pussy alone or something like that. I find her in the kitchen, where I knew she would be, wearing a nightshirt and thick socks. There are covered pans on the stove, and she's in the process of pouring two cups of coffee.

"Good morning." Right away, I'm relieved that she's not overly eager, giddy, giggly. But that's not her, either, is it? She's not one of those girls. She's not going to fall head over heels just because I was the first guy ever to eat her.

"Good morning. What's all this for?"

"For eating breakfast, obviously. Back when I was younger, I'd always have Sunday breakfast with my mom, at least when she wasn't working an early shift."

She shrugs before holding out a cup for me. "I figured I would bring the tradition back now that I can."

"So long as you didn't burn the bacon, I think I can learn to live with it." I can't help but eye her warily, though, as I take a seat at the counter. It's almost surreal, the idea of eating breakfast side by side in the same place where I went down on her last night. The memory alone is enough to stir things to life below my waist.

She slides a plate of food in front of me a moment later. Scrambled eggs, perfectly cooked bacon, toast. "This looks great," I murmur before sprinkling pepper over the eggs, then taking a bite. They're buttery and fluffy. "Are you sure you never took cooking lessons?"

I wish I hadn't asked that. Now all I can think about is how her old man wants her to take cooking lessons for her future husband.

She only laughs gently, unaware. "I've always been interested in cooking. I watched a lot of cooking shows, and I always used to watch my mom when she cooked. It probably drove her crazy, having me watch her, but she was always patient." I can't help but notice the warmth and affection in her voice whenever she mentions her mother. What a big difference compared to a father who throws money at her but not much else.

I should be used to her sudden shifts in topic by now. She has a habit of bouncing from one thing to another without warning. This time, she really surprises me. "Why did you leave me alone last night? And when can we do that again?"

Bad timing. I barely avoid choking on a piece of toast, waving her off when she jumps up like she wants to help. "I'm fine," I manage before taking a big gulp of orange juice. Once I'm sure I'm not going to die, I look at her. "Do you know what you're saying?"

"Do I look like I'm confused?" She pops a piece of bacon into her mouth, staring at me while she chews. I don't know if it's sexy or unnerving. Both?

"You know all the reasons that's a terrible idea."

"Why does it have to be?" She's so casual about it. That alone makes me wonder if she understands the enormity of what she's talking about.

"Mia, come on. We're talking about my job here. We're talking about your father castrating me if he ever found out. And he'd be furious with you, too. Are you really willing to take that risk?"

She makes a big deal about looking around, her head on a swivel, her eyes landing here and there. "Doesn't look like there's anybody here with us," she finally announces. "So, how would anybody know?"

I close my eyes, gritting my teeth, willing myself to be the smart one here. One of us has to be. "Mia, I know you're a virgin. I know you're probably in a hurry to change that."

"Don't patronize me," she spits, disgusted. "I know what I want. I've known for a long time. Pretend all you want that you don't want me too, but we both know that isn't true. I respect you wanting to be true to what my dad wants. I do. But he never needs to know."

The little tease runs her foot up my leg. "Does he? It can be between you and me. Why deny ourselves what we both want? Are you afraid you can't handle it?"

"Don't play games," I warn, though I don't bother pushing her foot away, either. She's winning me over, let's put it that way. How can I help it? My dick is doing the thinking for me, and right now, it's all in. No reservations.

Which means I have to call upon what little blood is still left in my brain. "I'm serious, Mia," I warn. "This is dangerous shit you're talking about."

"I know it can be." She goes back to her food, scooping some eggs onto a piece of toast. "But it doesn't have to be."

"You can tell yourself that all you want—"

"You know what?" She drops the rest of the toast onto the plate, swiveling around on the stool until she's facing me head-on. "Let's get this straight. I'm not some bubbleheaded, naïve little thing, no matter what my father thinks about me."

"I never said you were."

"Then why do you insist on telling me what I want? I know what I want. I know what's right for me. And you can't tell me it's been easy, the two of us living together all these weeks, both of us pretending we don't want what we so obviously do. Have you forgotten what it was like that night in my room? Will you ever be able to forget what it felt like to kiss me? Because I know I'll never forget it, and I don't want to. It's insane to think we could walk around and pretend it never happened!"

She has a point. And that's not just my dick talking. Most of the misery of the past two months has come from denying ourselves. I know in my case, my cravings for her can only be channeled into picking fights with her. Being jealous. Petty. That's not how I want to be.

I also don't want to be dead, which I'm afraid I would be if word of this ever got out.

"Zeke. Look at me." I lift my gaze to find her smiling. "Let's stop all this. Let's stop kidding ourselves. And let's stop believing my father would have any way of knowing about us being together. I know we can both be discreet adults. Right?"

She's right, you know she's right, just tell her so. I take a deep breath, like I can will myself into believing something I don't. I can make myself believe there's any way we can get out of this fucked up situation with her still being a virgin in the end.

She slides off the stool, standing between my legs. "You know what I want?" Her palm makes contact with my straining cock. "I want to know how to make you feel good. I want you to teach me to do to you what you did to me. It doesn't seem fair, with me having all the fun. Teach me. Show me what to do. I want to learn so much." She massages me in slow circles, and I have to wonder how often she's thought of this.

I catch her wrist and hold it still. "You're playing with fire," I warn.

"You don't have to tell me that," she whispers, her lip disappearing under her teeth. So fucking sexy. Innocence and sensuality all wrapped up in one perfect little package.

And she's handing herself to me on a platter. How insane am I to think I can fight against this?

"Let me touch you," she urges, still whispering. "Let me see you." With her other hand, she tugs at the waistband of my loose, flannel pants. I don't bother trying to stop her; it would be like stopping the sun from rising. This is going to happen no matter what I do to stop it.

"Let me help you." I hook a thumb into the waistband of my pants and my boxers and tug, giving her room to dip her hand inside and close her fingers around me. My breath catches before I moan in approval.

"It's so thick," she murmurs, looking down. She gives an experimental stroke, and I groan.

"Not too tight," I whisper, and she loosens just a bit. "And it's better if you can get it wet."

She's determined to surprise me today. Her eyes meet mine, locking onto me, and she raises her other hand before running the flat of her tongue from the heel to her fingertips. She wraps that hand around me this time, and I'm afraid I might come already. Either she has a very active imagination, or she's been watching porn. Either way, I don't care. It feels incredible.

"What next?" She pumps slowly, almost experimental. Watching me closely, seeing how I react. She's holding my whole life in her hands, and she doesn't know it. I would do anything for her, whatever she asks, so long as she never stops.

"Put it in your mouth. Get on your knees. I'll tell you what to do." Because fuck it, why not? It's a waste of time pretending this isn't going to happen. And I have imagined her sucking my cock too many times to keep from taking advantage of the situation. She wants to learn? I'll teach her.

She lowers herself slowly, still watching me. "Take off your shirt," I murmur, and the sight of her gorgeous tits dropping down from her nightshirt is a fantasy come true. Having her on her knees, eager, only wanting to learn. No holds barred.

"Put your lips over your teeth," I say. "No teeth. Relax your throat. It's not going to choke you, no matter what you think." I take myself in one hand, guiding the head over her lips. "I've wanted to fuck your mouth for so long." Color floods her cheeks, but she doesn't pull away.

In fact, the tip of her tongue darts out, and she catches precum as it oozes from my head. It's almost too fucking hot. "Go slow. Take your time." Sliding between her lips and into the warmth of her mouth is bliss. I have to focus on not losing it, or I might have no choice but to take her by the back of the head and fuck her until she gags.

And I will do that one day. But not yet.

She eases her way down, one inch at a time, until she finally has most of me in her mouth. "Now, ease your way back up," I murmur, stroking her hair. "Just like that. Don't part your lips. Keep that suction going. Use your tongue—press it against where the shaft meets the head. That's right, baby," I groan. She's a quick learner and eager.

I'm eager, too. I won't be able to hold on much longer, even with her taking it slow. If anything, it's that slow, sensual pace that has me ready to burst. "You're so good," I groan before withdrawing with a groan of regret.

"What's wrong?" Her eyes are wide, surprised. "I thought you liked it."

"I did," I assure her, one hand still in her hair. "But if we're going to do this, we're going to do it right."

18
MIA

I don't know who's in control of this anymore or if I ever was. I might have had to convince him, but he's the one who leads me to my room. I can't believe this is happening. That was the biggest gamble I've ever taken, and my legs are still shaking from nerves. But it worked. It actually worked, and he's turning to face me.

I can't believe he's standing in front of me like this, staring at me, taking in every inch of my bare skin. Goose bumps rise over my arms, and I shiver, but I'm not cold. In fact, my skin is flushed and getting warmer the longer I stand here, waiting.

"What do I do now?" I finally have to whisper. It sounds stupid, probably, but he knows this is my first time. I'm not trying to impress anybody.

"Right now? You could stand right there, and I could easily jerk off to the sight of you." He lowers his pants and kicks them aside, then takes himself in his fist. Watching him like this stirs something deep in my core, tightening it, spreading heat out in all directions.

And he's doing it because of me. Just because he's looking at me.

"Sit down." He kneels in front of me, and once I'm settled, he takes my tits in his hands. I can't help but thrust my chest toward him, offering more of me. All of me.

"Perfect, fuckable tits," he murmurs, flicking at the nipples with his thumbs. "One of these days, I'm gonna fuck these until I come in your mouth." I can only stare at him, breathless, wishing that time was now. Who knows if we'll ever have this chance again? He might regret it later—hell, I can admit, I might, too. I want to do everything I can now while I have him with me.

Or maybe it'll be so good there won't be any chance of either of us changing our minds.

He lifts one of my tits and replaces his thumb with his tongue, slowly circling the tip. I don't know what's better, the feeling or the sight of it. I could watch him do this all day. "That's nice." I sigh. My hand cups the back of his neck, and I hold him close. He groans softly, and I take that as a good thing.

"You deserve to be treated like a goddess." He delivers the same attention to my other nipple, sucking this time. He catches it between his teeth, and I moan helplessly, urging him on.

"That feels incredible. Oh, my God…"

I whimper a little when he stops, making him grin. "Already greedy."

"I guess it's because you make me feel so good." I had a feeling that would get him, and it does. His eyes widen a little, his grin spreading wider.

"If you think that's good, how about you let me taste you again?" He has me on my back before I can take a breath, my feet on the floor. He takes his time sliding my thong down, and I look down in time to see him lift the crotch to his nose. It's shocking and erotic, and I am so, so ready for him. I knew if it ever happened, it would be hot and exciting and a little scary, but I had no idea anything in the world could be like this. All I can do is wonder how much more there is. How much more we could do together if we had the chance with nobody around to stop us.

He drapes my legs over his shoulders, positioning me. I already know he's good at this, and I lie back again. It's amazing how much I already trust him. I know he won't hurt me.

"Has there ever been anything inside this beautiful pussy?" he asks before teasing my outer lips with the tip of his tongue. I can't help but seize up, gasping, then shuddering in pleasure. How am I supposed to answer questions when I'm on fire?

"No. Not inside."

"I'll get you ready, baby. You just lie back and relax." He buries his tongue between my lips, and relaxing is the last thing I can do now. Not when every stroke of his tongue against my aching flesh makes me writhe, out of control. I don't even mean to do it. My body has a mind of its own, finally able to express everything I locked up inside it all this time.

The pressure at my entrance is a surprise but not unwelcome. I don't realize I'm holding my breath until he raises his head. "Relax," he reminds me. "I'll start slow. I want you to enjoy it." Somehow, that's the hottest thing he could have said. The hottest thing so far.

He slides a finger deep inside me, and I smile, almost purring. "That's nice."

"So tight." His voice is strained. "I can't wait to stretch you with my cock."

"I want you to… I want you inside me." Who am I? Who's saying this?

The pressure increases, and I realize he's added another finger. He works them in and out in long, slow strokes. Every once in a while, he flicks his tongue over my clit, and I buck, hips shooting up off the bed. Again, again, and I realize he's teasing me when he chuckles.

"The fun I can have with you, princess." I don't mind hearing him say it. I actually like it when he says it while he has me like this.

"Think you could take one more?"

I can only nod, my lips pressed together, my throat going tight. My whole body is tensing up, including the muscles around Zeke's fingers. I'm going to come, and it's going to be huge.

"That's right. Be a good girl and come for me." He picks up speed until wet, slapping sounds fill the room. I'm sopping wet, soaking into the blanket, and a high-pitched whine is now coming from my mouth. I can't control any of it. I only know I'll die if he doesn't stop, and I'll die if he does.

I can hear his soft laughter as I start to come. "That's right. That's my girl. Show me how much you love this."

I have no choice but to do it, moaning until my voice breaks.

When I come to, he's licking me clean, then sucking me off his fingers. "I can't get enough," he admits. "You're so sweet."

"You really like it?"

"It drives me crazy." He stands, and I can see that's the truth. He's thick and long, and his head is swollen, purple, and dripping. He takes it in one hand, stroking himself, looking down at me. "You're sure about this? Because once I'm inside you, it can't be undone."

It's not just sweet. For all I know, sweetness is the last thing on his mind. There's more at stake here than just him and me. He could lose his job, and he's afraid I'll be the reason he loses it. I wouldn't do that to him, no matter what, but he doesn't know that.

"I'm absolutely sure. I want you."

That's all he needs to lean on one hand and guide himself to me with the other. This time, the pressure is stronger, verging on pain, but the pleasure is better. Stronger.

He rolls his hips and fills me, stretching me more than before, and that's it. I'm not a virgin anymore. And he's the only person I ever wanted to be my first. I open my eyes and look up at him to find him staring down at me. I smile a little, showing him I'm okay, and he pulls back to push forward again.

"So… fucking… tight…" He grits his teeth, tendons standing up on his neck like he's struggling. "So wet. Gonna make me come. Fuck…" But he doesn't. He holds back, and his steady rhythm slowly builds. A deeper, stronger pleasure than before starts to build along with it.

"Zeke, you feel so good…"

"Take my cock," he grunts before filling me again. "Take it all."

"Yes," I whisper while the warmth in my core turns to heat, ready to explode. "So good."

"Yeah… it is…" He lowers himself onto his forearms, and the extra pressure against my clit makes me gasp. That combined with his thrusts and the unbearable friction is too much. "Tight pussy. My pussy."

"Yes… yes…" I don't know what I'm saying anymore. I don't know anything. "Yours."

His eyes meet mine, only inches away. I could get lost in them the way I'm lost in this. In us. "I'm gonna come, I think…" My eyes squeeze shut, and I nod hard. "I'm coming, oh, God!"

He pulls out fast, and when I open my eyes and look up at him, his fist is moving frantically up and down his length. I'm still shaking and moaning his name when his cum splashes across my chest, then my stomach.

I know I should probably feel dirty, but all I feel is pride. Satisfaction. I can't believe it finally happened. And I already can't wait for it to happen again.

At first, though, I don't know how he feels. He goes to the bathroom like he did before and gets a washcloth. I guess if he's going to come on me, he might as well clean me up. And he does so gently but efficiently. Never once does he look above my shoulders. Is he going to get weird like he did last night? Will he walk out on me?

As it turns out, no. He makes it just far enough to throw the washcloth into the hamper before coming back to the bed, climbing in next to me, and getting under the sheets like he's ready for sleep. "Are you okay? Tell me the truth."

His tone contains a combination of caring and possessiveness. I can't decide if he's asking because he genuinely cares or because he feels like he's supposed to.

Either way, the answer is the same. "I'm fine. Really, better than fine."

"Good. Your first time should be good. It isn't for a lot of people."

"I guess not everybody gets as lucky as I did." I meant it sincerely, but he laughs anyway.

The laughter doesn't last long, and I knew it wouldn't. Now that it's over, we have to talk about reality. "Nobody can know about this. None of your friends. Nobody."

My head bobs up and down. I'd snicker and ask him to tell me another good one, but I just had sex for the first time and don't think this is the right time to get all sarcastic. "I won't say anything to anybody. Not ever."

He stares at me for a long time like he's trying to figure out whether I'm telling the truth. I must convince him because he nods. "Good. And obviously, nobody back home can know."

"You don't need to say that, believe me."

"So when we go home for break, we'll have to go back to the way things used to be."

"You mean hating each other."

He almost smiles. Almost. "Did we? I mean, I know I hated you, but how could you possibly hate me? I'm charming and friendly."

I know he's joking, but even if he wasn't, I'd probably burst out laughing anyway. "You are so full of shit."

"Admit it." He rolls onto his side, facing me, and I have to remind myself to look him in the eye rather than drool over his ridiculous body. Even now, relaxed, stretched out on the bed with the sheet barely draped over his hip, he's enough to turn me on all over again. I'm still sore, and I don't think I'll be able to do much walking today without wincing, but I'm ready to go again.

"Admit what?"

"You like my attitude. It gets you off, fighting with me." He grins, and I realize he hardly ever did before now. I barely recognize him. He even looks younger, and is that a dimple in his left cheek?

"So what if it does? Are you going to pick fights with me as an aphrodisiac or something?" I raise an eyebrow, challenging him.

"I don't need to fight with you to want to fuck you, Mia." He takes a long, slow tour of my body with his eyes. "All I have to do is look at you."

The low growl under his voice sends a shiver up my spine. "You're looking at me now." I don't take my eyes off him while pulling the blanket away from my body.

He licks his lips. "I'm in trouble, aren't I?" Something tells me he doesn't mind. I know I don't.

19
ZEKE

Maybe if I run fast enough on this treadmill, I'll outrun my guilt.

Maybe I'll be able to convince myself the past couple of weeks can be forgotten. That they haven't been a mistake.

That I'm not somehow happier than I've been in my life.

I don't deserve to be happy. I'm taking advantage of her. And eventually, she'll realize that.

My feet pound on the belt, sweat rolling down the back of my neck, my chest. I'm punishing myself, and I know it, but that won't stop me. Not when I deserve it. Not when I'm giving her so much less than what she deserves.

She's upstairs now, oblivious. She has no idea her future has been planned for her. That she's living in a fantasy. Reality will come crashing in eventually, and I'm not sure I want to be there when it does. That would be the cowardly way out, though. Destroying her, then disappearing before the fallout can hit me.

Just like I do every day, I tell myself to end things. Once I'm upstairs, I'll sit her down and tell her it's over. We can't do this anymore. I don't want her getting any ideas about feelings and all that shit. It'll be cruel, but it will get the point across. It will make her hate me, which is what I need her to do.

She's going to hate me eventually, anyway. Might as well get it over with now.

And once again, the same excuse I've given myself the past two weeks rings out in the back of my head. What if she's so hurt, she tells her father? I can pretend all I want that's not a real threat, that I'm not afraid of what will happen if he finds out. It just isn't true. And I can't get it through to her what a drastic reaction he'd have without revealing everything. That he's had people killed for much less than defiling his only daughter.

That would break her heart, too. It seems like no matter which way I look, no matter which path I decide to take, she ends up losing out.

All because I couldn't be strong enough to resist her. I let her down.

I pick up the speed, driving myself harder, faster. If I'm exhausted enough, I might be able to fight off the impulse to grab her the second I set eyes on her. That's how it always is. All it takes is a single look—or the smell of her perfume, or the sound of her voice—and I'm gone like some slobbering animal without a brain. That's what she does to me. Nobody's ever done that to me.

I don't even want to think about what that means. It doesn't have to mean anything, does it? She's hot. And she's available. It doesn't have to be any deeper than that.

Sure. Keep telling yourself that.

Finally, I reach the edge of my endurance, and I drop the speed of the belt to cool down. My legs are almost rubbery, and my lungs burn, but it's still not enough. I still feel like the world's biggest piece of shit for taking advantage of an innocent girl.

And dammit, I still want to ravish her once I get upstairs.

A cute redhead I've seen around the gym a few times gives me an approving look when we cross paths as I'm on my way to the fridge for a drink. I nod but leave it at that. Wouldn't life be easier if I did more? If I picked her up the way she obviously wants me to? If I had never been weak in the first place? If I had remembered my job and my duty? If I had put Mia's well-being before my own?

The most I'd have to worry about would be finding ways to sneak out of the condo while Mia wasn't paying attention. Heading over to the redhead's place for a quick fuck without being missed. The boss would chew me a new asshole if he ever found out I left his precious daughter alone, but I'd live to see another day.

And Mia might not end up with a broken heart. She'd be pissed as fuck, for sure. Hurt. Bitchy. She'd be the one to tell her father about me screwing around while on duty, now that I think about it. But she wouldn't have to live one day with knowing the man she gave her virginity to, who she so eagerly fucked so many times, had fucked her while knowing damn well there was no possible future for them. Knowing she was as good as sold off to the highest bidder and nothing about her future would be hers, ever.

Should I tell her the whole truth? Get it over with all at once? She deserves the opportunity to make her own decisions. I could help her somehow. Could help her think it through, make a plan to get away with her freedom intact without having to give up every last shred of herself.

And where would I go once I did that? If she got away, would I go with her?

She's not in the living room when I open the door. "Mia?" I hear footsteps somewhere—soft, rhythmic. "Where are you?"

Following the sound of the footfalls, I walk down the hallway and find her bedroom door partly open. She's in there, listening to music with her earbuds in, half undressed like she was in the act of getting changed when the song got to be too much, and she had to dance. The tight leggings she wears don't leave much to the imagination, and her lacy bra is see-through enough that her rose-pink nipples stand out.

I can't help but watch. It feels wrong to do it when she's unaware, but she would stop if she knew she wasn't alone.

How am I supposed to lay off her when everything about her seems built to tempt me? The way she moves, the sound of her voice, the feel of her skin. She haunts me day and night. Even my dreams.

Finally, I can't stay quiet anymore. I knock on her door before easing it open a little farther. "Hello?"

At least she can't accuse me of sneaking up and scaring her, even if she gasps with a hand over her chest. "You need to wear a bell around your neck."

"You need to stop listening to your music at deafening levels."

"Thanks for the advice." She looks me up and down, her nose wrinkling. It's cute even when she wrinkles it at me. "Good workout? You look like you took a shower."

"I need one, for sure."

"Do you always work out so hard? It's like you're punishing yourself. I mean, I work out too, but…"

If I didn't know better, I'd swear she could read my mind. Like she somehow knows why I pushed myself, why I've been pushing myself over the past two weeks we've been fucking like deranged rabbits. The boss has that tendency, too, of reaching into my head and pulling my thoughts out. Either that or I've been unable to deal with guilt for much longer than I knew.

"It's all that good food you've been shoving down my throat. I need to work it off." I pat my stomach, shrugging. "Don't like the sight of me all covered in sweat? Don't feed me so well."

"I like the sight of you all covered in sweat," she assures me with that impish little grin I've come to recognize as the precursor to something more. "It's just that I like being the reason you're all sweaty."

"Is that an invitation?" I take a step her way, then another.

"Oh, gross! Wash off your stink, at least!" She squeals an instant before sliding past me, running down the hall and into the living room, laughing the entire way. The sight of her ass jiggling is more than enough to strengthen my determination to get my hands on her. And my cock in her.

"Run all you want." I face her from the other end of the island, ducking right and left in time with her movements. "You can't get away. Not in your underwear."

"I can get back to my room and put on a shirt before you catch me."

"You sure about that?" I raise an eyebrow, grinning. "Try it."

She doesn't hesitate. Feinting right, then left, she finally breaks right and runs through the kitchen, reaching the hall a split second before I do. I try to make a grab for her, but she's too quick, flying barefoot down the hall and throwing herself into her room. She screams when I throw my weight against the door before she can get it shut.

"Get over here." I take her by the waist and pull her in close, making sure to rub my sweaty clothes on her. "Now you'll stink, too. Maybe we both need a shower."

"You're disgusting!" But she hasn't stopped giggling since I took hold of her, either. So I have to wonder how much she minds. I can't help but grope her a little now that my hands are on her. She's like a drug I'll never get my fill of.

Abruptly, her giggling stops. I realize it's because her phone's ringing, sitting on her desk. Her head swings in that direction because, of course, who can ignore a ringing phone?

"Oh, no." She breaks free of me and goes to it, blocking it from view.

"What's wrong? Who is it?"

She turns to me, eyes wide, the color gone from her face. "My dad."

20
MIA

I can't believe how hard I'm shaking. I think I'm going to be sick.

"Answer it," Zeke urges me in a strangled voice. "He'll be worried if you don't."

Right, but what happens when I answer, and he starts screaming at me? *Don't be stupid. He won't do that. He doesn't know what you've been doing.* No, maybe not, but why does it feel like he does? If he wanted me to spend the rest of my life feeling like he's watching, directly over my shoulder, he succeeded. It's actually kind of sick in a way.

"Mia." The way Zeke barks my name snaps me out of it. Right. I have to get it together.

"Hi, Daddy," I chirp on answering. A look at Zeke tells me I did a good job. I don't sound suspicious at all.

"Hello, sweetheart. You sound happy." *Sure, I was getting felt up by the bodyguard you sent to watch over me.* Yeah, that would go over really well. I should definitely start with that.

"No reason not to be." I pull on a jacket and step outside. The chill in the air feels good against my flushed skin. The heat in my cheeks starts to cool off. "How are you?"

"About as well as can be." So why is there a hint of regret in his voice?

"Are you taking care of yourself? You're not throwing all-night parties now that I'm not around, right?"

That gets him to laugh. "Not lately. Actually, sweetheart, I was more concerned with disappointing you."

For one heart-stopping second, I think, *this is it. He's going to tell me Zeke won't be my bodyguard anymore.* He'll give me one reason or another, some bullshit excuse like wanting to move him to a different job or needing him closer to home. Something like that. And when he does, I won't have any room to argue. I could say something about him making me feel safe, maybe, and about how long it took us to fall into a comfortable groove here. How I wouldn't want to go through that again, especially when I should be paying attention to schoolwork.

"What's up?" I ask when I realize I haven't responded. I need to shape up quick, or else he's going to ask if I've been doing drugs or something like that. He's always so suspicious.

But no, he's too busy being concerned about what he's about to tell me. "I'm sure you've been looking forward to coming home for Thanksgiving break. I know I've been looking forward to having you here. But it's looking like we won't be able to make that happen."

Well, talk about coming out of left field. "Oh. Okay." I lean on the railing, a little stunned.

"I'm sorry."

"No, I understand," I lie. Where is this coming from? "I'm sure I can stay here that week."

"Of course. It's not like you're living in a dorm. They're not going to shut down."

"Right, sure." Now I'm just saying words without really hearing them. "Is everything okay, though? Are you all right? You're not sick or anything, are you?"

He gives me one of those indulgent chuckles that sets my teeth on edge. If we were face-to-face right now, he would pat me on the head. "You are so sweet to be concerned."

"Well, I mean, it's kind of a big holiday. I figure there has to be a reason."

"And there is, but it's nothing like that."

"I'm glad to hear it." I pause, waiting to see if he'll explain. He doesn't. "So what's going on? Some big surprise you have planned for me?"

I didn't expect him to laugh, not the way he does. Like he's been found out. "How did you know?"

I stand straight, looking back over my shoulder into the living room. Zeke's in there, pacing with his arms folded. Our eyes meet, and I shrug. Is there something he knows that I don't?

Dad barrels over any questions I'm about to ask. "To tell you the truth, it has something to do with business. I'll be traveling and making arrangements for a deal."

Oh. That. Why did he think I would care about that? "I see." I should've known.

"We'll talk all about it when you're home for winter break. It's only another few weeks after that."

As if I don't know exactly when winter break comes up. As if I'm not practically counting the minutes. Some people sort of dread going home for break because it means giving up the freedom they've gotten used to while living at college. For me, it's the opposite. I won't have to get up for class, which means I'll be able to sleep in as long as I want. Dad would never bother me unless I needed to make an appearance at a function where he wanted to make a good impression. I hate that kind of thing, but at least I'd be able to get dressed up.

"Yeah," I assure him. "I'm looking forward to it."

"That's good to hear. I know I'm looking forward to it, too. It will be good having you home again." Sure, although we haven't been living together all that long. Sometimes, I wonder if he really feels about me the way he says he does. How can he? We still don't know each other all that well. Even after all this time, it's not like we have a warm, tender relationship. I guess I need to take his word for it and let it go.

It's just that I still remember so clearly how it felt to be really, truly loved by a parent. No, Mom didn't exactly have time to hang around with me all day. We didn't go shopping together unless it was for necessities. We didn't get our nails done or have spa days.

But the time we did spend together was ours. She focused on me. Even if we were sitting and watching a movie together, we were together. She wasn't on the phone, distracted. And when she asked questions about me, about my day, she listened to the answers. She asked because she wanted to know, not because she felt it was right.

She wasn't acting. That's it. It always feels like he's acting.

"I hope you're not too disappointed, though. I'll touch base with Zeke and make sure you have everything you need for any kind of dinner you want to have on Thanksgiving. I'm sure there has to be a restaurant around somewhere you could go to, or that might cater."

Zeke. Right. We'd be able to spend all this time together… All of a sudden, this is looking a lot better. "I haven't had a chance to cook a nice meal in a long time. Maybe I could give that a shot."

"That's an excellent idea!" He agrees with a lot more enthusiasm than I would have expected. "Sure, make whatever kind of meal you want. The sky's the limit."

"I will. And don't worry about it." I look over my shoulder again to find Zeke staring at me, his eyes full of questions. "I think we're going to be just fine."

I mean, I should thank him. He just gave me an excuse to spend almost a solid week with nothing to do but hang around here naked if I feel like it while Zeke does the same. Oh, gee, no. I'm giggling to myself by the time I go back inside.

"Well? What happened?" Zeke's eyes dart over my face. "You're not crying, so I guess that's a good sign."

"Everything is fine."

"What happened, though? Why did he call?" It's almost cute how anxious he is. I used to look down on him for his devotion—I cringe now, thinking back on it, but I can't deny how angry it made me, feeling like even he wasn't on my side. Now I know better.

Now I know his ass is in a sling even more than mine is. I don't want Dad to be angry with me, but it's not like I could lose my job over it the way Zeke would—at the very least. He always makes it seem like that would be the least of his problems.

"He said I shouldn't come home for Thanksgiving."

His eyebrows knit together instantly. "What? Why?"

"Something to do with business. I don't know." I shrug it off. "You would probably know better than I would, honestly. You know more about his business than I do."

"Not anymore. And even then, I wasn't exactly his right-hand man." He rubs the back of his neck, the other hand on his hip, staring at the floor. Deep in thought. "He's always got business. Why would that stop you from coming home?"

"Honestly? I don't even care."

"You don't? I figured you would look forward to having time off."

"Time off from what? From school?" I can't believe he's being so dense. "I won't have any schoolwork to do here, either, right?"

"That's true..."

I walk toward him with slow, even steps. "And you'll still be here. He didn't say he needs you to come home for anything."

"That's also true..." He's starting to get the message. Finally. A sly smile begins to spread.

"So what that tells me is that we'll have the days to ourselves. No classes. No project work. None of it. Just you and me." By the time I finish speaking, I'm standing directly in front of him, grinning from ear to ear. "I think I can live with that."

When he draws his bottom lip under his teeth, my pulse picks up speed. That's what he's capable of doing to me without laying a hand on me or even saying a word. It should be illegal to be this hot. This perfect. "I guess I can if you can. I wonder how we'll find ways to fill the time."

"I think we can come up with something together if we put our minds to it." I slip a finger under the waistband of his shorts. "Now, I think we were talking about getting you in the shower before we were interrupted, weren't we?"

He looks me up and down. "Who are you? Where is the little virgin I used to know? Asking me to show her what to do, how to please me?"

"I guess you were a good teacher." I back away, still grinning, and pull the nightshirt over my head before dropping it to the floor. The man has an excellent poker face, but not when it comes to this. Red hot lust sparks in his eyes a second before he follows, peeling off his sweaty shirt and dropping it next to mine. By the time he joins me in his bathroom, I have the shower running and am bending down to slide off my panties.

He takes me by the hips, grinding himself against my ass. "You get me so fucking hard," he grunts in my ear, his fingers pressing into my flesh like he wants to take control of my entire body. Like it's his, like he owns it. And if that's what he thinks, he's not wrong. I can't imagine anybody making me feel the way he does, knowing what I like better than even I do.

Instead of opening the shower door, he turns me around, still pressed against my back. We're facing the vanity, reflected in the mirror above the sink. There I am, stark naked, with Zeke holding me in place. "Look how fucking gorgeous you are." He lowers his head, and his lips skim over my shoulder.

I gasp, melting against him.

"Open your eyes," he suddenly mutters, his voice sharp. I hadn't even realized I closed my them—all I want is to lose myself in him. I want him to sweep me away so I don't have to think about anything or anybody but us. "Watch yourself."

"Watch myself what?" When his right hand leaves my hip in favor of wedging between my thighs, I know what. I gasp when his fingers brush against my clit, my head falling back against his chest.

"Watch what happens when I do this to you. Watch how beautiful it is." He nips my earlobe, and I shiver when that sensation combined with what he's doing to my pussy threatens to overwhelm me. My legs are already weak, but I force myself to stand. Whatever he wants, I'll do it because I know in the end, he's going to make me come. He's so good at making me come.

Is this what he sees when he touches me? My nipples harden, and my skin flushes. My face contorts until I hardly recognize myself. Who is that girl in the mirror? Sexy, sensual, mouth hanging open so I can moan his name. His free hand slides up my body, groping my tits before continuing further and wrapping around my throat. He holds my head in place, making sure I'm watching.

"There's nothing in the world like watching you fall to pieces." His dick is practically impaling my lower back. When I wiggle against it just a little, the way he groans makes me gasp with even deeper pleasure. Because it's not all about what he does to me. It's about what that does to him. What I am capable of doing to him.

He begins rubbing himself against me, the motion from his fingers speeding up. A strangled sob escapes my throat.

"Does that feel good?" he asks, like he needs to.

"Yes!" I gasp, leaning against him for support. "Yes, so good!"

"And do I own this pussy? Is this pussy mine?" Our eyes meet in the mirror, and fuck me, he's a beast. This isn't Zeke anymore. This is some primal force channeling itself through him. I should want to fight back, but I don't. That's the last thing I want. I want him to take me, I want him to use me, I want him to be as rough as he needs to be because that's what I need, too.

"It's yours," I promise, and I mean it with every fiber of my being. "Yours, Zeke."

He growls in satisfaction before burying his face in my hair. "Fucking right," he groans.

"I'm so close," I whisper, desperate, willing myself to get there. "I'm going—I'm going to—"

"Watch yourself," he demands when my eyes start to close again. "Or

I'll stop." Like he wants to prove it, his pace drops off until he's barely touching me.

"No!" I whimper, desperate for the release of this tension. God, I can't live with this. "Please, don't stop!"

"Then keep your eyes open." He meets my gaze over the top of my head, and it's the sexiest thing I've ever seen. Him watching me, me watching him. Both of us are in this together as he pushes me higher, higher, wet slapping noises coming from between my legs thanks to the juices running down the insides of my thighs. So close, so close—

"Oh, yes!" I watch in wonder, exhilarated, my body straining for one last second before a massive shudder wracks me, leaving me shaking and sobbing with relief. I fall back against him, weak and helpless, riding out the blissful waves.

But he's not finished yet. I haven't finished coming before he bends me over the sink and lines up with my quivering pussy. "Mine." He shoves himself inside me, taking me deep, making me gasp from the force and the depth.

"Oh, yeah," I moan, still riding the high. Instead of coming all the way down, it's like I'm on a plateau, stuck in that delicious in-between place. "I love the way you feel inside me." I look up in the mirror to meet his eyes.

He clenches his jaw, fighting hard against his own need to let it go. "Nobody will ever fuck you like this."

"Nobody!" I agree before gasping when our bodies crash together. There's something different about this. He's taken me hard, but this is fierce. There's something deeper going on, something I don't understand. But I feel it like a current running from him into me. Binding us together.

"Mine. Made for me. Only me."

"Yes!" This is all I want. This is all I ever want. Zeke inside me, filling me up, using me, and letting me use him.

"You have another one in you?" he asks, slapping my ass hard enough to make me yell. My head bobs up and down—I can't speak, I'm too out of breath—and he chuckles in approval. "Good girl. Let me feel it. Come on my cock, Mia."

The way he says my name is absolutely filthy. How can two syllables be filthy? But he does it, and it's so fucking hot, and oh, my God, I'm going to come again, I'm going to—

"Zeke!" I lean against the vanity, moaning his name over and over, but he doesn't let up. He takes me by the hips with both hands and hammers me hard, merciless, baring his teeth and snarling—ferocious. I love it. I love watching. I love seeing him come apart the way he makes me fall to pieces.

He pulls out just in time, a split second before a splash of cum hits my lower back. And I smile, strangely triumphant even though I didn't do anything special. It's the satisfaction of watching him find his pleasure in me. Knowing I can make him do that.

When he's finally spent, his head falls back, his breath coming in sharp gasps. "There's my second workout of the day," he manages before chuckling.

He then looks toward the shower. "I think now is the part where we get cleaned up."

I laugh with him because, yes, we both need it now.

Still, there's a tiny part of me, way in the back of my mind, that can't help but wonder why he seemed so angry. Was he getting something out of his system that I don't know about? And that possessiveness? It's sexy, yeah, but it didn't seem like he was trying to be sexy about it. It was like he actually meant it.

He's never been that way before this morning. Did something change?

Why do I get the feeling he knows something I don't?

21
ZEKE

"Can you peel these potatoes, please?" Mia turns away from what she's doing to the turkey long enough to jerk her chin toward the strainer, where she scrubbed a handful of potatoes earlier.

"You're assuming I know how to handle a peeler."

"You don't?" She looks my way, one eyebrow raised. "Are you serious?"

"No, I can peel potatoes. My grandmother taught me when I was a kid." Though it's been a long time since I've had to do it. "I was just screwing with you."

"Well, you can't blame me for taking you seriously."

"I've cooked before, remember?"

"Right. Boiling pasta and heating up a jar of sauce. A culinary masterpiece."

I take a swat at her ass before taking a peeler to the first potato. "Looks like you'll have to teach me a few things."

"Why not?" she counters. "You've taught me plenty." I can't argue with that.

I also can't believe how nice this is. Strange, different, but nice. I could almost believe this is a normal situation, that we're just two normal people making shit happen in a kitchen on Thanksgiving Day. Is this what it's like to live a regular life? It's the sort of thing I could get used to if such a thing were possible.

But it's not, and I have to remember that. No matter how much I don't want to, no matter how inconvenient it is. This is not my normal life. This isn't how things are supposed to be.

That's not going to stop me from enjoying it while I can. As much as I can.

The way she took this whole dinner thing seriously was almost touching. Narrowing down which dishes she would prepare based on the ones we both like most. Mashed potatoes were an obvious choice. Neither of us is crazy about stuffing, so we're skipping that. She insisted on cranberry sauce, and I agreed—but only if it's from a can. "I hate that fresh shit," I told her, and she did her best not to get too offended. I'm not trying to eat any actual cranberries. If there aren't marks from the can on it, it's not cranberry sauce.

That, some rolls, a vegetable—at her insistence—and we'll have a nice dinner. She even baked two pies yesterday—one apple, one pumpkin. She'd hate it if she knew how cute she looked, kneading the dough with a touch of flour on the tip of her nose. She walked around like that for at least an hour before catching her reflection in the microwave.

"When was the last time you had Thanksgiving with your family?" she asks all of a sudden. She has a tendency to do that, to hit me with a question I had no idea she was even thinking of.

I have to pause for a second and think about it. "You know, I can't remember."

"Really? You can't?"

I almost resent how sad she sounds. "Is that wrong?"

"No, of course, it isn't. It's not wrong. I'm just a little surprised, I guess."

"How come?"

She's quiet for a long second before laughing. "Because I'm naïve. That's why. There's your answer."

"I don't think you're naïve."

That gets her hooting with more laughter, louder this time. "Shut up. Yes, you do."

"About some things, okay. I'll admit that."

She rolls her eyes. "Gee, thanks." Meanwhile, she's loosening the skin on the top of the turkey with a bowl of butter and other stuff next to her on the counter. It's enough to make me want to gag. Only knowing how offended she'd be if I did stops me.

"What are you doing?" I ask instead.

"What's it look like? I'm getting the turkey ready." When all I do is stare, a little disgusted, she explains. "I mix butter with herbs and orange zest, then tuck it under the skin next to the breast." She takes a glob of soft butter and inserts it under the skin, then smooths it back in one long, slow motion over the top of the skin with her other hand.

"That's a little bit disgusting," I have to admit. If she only knew the worst of what I've seen—the aftermath of things I've done—she would laugh herself sick. Even I find it funny. I can turn a guy's head to strawberry jelly, but I can't stand the sight of turkey preparation.

"Just wait. It will be so delicious." She then slides me a knowing look. "Anyway, back to the subject. How come you didn't have Thanksgiving with your family? We never really talked about them."

"Did you ever think there might be a reason for that?"

I didn't mean to make her feel bad, but she blushes anyway before lowering her gaze back to the bird. "I'm sorry. You're right. I shouldn't assume."

"No, I shouldn't give you shit over the stuff you don't know about." I finish the last potato, leaving a pile of peels in the sink, then look around for a knife. I'm not going to be one of those guys who acts like he doesn't know what comes next. I've at least watched mashed potatoes getting prepared before. "It's just I usually had to work on Thanksgiving. So did my dad. And it was pretty much just the two of us for most of my life, except when I was real little and living with my grandparents."

"So your father worked—"

"For your dad and his family, yeah. For a long time. That's how I got this job." I look around. "You have a pot for these?"

"You know where the pots are," she reminds me. I do, so I grab one and fill it with water. She's not going to let me change the subject, is she?

"Anyway, we usually ended up keeping an eye on things while the family—your family—had their meal. There was always extra food leftover, and we always ate later with the rest of the crew on duty. Back in the kitchen, you know, wherever there was room."

"I'm sorry."

"For what?" I ask with a chuckle. "You don't need to feel sorry. To tell you the truth, I've never known it any other way, at least not that I can remember too clearly. So it's not like I lost out on anything."

"I guess you're right."

"How about you?" I nod toward the turkey before winking at her. "I get the feeling this isn't your first time."

"Honestly? It sort of is."

"What? How did you know how to do that?" I ask, gesturing toward the bird she's now tying up with twine.

"I watched videos, and I used to watch cooking shows on TV. We couldn't really afford a turkey for Thanksgiving. Sometimes we'd get a chicken or a free ham if the supermarket was giving them away—like, if you bought a certain amount of groceries, you'd get something free. We did the best we could with what we had."

She turns back toward her work with a little smile. "This is the first time I've ever been able to do everything I want. Like, I could just go crazy and buy all the ingredients my heart desired. That was nice."

And now I wish I had let her make her disgusting cranberry sauce from scratch. "So I'm not going to die of food poisoning or anything?"

"I'll do my best," she retorts with a smirk. Her whole life, she's done her best to make do with what she was given, and now she's been given so much. Strange how I used to think of her as a brat. She still can be, especially when she digs her heels in. But at her core, she's one of the most down-to-earth people I've ever met. And she still appreciates everything she's been given instead of taking it for granted the way other people do.

I go back to my potatoes, cutting them up and trying hard not to imagine a younger version of her cooking a pitiful little dinner.

* * *

MIA'S SLEEPING in my arms an hour after we went to bed, but I'm nowhere near sleepy. I can't even stir up any interest in doing more than lying here next to her.

I ate myself sick tonight. We both did. Sex was the last thing on our minds by the time we stumbled to bed after watching holiday movies. I still think it's too early for that shit, but she disagrees—and I knew better than to argue.

Besides, it made her happy.

And I think that's why I can't sleep. Why I have to carefully extract myself from bed, doing everything I can to keep from waking her up. She's out cold, though, snoring softly. She deserves it after all the work she put into making it a nice holiday.

I'm still too full and too uneasy. It's the uneasiness that gets me dressed in sweats with the intention of heading down to the gym. I'm not going to put in a full workout—I'd never get to sleep if I did—but at least a walk on the treadmill might help me think. I make sure to arm the alarm using the app on my phone once I'm out in the hallway. Once I get confirmation, I take the stairs down to the second floor, where the gym awaits.

It's a shame working out at this time of night is unsustainable. Otherwise, I'd be down here at one in the morning all the time. One of the TVs in the far corner is still on, playing The Weather Channel at low volume. That's fine by me since the rest of the gym is empty. I have the whole place to myself.

What am I going to do about her? And about myself? That's the question weighing on my mind when I start walking on the nearest treadmill. How am I supposed to balance how she makes me feel with the job I'm paid to do?

This was all a lot easier when I didn't know her. It was easy to want her and resent her at the same time. Most of the time, I resented her because I wanted her so much and couldn't have her.

Now, she's mine to have whenever I want. I know she's looking forward to the rest of her break, and so am I. It'll just be the two of us without distractions or interruptions, without having to pretend nothing is going on.

And that's the most dangerous part of all. The way I'm looking forward to having her to myself, just like I look forward to the end of her last class every day. I can't wait to get her back to the condo where we can be alone and drop the act.

Because it's not going to last. It can't possibly. I know it… and deep down inside, she has to know it, too.

Though we have very different reasons as to why we know it.

I crank up the speed on the equipment like I can outpace my guilt. Every time I fuck her, I turn my back on my duty. I'm supposed to be presenting her to her father as pure and untouched as she was when he sent us here. What's that old saying about not being able to put the toothpaste back in the tube? It fits the situation.

Even that, we can get around. She can pretend. I don't think they're going to be medieval about it. I doubt the boss would have her checked out by a doctor again. Even then, I know it's not possible to really tell if a girl is a virgin or not. It's all outdated shit.

But I've been betraying her. And that, I can't lie about. Every time she talks about next semester and next year and her plans for the future. Every time I listen quietly without warning her, I'm betraying her. Where's the line here? Do I owe her anything? I could easily brush this off, pretend this is nothing more than two people forced together who can't keep their hands off each other.

I'm not so sure that's the truth, is all. Because the more time we spend together—cooking, watching movies, even sleeping in the same bed—the closer I come to caring about her. Really, truly caring.

And more than anything else, that's the biggest mistake I could've made. I'm afraid it's too late now to do anything about it, though, that's the thing. It's almost enough to make me want to take a step back, to tell the boss I can't handle this anymore. I'm not cut out for the job, something like that. That she would do better with somebody else, one of the boss's other soldiers.

But they might be as dismissive of her as he is. They might break her spirit, and she's got enough of that coming to her in the future. The rest of her life, in fact. I doubt the husband the boss chooses for her will be a nice, kind, sympathetic sort of guy.

She's going to fucking hate me when she finds out I've always known what he has planned. I've had so many opportunities to give her the heads-up, too, and she'll remember every single one of them. Not only will she feel betrayed by her father, but by me, and how am I supposed to live with that? I've lost track of the number of lives I've taken, yet somehow, this is what gets under my skin the worst. This is what makes me wonder if I'm half the man I thought I was.

And what if I tell her and she tries to run away? I can't trust that she wouldn't pull one of her old stunts—only this isn't the same as sneaking out for a party. She could be taking her life into her hands if she runs. Unless I went with her, there would be no telling whether or not she'd be safe. Would it be better to let her absorb the betrayal upfront, knowing she'll at least be protected from harm?

No matter which way I turn, no matter how I look at it, I'm fucking trapped. And so is she.

And I can't pretend I don't care more about her than I do about myself.

After half an hour, I don't feel much better mentally, but at least physically, I've shed that heavy, bloated feeling. I slow down my pace, checking my phone for any alerts. Everything is status quo upstairs. After a brief cooldown, I turn off the machine and grab a bottle of water from the complementary stash before heading back up.

Maybe I'll have a talk with the boss when we go home for winter break. It isn't as if I have to come out and tell the man how unfair it is, the way he underestimates her. I can at least get a feel for what he has in mind. Who he has in mind.

A few major families have sons young enough to make a decent husband for her, at least on paper. I'm sure that's what he has in mind. A marriage that will look good for the press and the other families. One that will strengthen his position.

Part of me wonders if she wouldn't have been better off if he had never found her. But that would mean I'd never have met her, and I'm not sure I want to think about my life without her in it.

It finally hits me before I open the door leading out to the hall: I went and let my feelings get in the way. I wasn't even paying attention, but somehow it happened.

I'm still trying to grapple with this when I walk up to the front door.

And right away, I see the envelope sitting on the floor. Carefully placed and centered in the doorframe, it clearly wasn't dropped. It was positioned.

Before I touch it, I check my phone again to make sure nobody's opened the door since I left. Meanwhile, I dart back and forth down the length of the hall, though it's no use. Whoever was here is long gone.

I approach the envelope, my heart pounding. It could be innocent for all I know, but who leaves what looks like a card outside somebody's door in the middle of the night? Not to mention that half of the building holds college students who are home on break now. And it isn't like Mia knows any of the neighbors.

I pick it up at the corners using just my fingertips, examining every inch of the envelope before slowly easing the flap free. There's a plain, white notecard inside. Nothing else—no powder, nothing like that. All that's left is for me to extract the card and read the message.

It's short and sweet, and it sends my heart into overdrive. In big, block letters, somebody has printed four simple words.

YOU CAN'T PROTECT HER

22
MIA

When I wake up alone for the fourth night in a row, I can't pretend I don't know it anymore.

I guess some people in the world can sleep solidly. They get into bed, they close their eyes, they fall asleep, and they don't wake up again until their alarm goes off. Or, even weirder, they get up on their own. *Psychos.*

Me, on the other hand? I can't remember the last time I slept a whole night all the way through. Back in the day, I used to always listen for Mom to come through the front door, so I'd know she got home okay from her late shift. I guess it's one of those habits that stuck. Even though I have nothing to listen for now, I never sleep for more than an hour or two without at least opening my eyes and checking the time.

That's why I know that tonight's the fourth night in a row that Zeke started out in bed with me, then ended up somewhere else. I told myself I'd wait until he came back on Thanksgiving, but I fell asleep before that happened. In the morning, he was there, beside me. It's been the same since then.

And that's not the only thing different.

I sit up and check my phone—it's quarter to three, and I have no idea how long it's been since he left. I never pegged him as an insomniac. Maybe that's the problem, and he never mentioned it.

Or maybe something bigger is going on.

I hate to even think it, but I can't avoid what's been in my gut for days. Thanksgiving was definitely when things changed, no doubt about it. Everything seemed fine—great even. We had dinner, watched movies, and went to bed feeling good. Stuffed, but good.

By morning, everything was different. He can pretend all he wants to, but he's not a great actor. There's a stiffness to him now. Not quite the way he was before, but not the way he's been the past few weeks, either. It's almost enough to make me wonder if I imagined everything, even though I know I didn't.

But it's still easier to question my memory and experiences than to admit what's irking me.

I think he's tired of me now.

It's the only thing that makes sense. I was forbidden fruit. Because he couldn't have me, he only wanted me more. Now, I've literally lost count of the number of times we've had sex all over our home. Maybe I'm out of his system now. Maybe I made the biggest mistake of my entire life convincing myself we could keep this casual.

There's nothing casual about it for me. Not only because he's my first, either. I'm sure I would feel a certain way about whoever that person happened to be.

Zeke is different. He's not some random hookup. He's not some fumbling college freshman who managed to work his way into my pants.

And now, I don't think he wants me anymore. He hasn't even gotten handsy with me in days. I'm smart enough to know I didn't do anything wrong, but I can't help blaming myself a little. I shouldn't have gotten attached, and I know I did. But I've done everything I can to keep that from him. I don't want to scare him off.

I chew my lip, staring at the closed door. Should I go looking for him? Will he resent me if I do? He probably needs his space, right? Then again, I didn't invite him to stay in my bed. That's just something that sort of happened. I'm not trying to force him into anything, so I don't think it makes me needy if I wake up in the middle of the night and wonder where he went.

That's enough to firm up my resolve. It's enough to make me cross the room and open the door, to step out in the hallway and look around. There he is, sitting on the balcony of all places. Fully dressed, right down to that leather jacket. I don't think I'll ever smell leather again without thinking of him.

When I tap on the door, he flinches, his head snapping around. I hold up a hand, silently apologizing for startling him before opening the door. "What are you doing out here? Is there something wrong?"

He frowns, his brows a solid line over his eyes. Eyes that remind me of steel. They're that hard. I don't think he's ever looked at me this way before.

But just as suddenly as I notice them, they change. They soften. "Nothing's wrong. I just couldn't sleep."

"I hope I wasn't the one keeping you up."

"Now that you mention it, you were snoring like a trumpet."

"No, I wasn't."

"And how would you know?" He smirks a little, then gives in. "No, you didn't keep me up. I've never been a great sleeper."

Is that why you've been acting so weird? Have you had insomnia? The question is right on the tip of my tongue, but I don't dare ask it. Since when do I have a hard time expressing myself? He has me acting in a way that even I don't recognize anymore. "So what? You thought getting dressed and sitting outside in the middle of the night would make you sleepy?"

"The fresh air clears my head. And I figured what the hell, if I fall back asleep now, I'll feel like shit when it comes time to get up." That does make sense, even if I don't believe him. Something else is going on. I mean, I have class later this morning, but I haven't for days. Nothing to wake up early for. Yet something tells me this is how he's been spending his nights away from me. Sitting up, watching. For what?

I shiver, and this time, he scowls. "You shouldn't be out here. You're barely dressed." But he doesn't make a move either.

"Would you come in with me?"

He hesitates, his jaw working like he's frustrated, like there's something he wants to say but, like me, is holding back. "Yeah, I will. Otherwise, you'll give yourself pneumonia or something like that. And then what would I tell your father?"

Is that it? He did tell me a while back that Dad calls him all the time. "Is he giving you shit about me?" I ask once we're inside with the door locked.

"What do you mean?"

"Does he think you're being lax with my protection? Is that why you're sitting outside, watching?"

"No. He knows everything is fine here." He takes off his jacket, hanging it by the door before going to the kitchen for a drink. I follow him, hopping up on the counter. The marble is cold under my legs, but what's more important is getting to the bottom of what's bothering him. The fact that he hardly looks at me doesn't do wonders for my self-esteem, let's put it that way.

"What changed? You were so open with me. Is that the problem? You don't want to be open with me anymore?"

He shoots me a look like I'm crazy. "No. What would make you think that?" All of a sudden, he's very interested in the cap to his water bottle. Like it's the most fascinating thing he's ever seen.

"Let's start with the way you won't look at me for longer than a split second."

He shoots me a look from under his lowered brow. "Happy?"

"Thrilled. Thanks so much." He rolls his eyes, which only irritates me more. "You're not very good at hiding when something is bothering you. I hate to tell you that, but it's true."

"Is this a performance review all of a sudden?"

I have to fight like hell to keep from lashing out at him. He knows just how to push my buttons, doesn't he? "If I didn't know better, I would think you were trying to start a fight. Even though I haven't done anything worth fighting about except being concerned for you."

All that does is make him snicker. "I'm not the one you need to worry about."

Goose bumps race up the length of my arms. "What's that mean? Who should I worry about?"

"I shouldn't have said that." He leans his back against the counter opposite the island, facing me. Looking at me, finally. "I'm not trying to worry you or scare you. I'm just saying, I'm not worth you worrying about."

"That's not true." When his brows pinch together again, I add, "You're a human being. That alone makes you worth it." Oh, smooth. He won't think I've caught feelings for him at all, will he? I'm in so far over my head that I don't know what to do about it.

"I've been taking care of myself for a long time. That's all I mean. I can handle myself." He lifts his chin, eyes narrowing. "You're the one I should be worrying about. I'm here to take care of you, to look after you. And I'm starting to wonder if I've lost focus along the way."

So that's what this is about. I don't know if I'm relieved or annoyed or both. "It doesn't have to be complicated, you know. Just the fact that you're here, physically present with me, is enough. Don't tell me you've gotten all paranoid like Dad has." I try to laugh it off and make out like it's a joke, but he doesn't join me. Now, it's not just the marble that feels cold. I'm starting to feel cold inside, too.

Does he know something I don't?

"You would tell me, wouldn't you? If there was a reason for me to be concerned?"

There's looking somebody in the eye because you're telling the truth, and there's forcing yourself to look somebody in the eye so they think you're telling the truth. I should know. I'm pretty skilled when it comes to both. The fact that he doesn't blink or even breathe as he holds my gaze tells me it's the latter. "If there was something you needed to know, I would tell you."

"That's not an answer, and we both know it. But nice try," I add, shaking my head. He only chuckles and shakes his head right back.

"That's the truth." He tries harder to convince me this time, staring at me for a long time. Like he's daring me to argue. "I mean it."

"Okay. I believe you," I lie. Is this how it's going to always be? Tiptoeing around each other, practically speaking in code? I've never been one to back down from a fight—he should know that by now—but I don't want to fight with him anymore. I want things to go back to the way they were last week, when we both seemed, if not happy, at least content with the way things were for the time being. I had something to look forward to, something to be excited about when I opened my eyes in the morning. Just being with him, being able to touch him freely, to indulge the way I've wanted to for so long.

To see him smile. A real, true smile. He was starting to finally come out of his shell and share real, true things with me. And now that's gone, too. Like a turtle retreating back into his shell, and I don't know how to coax him out again.

"Well, if I'm going to stay awake through class, I think we should both try to get a little more sleep."

"I told you—"

"Fine, then I'll try to get more sleep. I'm not going to be able to if I'm worried about you sitting out on the balcony in the dark." Alone, I want to add, but I don't. He doesn't need to think I care more than I should. It would only make things worse.

I can tell he's getting annoyed and doesn't want to show it. His face is actually very expressive when he's not putting on a front for the outside world. Probably more than he realizes. "Fine. I'll go to bed, but I can't promise I'll sleep."

"See? Was it that hard to compromise?" That gets a real grin from him, anyway, even if it doesn't last long. It makes me think back to that first week, to the night he spanked me and opened up an entirely new world for my overactive imagination. The night we tried to compromise.

He strips down to his underwear before joining me in bed, both of us on our right sides the way we normally sleep. It makes me happier than it should when he wraps an arm around me and pulls me in close. I was almost afraid he wouldn't want to be near me, and it kills me that I was afraid. I don't want to care. I really don't. I'm only going to end up hurting myself in the end.

But I'm afraid it's too late to stop.

"Happy now?" he murmurs, which only makes me drive an elbow into his ribs. Not hard, but enough to get the point across. Then I snuggle in closer, fitting my body to his like we're a couple of puzzle pieces.

And I wait, eyes closed. Wanting to see what comes next. Never, and I mean ever, have we snuggled up with my ass against his dick without something else happening. He should at least get hard. He always does, even if he doesn't do anything about it. Though it's rare that he doesn't.

Nothing. Not so much as a twitch. Either he's got something on his mind or he's not attracted to me anymore.

"You know, I was thinking." His voice is soft, his mouth close to my ear. "How would you feel about me teaching you self-defense?"

Oh, and I guess I'm not supposed to read anything deeper into that, either. "Like how?" I ask, staring at the wall across the room.

"You know, moves you could use if you ever needed to. I can't be with you all the time, can I? Unless you like the idea of me following you into the bathroom when we're out."

Sure, this is all perfectly normal. Absolutely fine. "Yeah, if you want to. I'm happy to learn anything you want to teach me." I wiggle my ass a little, trying to be playful, even though my heart's not in it. "I mean, you've already proven what a good teacher you are."

He snorts, but there's no humor in it. "Okay. We'll start tomorrow."

"You mean today," I point out.

"Always needing the last word."

"Do you expect anything else by now?" He chuckles softly, and I think I feel the brief pressure of his lips against my head, but it's gone so fast I could have imagined it.

No matter what he says, now I know for sure.

There's some kind of threat out there, and it's directed at me.

And if I don't know what it is, what am I supposed to do about it?

23
ZEKE

There's one thing I can say for her: she's an eager student. Not that I didn't know that, but what we're doing now is a little different from what we do without our clothes on. Sure, she was a quick study when it came to learning how to fuck, but this is different. This is grueling, even painful at times.

And it's not easy for me, either. I wouldn't admit it to her since I want her to give these lessons everything she's got, but hearing her groan when she hits the floor or seeing her wince when she aggravates a body part that's already bruised hurts a little.

If somebody attacks her, they're not going to be merciful. Hurting her would be the point. I remind myself of this as I extend a hand to help her from the living room floor. "What did you learn that time?"

"Not to get in a fight with you?" She gets up slowly, rolling her shoulders. We've been at it for nearly an hour, and the strain is starting to show.

"Seriously. You have to take this seriously."

At least she's stopped asking why I'm so serious. "I have to plant my feet better, and I have to pivot with purpose." She puts her hands on her hips, breathing heavy.

"That's right. It's not enough to throw your weight behind your movement. You have to know exactly why you're doing it and its purpose. That way, you can focus. Otherwise, you're flailing around like a fish, and you end up hitting the floor."

"This would all be a lot easier if you would let me do what I want to do." She stands with her back to my chest, positioning my arm across her as if I grabbed her from behind. "I call it the sandbag."

"And what is the sandbag?"

"This." Suddenly she goes limp, dead weight, dragging me down with her. "See? I knock you off balance. I surprise you, and isn't the element of surprise half the battle?"

"I never said that. And I never would." Still, it takes effort not to laugh. "I don't think we'll be using the sandbag anytime soon." I put her back on her feet, and she scowls.

"Whatever. I'm going to patent that move. Or trademark it or something, whatever applies."

I would laugh it off if the memory of that note wasn't so clear. *You Can't Protect Her.* It's been more than a week since I found it, and there haven't been any follow-ups since. A random threat? From whom, though? Considering I was unaware of the boss having any enemies around here in the first place, it's been a long, sleepless ten days. And I still can't come up with an answer.

All I can do is prepare her as best I can—but the line between preparation and scaring the shit out of her is thin. I have to be sure I don't cross it, or I'd run the risk of having her shut down on me.

"So?" She bounces on the balls of her feet, bubbling with excitement.

"So what?"

"You know what." She scowls before poking me in the chest. "You promised if I did a good enough job today, we would do something cool. Considering I feel sore from head to toe, I think I did pretty well."

"Pretty well? I knocked you on your ass."

"But I tried hard, didn't I? And you can't pretend I'm not getting better." She's got me there. She might not have a lot of physical strength, she's quick, and she understands physics. You don't have to be the strongest so long as you know how to leverage the strength you have.

Still, I pretend to think about it, letting her stew a little. When she's as close as she's going to come to boiling over without actually doing it, I give in. "Okay, let's get showered up, and we'll do what I had in mind."

"It's not sex, is it?"

"And would that be so bad?"

"I'm just saying, is it something besides that?"

"Yes, and I'm going to try not to take it personally that you're so concerned." She only rolls her eyes before following me. I massage her shoulders, letting the hot water loosen them up for me. By the time we're finished, she's in considerably better shape.

And I'm considerably hornier, but then she always has that effect on me. It doesn't matter what we're doing, where we are, the time of day. There's never a time I don't want her.

There's something worse than that, though. I want to make her smile, and I think I might be able to do that today. "We're going to take a ride on the Harley," I announce. "There's a great spot around half an hour from here. I checked it out on the map and looked at the pictures on Google Earth. I think you'll like it."

She smiles, happy, but I can still see a touch of uncertainty in her eyes. She doesn't quite understand what the big deal is. But she will.

It feels too good, riding with her behind me, her arms around my waist. Her weight against my back. I could almost imagine things always being like this—and I know I need to stop. It's no good, allowing my imagination to run away like that. It's only going to end up biting me in the ass when the inevitable happens, and she moves on with her life. It's going to happen someday. Her father's going to find her a husband.

And every day I let pass without warning her is another day I've betrayed her. There's no question in my mind that's how she'll take it. I can't even say she would be wrong.

We reached the lake around three o'clock, meaning we have a couple of hours before it gets dark. The campground is virtually deserted at this time of year, giving us all the privacy and safety we need.

She gasps when I pull to a stop on the shore. "Wow. It's gorgeous out here." And it is. Peaceful, the water still as glass. The sky is the kind of deep blue it can only be at this time of year. I never much thought about it before now.

And when she turns to me with a smile, I'm fairly sure my heart stops. It takes so little to make her happy, unlike the bratty façade she put up to protect herself when she first came to live with her father. "It's incredible. What made you think to come here?"

"That's easy." I put the kickstand in place before swinging a leg over the seat. "I'm teaching you the basics of riding a motorcycle."

"What?" She's loud enough to drive a few birds out of the trees, but she doesn't notice them since she's busy gaping at me. "You're going to let me ride your bike?"

"Slow down," I murmur, chuckling. "I'm going to be behind you the entire time. I would never step back and let you careen off into the water."

"Thanks for all the faith you have in me." But she can't pretend she's not thrilled.

"I just want you to pay attention. There may come a time when you have to make a quick getaway, and I want to make sure you at least know the basics if the Harley's all you have at your disposal. Know what I mean?"

I can tell she's troubled at the way I put that, but I can't coddle her forever. "Got it. Teach me."

I do, giving her the rundown of the basics. The intensity of her attention is almost cute. She wants so much to do well. By the time I tell her to get in position, she's chewing her lip, caught between excitement and apprehension. "I'm not so sure."

"You're going to be fine. Remember, I'm right behind you. If you freak out, I'll help you." I mount behind her and repeat the instructions on how to use the throttle and brake. "The Harley comes with anti-lock brakes," I assure her. "Still, take it easy. Don't twist too hard. You'll figure out the pressure. And don't panic and hit the brake too hard."

"Okay, okay." I can tell she's overwhelmed, but I couldn't be more proud that she still wants to try. We shoot forward, and she squeals.

"Relax," I remind her. "You're doing fine." Still, I'm ready to reach out and take control at any second. "I'm right here. You can do anything. I have faith in you."

"Really?" Her voice is soft, sweet. We pick up speed.

"Focus," I remind her. This isn't the time to swoon.

And she does focus, and after an hour, she's more confident. We ride around the perimeter of the lake, taking our time, and it's amazing to witness her attitude shift. She's not so stiff anymore. She actually laughs a few times.

I'm so proud of her. Dammit, what the hell am I doing?

"That was amazing!" We stop at the place where we started, and she's very careful to cut the engine before lowering the kickstand. "I feel incredible. Like I can do anything."

She leans back against me with a sigh. "Thank you."

"You're welcome." I slide my hands up her thighs before wrapping my arms around her, holding her close to me. We're looking out over the lake, the sun setting, and I take a deep breath. Soaking it in. Part of me wishes we could stay this way forever. What's happening to me? I don't think things like that. I usually laugh at people who do.

Right now, though, the last thing I want to do is laugh.

When she turns her head, her lips grazing my jaw, I get the feeling she feels the same.

I wedge a hand between her thighs, glad she chose leggings today. "What are you doing?" she whispers, shocked.

"Nobody can see us. Nobody is here." I apply pressure with my fingers, and she gasps softly. "Don't tell me your blood's not pumping. Don't tell me it doesn't feel good."

"But we shouldn't…" Her body's reaction tells a different story, though. She doesn't stop me from slipping my hand between her pants and her skin. She's soaking wet, buzzing from the high of her first ride.

"You know you want to," I whisper, nibbling her earlobe as I begin to finger her. She angles her hips to give me better access, and I chuckle. "I thought so."

"What are you doing to me?" I could ask her the same question. Instead, I take my time licking her throat, sucking, scraping my teeth over the place where her pulse flutters. No matter how tight she presses her lips together, she can't hold back a moan.

"So sweet." My cock is hard as a rock, and I grind it against her ass, groaning when she pushes back against me. Urging me on. She can pretend all she wants to be a good girl, but deep down inside, she loves this. Loves the side of her only I can bring out. Loves being bad with me.

"Lean forward." She places her hands on the grips so I can ease her leggings over her ass. She gasps when the cool air hits her warm cheeks, which I massage with both hands. One day I'll take her ass—but for now, I'm satisfied with the idea of sinking in where it's wet and warm and so, so tight.

I glance around once before freeing my cock, lining up with her waiting cunt. I drag my head through her wetness before impaling her.

"Oh my God," she moans, her head falling forward, her hips moving in time with my slow, deep thrusts. "That is so good. So… so good…"

"Yeah, baby." I place one hand on her shoulder and the other on her hip, holding her steady. "Tell me how good it feels. Show me." She moans, lost, moving faster. I slow down, letting her take what she wants. Letting her feel powerful while I have the pleasure of watching her slide up and down my length. My cock is coated with her juices, glistening in what little sunlight is left.

When her muscles begin rippling, I know she's close. I reach around, cupping her plump little mound, working my fingers against her clit. "Come for me," I grunt. "Squeeze my cock. Come on it." She does as she's told, barely holding back a broken sob before almost collapsing in a fit of spasms. I hold on, closing my eyes and willing myself not to let go. Not yet.

She makes a surprised sound when I withdraw and swing my leg over the seat to stand beside her. "Suck me off," I growl, one hand on the back of her head while I feed her my cock with the other. She barely has time to part her lips before I push my way deep into her mouth, hitting the back of her throat hard enough to make her grunt.

But she takes me eagerly once the surprise wears off, tightening her grip around my shaft, her cheeks hollowing out while her head bobs up and down. She knows just how I like it, pressing her tongue along the underside, taking my entire length. "Good girl," I murmur, groaning when my balls lift, my body tensing in preparation. "You're so good to my cock." She moans in response, only heightening the sensation.

My body jerks from the force of my release, and she still takes it, swallowing spurt after spurt of cum as I unload in her mouth. I've never met a woman who wasn't at least hesitant about swallowing, but she does it eagerly. I don't know whether it's because she wants to or thinks it will please me. Either way, I'm not complaining.

When I withdraw, she looks up at me with a smile. Like she's proud of herself. "It's been a day of firsts, hasn't it?"

As perverse as it is, the sight of her happy little smile at a moment like this goes further than anything else has toward breaking my heart open.

I am too far gone over this woman.

Yet all I can do when I look into her eyes is remember that note and the threat behind it. It was one thing to protect her when only my job was at stake.

Now? I'm afraid my heart might be in on it, too.

24
MIA

"I'm glad I found the papers in Dad's office," Posey announces from the dressing room next to mine. "That way, I can practice my excited face in time for Christmas."

"Who wouldn't get excited over getting a luxury car for Christmas?" Zoe asks from the dressing room on my other side. "I wish my parents would spend that much money on my Christmas gifts. They're too busy buying things for themselves and each other." Considering Zoe drives a BMW, she's not exactly hurting.

"Seriously," I add, turning around to zip up the dress I'm trying on. "You could do a lot worse than a Lexus."

"Yeah, yeah, but he didn't even pay attention to the model I wanted. And he added on a bunch of safety crap I'm not even interested in." It's funny. Posey is one of the smartest, most levelheaded people I've ever met. But when it comes to things like this, she's exactly what I always used to imagine rich people acted like.

"At least your parents let you drive," I mutter, opening the door to my room and heading over to the three-way mirror to check myself out from all angles. At least Dad warned me about the big, swanky Christmas party he'll be holding in a couple of weeks.

I wonder if he'll think red is a good color. It's a festive red, deep, almost burgundy. Not like a stop sign or anything. It's cut straight across my chest, exposing my shoulders, but with long sleeves and a full-length skirt. I can't imagine he would raise any objections.

Zeke is in kind of an awkward position. I almost feel bad for him. He can't come into the dressing room area for fear of being called a pervert and possibly getting kicked out of the store, but he has to stay close enough to watch over me. I see the tips of his heavy, black boots just outside the doorway dividing us from the rest of the store.

The girls are still putting their dresses on, bitching about the cars their parents bought them, so I scoot over to where he'll be able to see me. "What do you think?" I whisper, doing a slow turn.

He looks to the left. He looks to the right. His eyes land on me again.

He grins in approval. "I can't wait to tear that off you with my teeth," he whispers. "And I can't think of a reason he wouldn't like it. You'll make him look good."

Right, because that's my only use. Making him look good. I feel a bit deflated walking back to the three-way mirror, checking myself out again. Maybe I should add a festive bow to my hair so I really look like a gift Dad can put under his tree. Something pretty and shiny to catch the eye of guests walking from room to room.

I'm too busy sulking silently to notice when Posey opens her door. She's in something cute and slinky and sexy, her New Year's dress. Apparently, her grandfather throws a hell of a party with big, popular musicians and New York's best chefs catering the event. It's the sort of thing that gets written about in newspapers.

"Hot," I confirm when she steps up next to me. "I wish I was as tall as you. You can carry off a look like that, but I can't."

"Please, like you don't look like a million bucks in this. Give me a spin." I do as she asks, and she whistles appreciatively.

Until she sees my shoulder blades, that is.

"Are these bruises?" she whispers, touching a finger to one of them. They're more than a week old, and now I wish I had worn my hair down to hide them. I'm sure their ugly, greenish-yellow color is disturbing.

"Oh, yeah. I told you I've been taking self-defense lessons."

She narrows her dark eyes. "What was the first lesson? How to get thrown on the ground without panicking?"

"Actually, that was lesson three." I try to laugh it off, but she's in no mood. "Yeah, that's how I got these. I was learning how to fight off an attacker if I get knocked onto my back."

"What are you talking about?" Zoe appears, wearing a silver dress that makes her look like a Christmas ornament. She's got the curves for it. "I might dye my hair green for the holiday. Still trying to decide."

"Damn. You remind me of one of those pinup girls from the fifties." I fan myself, laughing. "Seriously hot."

"Yeah, this is my favorite one so far." She looks at Posey, obviously waiting for her opinion, but Posey is too busy staring at me. "What did I miss?"

"For one thing…" Posey points at my bruises, and Zoe gasps when she sees them.

"Stop it," I whisper. The last thing I want is Zeke overhearing. "I told you, I'm taking lessons. It's my dad's idea," I add. It's not like they don't already know how protective he is.

"And what does that include? Getting your ass kicked?"

If they think that's bad, they should see the bruise I had on my ass thanks to losing my balance when I tried to knock Zeke off his. I hit the floor hard that time and had to sleep on my stomach for two nights.

"Don't do that," I beg them when I see the look they exchange. I know exactly what they're thinking, and it's driving me crazy. "Seriously, ask Zeke if you don't believe me."

"Sure. How do we know this wasn't what he told you to say?" Zoe looks like she's ready to cry.

I turn to Posey, who knows a lot better than Zoe about what's going on. I haven't told either of them about the way things are between us now, but at least Posey knows about some of the background. "Would you tell her? It's not like that between us."

"Yeah, I know, but…" She shrugs with a wince. "It's not like you'd be the first girl who got abused by somebody she's living with."

"I can't believe this. Seriously." I back away from them, shaking. Not because I'm hurt, not because I'm scared, but because I hate that they don't believe me. And I hate I can't come straight out and tell them everything. All of it.

But if there's one unbreakable rule, it's that I can't breathe a word about it. Not about sleeping with Zeke and not about his sudden concern over me. And that sucks because I do want to tell them. I want to be able to confide in somebody. I can't even tell Blair, not really, even though she's at a different school, and it couldn't possibly make a difference. Zeke made me swear.

What am I supposed to do with all this anxiety I feel? Do I have to keep it all bottled up inside me?

* * *

"What's wrong with you?" Pete, Dean's roommate, nudges Posey when she doesn't laugh along with the rest of us at a video Brad played on his phone. The restaurant is pretty empty except for us. That's probably a good thing since we're not exactly quiet.

And it's driving Zeke crazy. Every time I glance his way after somebody bursts out laughing, I see the way he cringes. It's enough to make me laugh some more—though I'm sure he'll punish me for it when we get home, which is more like funishment, anyway.

Nobody would guess he has a sense of humor without knowing him the way I do.

But you're not supposed to know him that way, right? Right. I have to remember that. It's so hard sometimes, trying to keep track of what I can and can't let people know.

Posey tries to play it off, but not without glancing at me first. Nothing. I guess I'm distracted."

"Sure, you have that presentation at the end of the week." Pete's really trying hard to win her over, it's obvious. Now he's trying to show an interest in the thing that interests her. I exchange a look with Zoe, and we have to look down at the table before we start laughing.

"Oh yeah, that too." Zoe pouts. "I'm going to be so sad when I don't have an excuse to see you guys anymore."

"Just because we won't have class together anymore doesn't mean we can't be friends." I reach out and squeeze her hand. "Besides, it's a small school. I'm sure we'll see each other on campus all the time next semester."

"Which classes are you taking?" We start talking about that while the guys pick at what's left of an appetizer platter. Big surprise, they ate most of it. But we have to look good in the dresses we bought, too, and I, for one, don't need to shove any more boneless wings in my mouth.

Posey's still pretty quiet, though. Part of my attention is on her, no matter how I try to ignore her pensive expression. She keeps tapping her fingers on the table, chewing her lip. And more than once, I've caught her looking toward Zeke, sitting at a table for two on the other side of the dining room. He's not paying attention to her, focusing on his burger and onion rings instead.

I would call her out on it, but that would only make things more awkward. Especially with Dean, and we both know his feelings toward Zeke. And vice versa.

I lean in closer to Posey. "Come to the bathroom with me," I whisper before grabbing my purse and standing. I need her on my side right now. We head back, with me passing Zeke on the way. All he does is exchange a look with me before going back to his food. But he's not fooling anybody. I know he'll be watching the table while listening out for any signs of trouble from me. I wonder if he ever lives in the moment without having to question or worry.

As soon as we're alone in the otherwise empty bathroom, I fold my hands like I'm praying. "Please, can you drop it?"

"I'm sorry, you're my friend, and I don't like—"

"I'm telling you, there's nothing wrong. For some reason, my dad is more paranoid than ever," I whisper. "That's why he has Zeke teaching me to defend myself. And that's the entire story. And nobody's said anything, but I'm wondering if that's why my dad didn't want me to come home for Thanksgiving. Because there's something bad happening, or there was."

Her shoulders sink a split second before she sighs. "I didn't think about that. That does make sense. But you're going home for Christmas, right?"

"Yeah, as I said, I guess whatever it was blew over. Unless he has another surprise in store for me, and we're going someplace else for the holidays. I really don't know. But I swear, there's nothing shady or sketchy going on."

She reaches out for a hug I gladly give her. "I'm sorry. I didn't mean to make it seem like I was—"

The door bursts open, and Zoe appears, flushed and out of breath. "Come quick. They're going to fight."

"What?" I push my way past the girls and run out to the dining room. The tables are empty now.

"Outside," one of the servers tells me, pointing at the door leading to the parking lot. I make a run for it, getting outside in time to see Zeke and Dean standing face-to-face, fists clenched.

"You don't know what the hell you're talking about," Zeke warns in a low, dangerous growl. "Why don't you step off, little boy, and go back to eating your food?"

Dean is stone-faced, his eyes glittering. "You fucking hit her, didn't you? You're calling me a little boy? When you're the one putting bruises on her?"

I whirl around to face Zoe. Her face is deep red. "I'm sorry, I shouldn't have said anything." Great. There I was, thinking Posey would be the problem, and it was Zoe who opened her big mouth the second we were away from the table. I should have asked them both to come to the bathroom with me.

At the same time, it's not her fault. It's probably Dean's. I can't imagine Zeke would start anything with him unprovoked. "Stop it, right now!" I shout, marching over to them. "This is stupid. Dean, you don't know what the hell you're talking about."

"And you would defend him?" he demands, red-faced and spitting. "Are you fucking serious? Or are you that brainwashed?"

"Don't talk to her that way," Zeke snarls, getting in his way so he can't see me without craning his neck. "This is between you and me, asshole. And it's been coming for months."

"Damn right," Dean agrees, taking off his hat and tossing it to the ground. Oh my God, he actually thinks they're going to fight.

And so does Zeke, who is now stripping off his jacket. It's like a nightmare. I'm standing here, watching this unfold, and I don't seem to be making any difference in the situation. I'm powerless. I might as well not be here—ironic because this is all supposed to be about me.

"Please, don't do this!" I try to force my way between them, facing Zeke, shaking him in a desperate attempt to get him to look at me. If he would only look at me, I might be able to calm him down. Now some of the waitstaff are standing on the other side of the glass doors, and one of them is holding a phone to record what happens. Terrific.

"You need to get out of the way." Brad takes hold of my arms and pulls me back like he's afraid I'm going to get caught in the crosshairs once fists start to fly. It's all happening so fast, I don't know what to deal with first.

"Get your hands off me," I snap, fighting to get myself free.

"Just let them get it out of their systems."

"I can't do that." When he won't let me go after, I try again to break free, and he leaves me with no choice—especially when Dean shoves Zeke hard enough to knock him back a step. All Zeke does is laugh, but it's a dangerous sound. Scary enough to make the hair on the back of my neck stand up.

And that's why I stomp on Brad's instep as hard as I can. He howls, probably more in surprise than pain, but it's enough to loosen his grip on my arms. I pull the right one free and drive an elbow into his sternum. This time, he doubles over, the wind rushing out of his lungs all at once. It's the most basic move, but at least I now know it's successful.

"Stop, stop!" I throw myself between them, my back to Dean. "Please. Would you look at me? You know this isn't right. You can't do this."

"Don't tell me what I can and can't do." I don't even know if he actually hears me or knows it's me begging him. He's locked on Dean. "He knows what's coming to him. He's been begging for this."

"Come on, then," Dean mocks. "Or do you want your girlfriend here to fight your battles for you?"

"That's enough." I turn around, ready to murder him. I hardly even recognize him right now. He's not the sweet, almost goofy guy who always has to make jokes. He wants blood. Zeke's blood.

He has no idea who he's dealing with, though, and that's the problem. "He'll seriously hurt you," I whisper urgently. It's not like I want to offend his male pride or whatever, but it's the truth, and he deserves to know it.

Dean's face falls a little, and I know it was the wrong thing to say—though if it stops a fight from breaking out, was it really? "So that's really how it is?"

"Yeah. It is," I say, my heart sinking. I don't think we're talking about the fight anymore. Not entirely.

His jaw tenses, and his nostrils flare like he wants to explode, but he manages to hold himself back. "Fine. Got it. You're not worth the effort." He spits on the ground close to Zeke's feet before grabbing his hat off the ground. "For lunch." He tosses a handful of twenty-dollar bills on the pavement before shooting me one last look.

A look that brings only one word to mind: hatred. He hates me. Was he ever who I thought he was?

And when Zeke growls behind me, I realize I'm in trouble with him, too. Can I ever win?

"We're going to have a talk when we get home about embarrassing me in front of people," he warns. "I think we should head in that direction now."

I can only brace myself for what I know is coming—even though I doubt there's any way I can prepare for his wrath.

25

ZEKE

We don't say a word the entire way back to the condo. I'm afraid that I won't be able to stop once I start. I might even end up driving us off the road, and then where would we be? Anything I have to say can wait until we're alone.

Which means my rage only has time to grow bigger. Hotter. More intense. Who the fuck does she think she is, telling me what to do or who I can fight? She doesn't make my choices for me. And she sure as fuck doesn't do it while we're in front of people. Why not cut off my balls and carry them in her purse?

Judging by the way she sits with her arms folded, staring out the window, I'm guessing she feels the same way. I've never seen her furious enough to shut her up. It's like we've reached a new level of how far we can push each other.

We walk silently from the car to the elevator and take the ride up just as silently. I can feel her seething, the energy radiating from her. Something is going to explode.

And it does once we're inside with the door locked. Rather than set the alarm straight away, I choose instead to shove her up against the door. "Who the fuck do you think you are?" I growl, leaning down close to her face. "Telling me what to do. Bossing me around. I'm not some bitch you can control."

"Who the fuck do you think you are?" she growls back. Her chest is heaving, her pulse fluttering wildly in her throat. "The big, bad man. Like a fucking animal without enough common sense to avoid getting in a public fight. You're supposed to be protecting me, not drawing more attention. Right?"

"Of course. That's all you fucking care about. The attention. How it would make you look."

"You don't have the first fucking clue what I care about." She swallows hard, her eyes darting to my mouth and back again. "Did you ever think maybe it was hard for me to see you about to fight over me? Do you know how shitty that made me feel?"

"So I was supposed to take it?" I lean in closer, so close our bodies touch. I'm not sure how much more of this I can take before I have no choice but to rip her clothes off. "Let him goad me into a fight and pretend it didn't matter? News flash: that's not how I operate."

"Because you're the big, bad alpha. Right?" She manages to find room to slide her hands between us and then pushes against my chest. "Is that supposed to impress me?"

"I don't do things to impress you." She gasps when I take her by the throat, tipping her head back. Her beautiful eyes shine with a wild light. "As for the big, bad alpha, I think we both know it doesn't take much to control you."

"Get your hand off me." It's a whisper, barely audible. I'm not squeezing, only holding her firm enough that she can't get away. When I do apply a bit of pressure, though, her eyes widen further.

"Don't pretend you don't want me to touch you." With my other hand, I skim her body, taking in the fullness of her hip and her tits. "Don't act like you're not dying to be fucked."

All it takes is the slightest upward tick of the corners of her mouth. She wants this. She wants me.

I spin her in place so fast she barely has time to make a sound. With one quick, violent tug, I pull her jeans down around her knees. Panties, too. "You like it like this?" I whisper next to her ear, pinning her in place with my body while I pull out my cock. It's aching, dripping, ready for her.

"Just do it," she pants. "Just fuck me. Now." And when I do, when I drive myself into her, she gasps.

"You want your little boyfriend to do this to you?" I ask, fucking her hard. Merciless. Punishing her. When she doesn't answer right away, I slap her ass cheek hard enough that my hand stings. "Huh? You think he could do this? You think he could fuck you this way?"

"Just you," she whispers.

"That's fucking right," I growl, pulling her head back when I take a handful of her hair. "Just me. He wants to do this to you. He wants to fuck you like this and make you scream the way I do."

"I don't want to talk about him." She cranes her neck, looking me in the eye. "I just want you to fuck me."

And I do, my hips sawing back and forth, my cock plunging in and out. She grunts like an animal every time our bodies meet, her ass jiggling when I slap against it. I look down, transfixed, watching my cock disappear inside her again, again, and every time it does, she lets out a squeal. Her first orgasm comes quick, her hands pressed against the door, fingers curling while her already tight cunt grips me like a vise. I have to slow down, or else she'll take me with her. And I'm not finished yet.

She slumps a little when I withdraw, leaning against the door for support. I kick off my jeans, then take her in my arms, carrying her to the island between the living room and kitchen and placing her on one of the stools, facing me. If she's going to use those nails of hers on something, I want it to be on my back. Not the door.

"Say it again," I grunt, entering her. "Who do you want fucking you?"

"You," she sobs, dragging her nails over my shoulders, my back, while I take her hard. Unforgiving. The deep, driving need to break her, to win, sweeps everything else out of the way. She needs to know who's in control. Who calls the shots.

When she breaks the skin, I suck in a pained breath—but if anything, it only heightens the sensation, pushing me closer to release. "You want to hurt me?" I grunt before slamming into her again. "Do you want to leave your mark on me?" She responds by raking me again, then driving her nails into my ass cheeks and pulling me deeper.

I'm completely lost in sensation. Lost in her. In the unimaginable feeling of being inside her, using her body, letting her use mine.

"Come inside me," she whines as her tunnel tightens, squeezing me again. "Come in me. Please."

That's all it takes. My thrusts lose their rhythm, my hips pumping frantically. She closes her eyes, her head dropping back, and I run my teeth over her neck when the edge comes rushing up to meet me. To meet both of us. She screams loud enough to make my ears ring, but I hardly notice, too busy filling her with cum.

When it's over, when I pull out, I look down to see our mixed fluids dripping out of her with every spasm of her muscles. I'm almost transfixed by it before stepping back, grabbing something to clean her up with. I've never let myself get carried away like that.

But she seems happy when I rejoin her. "I've been on the pill for more than a year," she informs me. "Mail-order prescription. I can't believe you didn't know that."

Good to know now that I shot my load. "Does your father know?" I ask as I wipe her clean. Not exactly who I want to be thinking of right now, but I didn't bring it up.

"Do you think it would be a surprise to you if he did?" Good point. We piece ourselves back together, the tension now gone, though there are still too many unanswered questions to count. I grab us both some water while she recovers, sitting on the stool again and leaning against the counter like she's wiped out. I can't pretend it doesn't make me the slightest bit proud, being the reason for it.

Still, I can't let it go. It will eat at me like an ulcer unless I say something. "You still haven't told me why you broke up the fight. Not really."

She rolls her eyes more dramatically than I think I've ever seen. "Why are you stuck on this?"

"Because it struck me as strange. I can't help it. I need to know."

"There's nothing to know. Why can't you get that? Why do you keep having to try to turn this into something it isn't?"

I don't know. That's the thing. There she is, barely recovered from the punishment I gave her, hair mussed, and her makeup smeared thanks to me. We've been as physically close as two people can be, yet it's still hard to open up. I wonder if it will ever be easy. Probably not.

Eventually, she realizes she's not getting away with avoiding the question. "Because it wouldn't have been fair. You're much bigger and stronger than he is. You would have kicked his ass and humiliated him and only pissed him off more. And you could have gotten in trouble for it."

Her concern for him sickens me. "You think I care about his ass getting kicked? Trust me. Once I kick a guy's ass, it stays that way."

"That's very cute," she informs me with a smirk. "But that's not how life actually works. I would still have to face him in class, and we have our presentation coming up. How uncomfortable would that have been? Do you think he would have been able to deliver his part of the presentation while you were sitting there in the back of the room? The guy who kicked his ass in front of his friends?"

Sometimes, it's like I've never really looked at her before. There's so much more than meets the eye. "Are you saying you stopped us from fighting because it would've affected your grade?"

"No! I was thinking about how it would make him feel. And yeah, it would make me feel like shit, too. Guilty. Jittery." She lowers her brow, and I swear I'm looking at her father right now. In some ways, they are too much alike. "And you're conveniently ignoring the part where I said I didn't want you to get into trouble."

"Who says I would?"

"You mean to tell me he wouldn't go straight to the cops? There were witnesses. And with a record like yours…"

It's not easy hearing that without laughing. That's what she's worried about? "Who says I have a record?"

She can't hide her surprise. "You don't?"

"I never took a collar."

"How is that even possible?"

"What the hell do you think I do for your father?" Her eyes drop to the countertop, which is all the answer I need. "If I got caught doing that, I wouldn't be standing here with you right now. Would I?"

"But have you?"

I lift my chin, staring at her. Daring her to say it. "Have I done what?"

"Have you killed anybody? There. I said it. Happy?"

"Thrilled. Thanks so much."

"Well?" I know better than to think she's ever going to let this go. It was bound to come up eventually. She must've asked herself before now if I've ever gone that far.

That's why I'm honest. No sense in lying. "Yes. I have. I have killed people."

She gulps but takes it well. "To keep him safe?"

I nod, though it's not as simple as that. "In his line of work, he makes a lot of enemies. And plenty of greedy people would do anything to get what he has. They don't want to put the work in, though. They want to take it from him. And sometimes, they won't listen to reason. It really is that simple."

"Simple? There's nothing simple about it." She wraps her arms around herself. "You're talking about taking people's lives."

"What would you rather have me do? Stand back and let them take his? Or yours?"

"Mine?" Her arms tighten, and now she's trembling. I shouldn't have said it. She asked, and she needs to know this isn't a game, but I hate seeing her like this.

"Why do you think I'm here with you? I'm not saying there's ever been a threat on your life. For the most part, he's kept things quiet when it comes to you. His friends know, his associates, but that's about it. And that's deliberate. That's why he didn't have you change your name to Morelli when he brought you in. That's for your safety. Do you understand?"

"So he isn't being overly paranoid."

"I'm afraid not. I wish it was as simple as that, I do."

"So do I." She tries to laugh, but the effort falls flat. Maybe somebody who doesn't know her as well as I do now would buy it. "This is a lot to swallow all at once."

"I know it is. And I'm sorry you have to hear it like this, I really am. But it's better that you know."

She nods, eyes downcast, and I have to wonder if something didn't just get lost. I would think she'd feel more confident than ever, knowing the man protecting her will do whatever needs to be done should her life ever be in danger.

I hope the time never comes that I have to prove it.

To lighten the mood, I ask, "So you weren't just a little bit worried about me out there? That I would get hurt?"

She giggles, and I can't pretend it isn't gratifying. "Right. Like he could do anything to you."

"I don't know. I mean, I hate to say it, but he's bulked up a little bit this semester. There's more muscle on him than there was back when classes started."

"Is there?" She shrugs. "I didn't notice." It looks and sounds like she's telling the truth, too. I wish he was here so he'd know for sure he doesn't have a chance with her. Nobody could do to her what I do.

And nobody could protect her the way I can.

As I walk to the bathroom, I can't help but remember that note, the only one left in front of the door. *You Can't Protect Her.* The memory leaves a sour taste in my mouth, even with Mia following and leaving a trail of clothing in her wake.

As much as I believe I can—as much as I have to, with every fiber of my being—I can't help but hope as she steps into the shower along with me that I never have to prove it. Because that would mean her life was in danger.

And I don't know anymore how I could live if that was ever the case.

26
MIA

I was a total asshole. I'm sorry. Stress from finals, all that shit.

I get it, I type out before glancing up at Zeke. He's busy driving, humming to the radio, and tapping his fingers on the steering wheel. It's nice, seeing him like this. He's relaxed, almost happy. I know he's looking forward to his long rides on the Harley, one of the few things Dad lets him do once I'm in for the night. He shipped it back to the house a few days ago rather than leave it in the garage at the condo. I wouldn't want to leave it sitting around either, not if I was ninety minutes away on a good traffic day.

It's a shame there's no way Dad would ever let me go for a ride with him because I would love nothing more. But we have plenty of time for that once we get back.

And then you were so cool during the presentation. Nobody would ever know anything happened.

Yes, and I had to get Zeke to swear on his motorcycle he wouldn't start anything during that final class—and that if Dean did, he would walk away rather than fight back. They both behaved themselves, and I'm still grateful.

That's what needed to be done, I tell Dean, typing on my phone and glad I'm sitting in the back seat so Zeke can't see. *It's all over now.*

The fact is, I want to continue my friendship with Posey and Zoe, but I wouldn't care if I never saw Dean again. I will, I'm sure, but it's not like I'm going to seek him out on campus. Any chance we ever had of being good friends was ruined when he looked at me like he did that day. He was so nasty, too. I'm willing to forgive and forget a lot of things, but that?

Are you home yet? he asks.

Not yet. On the way. Are you?

Yeah, I left first thing in the morning. Then another message. *I'm meeting up with somebody later, too. I'm looking forward to it.*

I bite back a knowing laugh. So this is how it's going to be, huh? He wants to make sure I know I'm not the only fish in the sea. *Yeah? Somebody special?*

"Everything okay back there?" Zeke looks at me in the mirror, and though I can't see his entire face, I know he's smiling by looking at his eyes. Right now, their gray is soft and comforting.

And as much as I love to see that, it's a problem. "Hey, careful. You can't go around smiling at me while we're at home. You have to go back to being your grumpy self." I scowl at him as an example.

"Right, what was I thinking?" He rolls his eyes before lowering his sunglasses, then he grunts. "Better?"

"That's more like it." Sure, we're joking about it, but we both know how serious the situation is. Nobody can find out about us.

It's going to be an interesting break, finding ways to sneak around. And I'm not going to waste energy telling myself we won't, like we'll be able to keep our hands off each other the next three weeks. I'm sure there will be plenty of opportunities.

There's a new message from Dean. *It's one of those things that kind of got left hanging a while ago, and I'm hoping we can get things moving again.* He sends an emoji, too, a hand with fingers crossed. I send it back to him.

Almost home, I tell him. *Good luck. I'm sure we'll talk before the holiday.*

"You ready for this?" Zeke asks, and I nod enthusiastically. I might have dreaded going home if it wasn't for him. No, he's not going to outwardly break any of my father's rules, but I'm sure I'll be able to bend them a little. Plus, Christmas. Who doesn't love Christmas?

My phone buzzes. I didn't expect Dean to have the last word. *By the way, I meant to tell you something. I found a bunch of stuff when researching our project that I thought you might be interested in.*

I send him a question mark in response. "What's up?" Zeke asks. He's always watching, isn't he?

"Nothing. Just talking with Blair." I don't like lying, even about something as dumb as this, but what's the alternative? I don't want him getting pissed and driving us off the road only a few miles from home.

I sent it to your school email. I didn't want to include it in the project because I didn't want to freak you out. Well, that doesn't sound good. What could he have found that would freak me out?

Was it about my father? No, that's not possible. Besides, we don't even have the same last name. Even if my suspicions are correct and Dad is into some shady stuff, Dean couldn't have made the connection. *Let me guess, it's something about Scarface, right? I'll have to check it later.*

"Here we are," Zeke murmurs. "Let's get serious."

"Yeah. We have to get into character." I shake out my arms and hands, rolling my head from side to side. "I hate you. You're the worst. I want to curb stomp you."

"Wow. That rolled off your tongue way too easy. Should I be concerned?"

"I hate how good you are at eating me out," I continue.

"Whoa, careful."

"And your dick is way too big."

"I wouldn't argue with that, but..."

"I hate when you make me come until I pass out."

"Enough, princess." He grins at the way I growl in response. "You deserve it. Fucking tease."

210

I guess I can accept that.

Rolling through the front gate of the compound is a strange sensation. It's still not the warm, fuzzy feeling place home should be, but it's getting there. I hope one day it will be. Zeke still looks happy even with the aviators, but I won't bother warning him about it because it only makes sense he would be glad to be back. In some ways, this is more his home than it is mine.

Dad meets us outside, arms outstretched. It's almost like we're a normal, happy family—except for the bodyguards to either side of him. "There she is! My beautiful girl." I have to admit, it's nice. Heartwarming. I didn't expect such an enthusiastic welcome. For a moment, I can almost pretend we're a regular father and daughter. Not that I would know what that feels like in real life, but I know how I've always imagined it being.

He then shakes Zeke's hand. "I want to see you in my office right away. I have a few things I need to discuss." Of course, because business is never too far from his mind.

He turns back to me, an arm around my shoulders while he leads me into the house. The tree in the entry hall is mind-blowing, covered in red and gold ornaments, and bright enough, it might be visible from space. "I'm having a dinner party tonight."

I knew he would bring me back into his social world, but I didn't know it would be this immediate. I know better than to complain about hoping we'd have a nice family dinner tonight, something quiet where we could catch up. He's not interested in that. "Dress code?"

"Something nice. You have plenty of dresses that will do fine. But keep it modest, of course."

Like that doesn't go without saying. "Of course." He leaves me at the foot of the lavishly decorated stairs before crooking a finger to beckon Zeke. Zeke glances at me before following.

So much for the happy reunion. I guess I should consider myself lucky I was personally greeted in the first place. Some of Dad's staff are unloading my bags and carrying them up to my room. I follow and tell myself it's better this way. I'll have a little bit of privacy before getting grilled over how the semester went and what my plans are for the spring.

Strange how this bedroom still doesn't feel like mine, but the one at the condo is starting to already. I wonder why. Is it because the condo feels like ours: mine and Zeke's? I didn't choose any of the furnishings, none of it, but it feels more like home than the lavish room Dad splurged on here at the house.

I need to stop sulking and fast. Especially if we're having people over tonight. It goes without saying I'll need to be on my best behavior, the perfect credit to my benevolent father. Or something like that.

I start to unpack, eyeing up the dresses in my closet. I have plenty to choose from. He's right about that. I need to remind myself how generous he is and how lucky I am. He didn't have to go to the trouble of making sure I had everything I could ever want. Even if everything comes with conditions.

Once I'm finished putting my clothes and toiletries away, I unpack my laptop and set it up on my desk. It'll be nice getting away from it for a while. I'm tired of carrying it around everywhere I go. Then again, I can't imagine having to lug around textbooks for every single class. How did people survive that back in the day? They probably all need chiropractors by now.

I wonder what Dad and Zeke are talking about.

It seems like I can't distract myself enough. Why did Dad want to talk to him right away? It doesn't have anything to do with me, does it? Us?

How could it? Nobody, not even the best actor in the entire world, could pretend to be as friendly and warm and welcoming as Dad was if he was waiting to strike. Like a snake in the grass. There wasn't so much as a hint of tension or anger.

He's probably going over ground rules for how to guard me now that we're back home. Then again, I doubt it would take long. Don't let her go anywhere, don't let her go anything. Pretty simple. I flop into my desk chair, wishing Zeke would knock on the door to signal the end of their meeting. The sooner he's finished, the better for my anxiety.

I need to get over this. We talked about it last night after we finished packing. We have to pretend everything is normal. We can't let guilt eat at us because that's when mistakes are made. And while Dad is usually too busy with business to pay attention to every minute of my life, there are eyes everywhere. And no telling who might want to gossip.

I need another distraction. Opening my laptop, I pull up Facebook and scroll through pictures for a while. Posey is already in Manhattan at her grandfather's place, where she'll be spending the holiday. There's the tree at Rockefeller Center, with Posey and her family smiling in front of it. She complains about them a lot, but at least her parents are present for her.

She's really lucky. I mean, so am I, but still.

What is taking so long? Dammit, I'm going to go nuts.

I keep scrolling until I come across a post from Dean. That reminds me of the conversation we had back in the car. I don't really feel like rehashing all the work we put into our project, but I am kind of curious about the materials he says he sent to my school email account. I'm sure he'll ask me about it the next time we talk, so I might as well look and see what he's referring to. Even if opening my school email is the last thing I want to do on my first day home on break.

His message is right at the top. I click on it, then click the links in the body of the message.

At first, I don't understand. Articles, a handful of them, some dating back fifteen years or so. I skim one, then the next one, and I'm starting to get the feeling this was all a ploy to have another reason to touch base again. Like texting somebody and pretending it was an accident later on, all for the sake of getting their attention.

It's the third article that lands like a bomb.

I lean in, eyes wide, mouth hanging open.

Before long, the words start to blur, thanks to the tears welling up and spilling over onto my cheeks.

No way. It's not possible. This has to be a joke.

But I'm not laughing.

27
ZEKE

"Naturally, there are certain questions I don't want to ask directly in front of Mia." The boss lets out a booming laugh as we enter his office. I want more than anything to be with her, not with him, but that's how things have to be. For both our sakes, but mostly for hers. Amazing how my whole mindset has shifted. It used to be my neck I was looking out for.

"Of course. But not to worry. Everything's been smooth sailing." I hope lightning doesn't strike me dead on the spot. Grandma always used to warn me about that if I lied too much.

"I knew I could count on you. You know, in a lot of ways, you're like a son to me." He walks over to the bar set up across from his desk, an antique cart trimmed in brass. A lift of his eyebrows in my direction is a silent question. An offering.

"No, thank you. I'm on duty." I stand with my hands clasped behind my back, as usual.

He laughs again, waving a hand. "We don't need to go through all that right now. You've been on duty nonstop for the past four months. You can relax a little."

"Thank you, sir." I accept his offer of bourbon, and a minute later, he hands me a glass, then touches his own to it. He's in a very festive mood today. Then again, with all the decorations all over the house, I guess he can't help it. I've never seen it decked out like this before, with a tree in every room we passed.

"To successful partnerships." He drains half the glass, smacking his lips with a satisfied smile. "I haven't felt this hopeful in a long time, Zeke."

Obviously, I'm starting to wonder how many drinks he's already had today. He's practically floating, bouncing on the balls of his feet. It's enough to make me suspicious. This is not a man who goes around feeling joyful and positive. It's enough to make me wonder what's changed since we left.

"I'm glad to hear that, sir." He goes to his desk, and I follow him. After gesturing for me to take a seat, he sits in his leather chair and leans back with a sigh. I settle into my chair, though I'm not quite as ready to get comfortable as he is.

Something's off. I didn't get to be as good as I am at my job without honing my senses and trusting my instincts. That, plus the many years I've known him, tells me he's about to drop a big piece of news.

And he doesn't disappoint. "This party tonight. I'll need you to be there, guarding Mia."

I eye him up over the rim of my glass. "You think there'll be trouble?" I ask before taking a sip of the smooth liquor. It burns a familiar, welcome trail down my throat, warmth spreading in my chest.

"Nothing like that," he assures me. "You'll be more of a silent message. A reminder."

"Hands off?" I suggest with a wry smirk.

"Always," he agrees, chuckling. "But also a reminder of the excellent care that was taken with her all semester. Anybody takes a look at you, and they'll know for sure no swinging dick got anywhere near my girl."

None except mine. That's not even the worst part of what he's saying. Is this how all fathers treat their daughters? It can't be. From day one, he's been obsessed with keeping her a virgin. Do people truly care about that so much? It's bizarre and way over the line between healthy and twisted.

Why would anybody at this party care—

Oh, no. Why didn't I see it? It was right there in front of me. Thanksgiving. Business arrangements, travel. And a dinner party tonight, coincidentally the day Mia returned from school.

A jangling noise reaches my ears, and I realize it's the ice in my glass. I will myself to be still, to stop shaking. "You know I'm always here to handle whatever you need."

"Lucky for you, you won't have to worry about it much longer." His smile is indulgent and maybe the happiest I've ever seen from him. "You've done excellent work, guarding my most cherished possession. By summer, she won't be your problem anymore."

"Do you plan on kicking her out?"

He bursts out laughing. "No—well, not quite kicking her out. The wedding is in June."

I know what he's saying, but still, there's a part of my brain that won't accept it. "Whose wedding?"

His head snaps back with a look of disbelief on his face. "Mia's, of course! I told you that was always the endgame. Now, everything's settled. The contract's been signed, and everything is in place."

Focus. Calm. How the hell did I manage half the jobs I've pulled off in the past ten years if I can't handle this? Even my father wondered how I could be so icy and detached while planning to stalk and murder the boss's enemies. He didn't have to worry about it long since somebody took him out when I was eighteen. And in the seven years since, I've only got harder.

Now? The idea of a wedding has me fighting to keep a straight face. He's actually doing it. I can't believe he's doing it this soon.

"I don't have to ask whether she knows," I murmur, gripping the glass for all it's worth. It's all that's holding me together, the feel of it in my hand. The ice's cold flowing into my palm and my fingers. I focus on it, struggling to contain my reaction.

"I planned to tell her before the party. She'll meet her husband tonight, along with the rest of his family."

"With all due respect, it might be easier on her if she finds out well in advance of the party."

He arches an eyebrow, his smile sliding away. "Explain." I've heard that sound in his voice before, and it doesn't bode well. But fuck, I have to do something. I have to keep her in mind, even if he won't.

"You know how emotional she gets," I explain, rolling my eyes. I hardly know what I'm saying. It's like another part of my brain kicked into gear to protect me from stepping over the line and ending up with a bullet in my brain. "You don't want her throwing a fit in front of your guests. Not a great first impression."

His eyebrows shoot up. "See? This is why I rely on you. You're right. I don't want her causing some big, emotional scene. She'll probably have a lot of questions and maybe some worries."

You fucking think so? Genius. "I'd be glad to go up to her room and let her know you want to see her." I'm practically out of the chair already, my body straining to break free, wanting to burst out of this room and run up the stairs. To throw open her door, pick her up, and make a run for it.

"Not yet." He checks his watch. "Give her a little time to settle in first. I'll need you to stick around close to her room in case she gets any ideas about throwing a fit up there. I need her on her best behavior for this."

"Naturally." I'm like a robot, churning out what I know he wants to hear. My mind is miles away, conflict raging like a storm in my skull. What do I do? I didn't know it would be this soon. I thought we had time. "What does this do to her plans for next semester? She's already registered for classes and all that."

"If it's that important to her, she can finish out the year." What a fucking prince. "So long as she promises to behave herself and to keep herself in good shape for the wedding. She'll have wedding planning stuff to handle along with her schoolwork, of course." He shrugs like it's all too far beyond him to give it much thought.

Suddenly, he hits me with a hard stare. "I trust she's returning to me in the same condition in which she left?"

No need for an explanation there. I nod before taking another swig of bourbon. I hardly taste it now.

"That's good. I wouldn't want to renege on one of the conditions of the contract."

Good thing I've already swallowed, or I'd end up spitting expensive bourbon on an even more expensive desk. "That was one of the conditions? That she be… you know…"

"Untouched. Pure." These people are fucking sick. He makes it sound totally normal to be this obsessed with his daughter's virginity. "Her future husband wants to be sure she's saved herself for him, and only him."

"Would it be out of line to ask who she's been… promised to?" I came dangerously close to using the word *sold*. If I'm not careful, I won't live long enough to warn her about what's coming.

"Philip Rinaldi's son, Eric. He's been to the house before."

Yes, and I remember exactly who he is—and the sour taste he left in my mouth. Nothing I can put my finger on. I just got a bad feeling about the guy. He's around my age, maybe a couple of years older, and unlike Mia, he's been raised in this world.

And evidently, he has certain expectations that I'm sure were drilled into his head by his father and the other men around him.

Eric Rinaldi. It will be him sharing her bed. His children she carries. His name she'll have to moan night after night even if her heart's not in it. When I imagine her under that greasy sonofabitch, my teeth grind together hard enough that I'm afraid the boss will hear.

I can't let that happen. There's got to be a way out for her.

But not if I want to stay alive.

"I know what's bothering you."

My head snaps up. I hadn't realized I zoned out. "Pardon?"

"You look troubled. I know why." He sits up straight, pulling the chair closer to the desk. Folding his hands on top, he looks me straight in the eye. "You're wondering what this means for you. Of course, the Rinaldis will want to furnish Mia with a security detail. They offered the option of taking you on as part of their crew, but I knew you wouldn't want that." That last line falls heavy, full of meaning. Even if I wanted to go, he wouldn't let me. It would be a betrayal, even though the families would now be joined if only on paper.

He takes my silence as agreement. "I want you to know you have nothing to worry about. You'll always have a place here, in the family. Having you return to your old job duties would be kind of a demotion now, wouldn't it? That's why I want you as head of my security detail."

"Head of security?"

"As of right this minute, yes." His smile reminds me so much of Mia's that it's uncanny. "And with that comes a raise. You deserve it. You've done well. I'll want you at school with her in the spring, but I'll keep you abreast of matters as they come up around here, so you'll be up to speed by the time the semester is over, and you transition back to your role with me."

I know he wants me to thank him, and ordinarily, I would do so without thinking. This is a big promotion, something I thought I wanted before everything I wanted flipped on its head. I can't even enjoy it. I don't know if I'll be able to enjoy anything again. Not with the fact of another man taking what's mine hanging over my head all the time.

She's not yours. She never was. And I was nothing but a fool to think she would be.

I hear her running down the hall before I see her. How I know it's her, I can't say. I only know it doesn't come as a surprise when she runs into the room.

Her tears, however, do surprise me. I stand, as does her father.

She glares at him, shaking. "How could you? How could you lie to me? What have you done?"

28
MIA

It's all been a lie. All of it. And I was stupid enough not to see it.

"Sweetheart, what's happened?" My father makes a move, walking around his desk, but the idea of him touching me is enough to make me want to throw up. I back away, shaking my head.

"No," I sob. "Stay there." And there's Zeke, holding a glass of liquor. What were they doing, sitting around and having a toast? "Did you know? You're a part of this, aren't you?"

His face falls, one of the rare times I've managed to catch him off guard. "Part of what? No, I didn't know exactly—"

"Save it. I don't want to hear any more of your lies." I swing around, turning back to Dad. "From either of you. How could you lie to me? All this time."

"You did say she would get emotional, didn't you?" Dad glances at Zeke.

"You were talking about me? Planning how to deal with it when I found out what really goes on here? What you do for a living? How you've made all this money?" I'm shaking so hard it's amazing I haven't shattered into pieces. Even my teeth are chattering.

All those articles. All those hints, allegations, payoffs to keep the Morelli name out of the courts. My father, the man whose DNA I carry, is responsible for death, misery, horror. Sex trafficking, drug trafficking, money laundering. All of it. Dean found all of it when he was researching, and that's what he didn't want me to know. That's what he tried to shield me from.

Because unlike the men standing in front of me, he actually gives a damn.

Zeke blinks rapidly, his head snapping back like he's surprised. "Wait a second. What are you talking about? The business? The family?"

"What else would I be talking about?" I scream. It feels good to scream, but not good enough. It doesn't ease the pain in my chest. Is it possible for a heart to literally break?

"Just take it easy." He sets his glass down and holds his hands out like he's not a threat. What a joke.

"I can put two and two together, you know. How many people have you killed for him?" Tears drip from my chin onto my shirt, and my nose is running. I run my sleeve under it, not caring how it looks. I don't care about anything anymore. "I can't even look at you without wanting to be sick."

"Mia, sweetheart." At least my father has the decency to look pained. "I never wanted you to find out, but especially not this way. Not until you could be eased into it. Nobody expects you to have anything to do with that side of the family, not ever."

"I sure as hell hope not!"

"But this is the sort of thing you're going to have to learn to deal with once you're—" He's cut off by Zeke, who violently clears his throat. They exchange a look that can't mean anything good.

"Once what?" I bark. "What else haven't you told me? What else do I have to be the last to know?" I have to get out of here. I can't even look at them. How could I have been so blind? Of course, the man makes his money in all kinds of shady, immoral ways. Why else would he keep it from me? Why else would he have so many powerful, wealthy friends?

222

Not to mention the security. How often have I deliberately turned a blind eye because I didn't want to know?

It's Zeke who speaks first. Zeke, who, even with my vision blurred by hot, furious tears, looks like a whipped dog. "Once you're married to Eric Rinaldi, the son of another prominent family."

No. This isn't true. I'm not hearing this. I fell asleep, and this is a dream. A nightmare, an absolute fucking nightmare. The worst I've ever had, which is saying something. I wrap my arms around myself, feeling as lost and small and terrified as I've ever been. "I'm not getting married. I'm not marrying anybody! What are you talking about? Who is Eric Rinaldi?"

"This isn't the way I wanted to tell you," my father murmurs. At least he has the decency not to act like this is a happy conversation. At least he's not completely dismissing me the way he usually does. "But tonight, the Rinaldi family are coming for dinner, and you will meet your soon-to-be husband. The marriage contract is already finalized. By the end of June, you'll be Mrs. Eric Rinaldi, and our families will be joined."

"But I won't. I can't! You mean you sold me?"

"Don't be childish." There it is. There's that dismissiveness. "This is the way the world works. Yes, you are my daughter, and with that comes certain responsibilities. Such as marrying the man I've chosen for you."

"But Dad." I can't find the words. Who could? "I don't know him. I don't want to get married, not yet. What about school?"

"School served its purpose. You met people, enjoyed yourself, and did well in your classes. And you'll have the whole spring to do that again. But come June, you will be married. You'll be Eric Rinaldi's wife, and you'll be expected to perform as a wife performs."

Oh.

It's like the final piece of the puzzle falling into place.

"That's why it was so important to you that I be a virgin, right?" Bright spots of red pop up on his cheeks. I don't know if he's more embarrassed at being found out or at me coming out and speaking plainly. "Because I have to be the good, virginal little wife, right?"

"Mia…" Zeke murmurs. If I didn't hate him with every ounce of my being, I might actually listen. As it is, all I do is glare at him, gratified that he at least has the decency to look embarrassed. He should be embarrassed.

"And you knew about this, too, didn't you?" It's like I've never seen him before. I don't even know who he is now. "Didn't you? You've known all this time that school was a joke. He never had any plans to let me graduate. I was going to be married and sent off to somebody else's house. Right?" My rage grows with every word until I'm practically screaming.

And he takes it without so much as a single flinch. That's how I know I'm right. He won't even bother arguing or defending himself because there is no defense.

"I've said this before," I tell him in a low voice, ignoring my father for the moment. "But this time, I mean it with my whole heart. I hate you."

His eyes close for a second, and I know that hit him hard. Good. That's not even anywhere close to what he deserves.

Dad sighs before clapping his hands together like he does when he wants to change the subject. "Mia, we can talk about this. We can smooth this out."

I don't want to hear a single word he has to say. I don't want to hear anything from either of them. I can't even be in the same room with them.

First, though, I want to get one thing clear. "Your plan is useless," I inform my father, holding my head high. I don't care. He won't see me tremble anymore.

"What does that mean?"

I see Zeke out of the corner of my eye, and the way he tenses all over tells me he knows where this is going. I wait a second, drawing it out, and I hope the tension kills him.

"It means I'm not a virgin anymore. I've already had sex. Lots of it, in fact. So this Eric Rinaldi isn't going to get his little virgin bride, after all."

His face goes from slightly red to almost plum purple. "That's not true! That can't be true!"

"Who says it can't be? Face it. I'm not who you wanted me to be to make your little deal work." And it was Zeke who did it. It's right there, right on my tongue, ready to tumble out into the open. It would be the ultimate revenge, wouldn't it?

But I can't. Even now, I can't do it. Even though I have every right in the world.

I take one more look at my father's stunned expression before turning around and running for it, sprinting back down the hall and up the stairs. I lock my door, though I know if anybody wanted to get in, nothing would stop them.

I have to go. I need out of here, now. No way am I going to let him use me this way.

And Zeke. Why did he have to do this to me?

I reach my bed, and my legs threaten to go out from under me, but I can't let that happen. Once I'm away from here, I can cry my eyes out until my body shrivels up and blows away like a dry leaf. I don't care. But that can't happen now. I have to hold it together long enough to find a way out.

But how?

My mind races. I don't have the keys to any cars, and I seriously doubt anybody would give them to me if I asked. Blair? She should be free for break by now, right? Even if she isn't, maybe I can convince her to come and get me. There has to be a way I can sneak out. While everything is getting fixed up for the dinner party, I could slip out.

The fact is, I need to believe I can. I need to believe I have some measure of control over my life.

Rather than taking everything with me, I pack a few essentials, throwing everything I just placed in my bathroom back into a bag. And he wanted me to dress up tonight. Like he was getting me ready to go up for auction—no, not quite, because the auction is finished. I'm already sold.

Only when I grab my laptop, one additional option comes to mind.

And wouldn't it piss Zeke off to no end if he knew how I chose to get away? When I think of it like that, it's almost too perfect.

I sit down, fingers flying over the keys. *Please tell me you're around. Please tell me you're available.*

Dean answers right away, to my relief. *Yeah, I'm just hanging out. What's up? Are you okay?*

No, I don't think I've ever been less okay. I listen for any sound out in the hall, but everything's silent. For once, Zeke has enough sense to stay the fuck away from me. I would claw his eyes out if given the chance.

What happened? Do you need help?

Yes! I do. Can you please come? I can meet you out on the road that runs alongside the compound. I give him the address and cross my fingers, praying he'll come through. I need him to come through.

Whatever you need. I'm not far away. I can be there in five minutes.

Some of the pressure on my chest loosens, and I'm finally able to take a decent breath. *Thank you so much. I owe you my life. Please, hurry.* I can tell him all about it once we're in the car. And I can thank him for opening my eyes.

Because the person who was supposed to care about me—who pretended to anyway—didn't think he needed to. He figured it would be okay to lie to me, over and over, so many lies I don't know if anything he ever said was the truth. How could he do that? He knew I would be married off to some stranger all this time, and he never even gave me a clue.

He fucked me. He slept next to me for weeks.

He protected me.

But he couldn't protect me from this because he didn't want to.

I finish packing up my things and take one last look around the room before creeping down the stairs.

At least he won't have to worry about protecting me anymore.

29

ZEKE

She hates me. She would've killed me where I stood if she had the chance.

She's said it before, but this time, she meant it. I would have known that without her saying it.

"Do you want to tell me what the hell that was all about?" the boss bellows. "You mean you let her run around and fuck random boys at that school? What the fuck did I hire you for? You knew I needed her pure. I told you so, explicitly."

She could've thrown me under the bus, which is exactly where I deserve to be. She left me out of it, no matter how much she didn't want to. I hate that the way she spared me gives me hope.

But there's no guarantee she won't eventually spill the truth if he pushes her hard enough.

"She's lying," I mutter, staring at the open door. I can just imagine her up there, screaming into a pillow, sobbing in the middle of her bedroom floor. If it wasn't for her father, I would've followed her. I would have fought to make her see the truth somehow. I wasn't plotting against her.

But dammit, I didn't do a single thing to help either. It's practically the same thing.

"She's lying? And you know that how?"

Once again, I'm reminded of the similarities between father and daughter. He sounds just like she does when she's indignant, demanding. To think, he didn't raise her, either. Nature versus nurture. Thank you, Intro to Psychology.

I turn slowly, willing myself to keep it together until he lets me go. "I know it because she hasn't been out of my sight. Because every time the front door opened or closed, I received an alert telling me so. She never snuck out. She was never alone with a boy, ever."

This is dangerous territory. Eventually, he's going to come to the natural conclusion that I was the one fucking her. Unless I can convince him otherwise.

"Then why would she say that?" He slams the side of his fist against his desk. "Where would she come up with that?"

"She's upset," I remind him as quietly and evenly as possible. "Just like we knew she would be. That's why I recommended she find out about the engagement before the family gets here, remember? This is exactly the kind of reaction I expected." Fuck me, how am I still standing here? Pretending I'm on his side, talking about her like she's nobody. The way he does. It's the only way to get through to him, sure, but it makes me sick, the way I have to coddle him.

It's enough to bring his face back to a somewhat normal color anyway. There was a moment there I was afraid he would have a stroke on the spot. Still, his fists are clenched, his breathing erratic. "So you're saying she said it to get back at me?"

"Why else? She was throwing a tantrum." Forgive me, Mia. I have to say something to convince him.

"Yeah. She's pretty good at that." He runs a hand over the top of his head, blowing out a huge sigh. "Well, she won't be my problem much longer. Rinaldi can handle her from here on out. I only hope he has the stomach for it."

And that's it. That's all he cares about. Not how Rinaldi will treat her. He doesn't care if her husband is understanding or abusive—though I have no doubt he'd rage and scream and throw things across the room if she ever showed up at the house with a black eye. It wouldn't make a difference. Nothing to upset the alliance between the two families.

"You know, sir, if I may." He lifts a shoulder, still cooling off. "With all due respect, she's worth a lot more than you give her credit for."

He snorts, but the sound cuts off when he realizes I'm not kidding. "What do you mean?"

"For one thing, she's probably heartbroken knowing she won't be able to go to school anymore. She takes her work seriously. Straight A's in all classes. She was proud of that, and she wanted you to be proud."

"What the hell do I care? I didn't go to college, and I turned out just fine."

"Understood, but still. She had plans of her own, and you never gave her any idea of your plans. You blindsided her. And don't forget, before you found her, she was used to taking care of herself. Her and her mom."

He stabs a finger in my direction. "I took her out of the gutter, in case you forgot. Did she? Because I can put her right back there again if that's how she'd rather have it."

"She's independent," I murmur, hoping to calm him down. "I'm sure she inherited that headstrong attitude from you." I don't even know what I'm doing. I've never so much as breathed anything that sounds like a disagreement with anything he has to say. There's never been any reason to disagree with him. He's the boss, I followed orders. End of story.

She changed everything. Including me, who I am. I see that now.

"So what you're saying is, I should've asked her opinion? We both know where that would have gotten me. She's impossible."

"I know. But she's also smart. She has a mind of her own. Going from making her own decisions to being told who she will marry and when. All this time, she had no idea you were even thinking about arranging a marriage…" All I can do is shrug and hope he doesn't blow my brains out on the spot. Frankly, I wouldn't care if he did at this point. What the hell good is anything if I don't have her? I'd rather take my last breath right now than watch her being forced to marry a man all because of his last name and his connections.

"I'm not about to apologize. I didn't lose my balls, you know."

"Nobody expects that. But maybe, if you approach her with a little more empathy, you'll get a lot further. She only wants to feel like you're listening to her."

He returns to the bar cart, chuckling wryly. "How did you get so smart about this shit? Were you paying attention during class?"

"Yes," I admit, struggling to suppress the need to knock him on his smug ass. "But that's not all. It's living with her. I had to learn how her mind works so I could anticipate her reactions."

He's quiet for a moment, pouring himself a drink, not looking at me. And at that moment, I think, is this it? Is this where he finally realizes the mistake he made sending me to Blackthorn Elite with his only daughter?

"Since you know her so much better than I do," he murmurs before replacing the bottle of bourbon, "what happens next? I can't have her blurting out shit like that tonight at dinner, that's for sure. We have a few hours to get her to come around and agree to behave herself."

Right, because no matter what, nothing will stop his arrangements. He used the word contract, and that's not a word that gets thrown around carelessly in our world. Agreements have been made. Expectations have been set. I highly doubt the Rinaldis would be understanding if they found out the bride-to-be got cold feet.

"I'll go and talk to her," I suggest. "Maybe I can get her to come back downstairs."

He snickers, looking at me like he wouldn't want to be in my shoes for anything. "Didn't she just say she hates you?"

"She's said it at least once a day the past four months." His laughter is like nails on a chalkboard. How can he sound like that? Not only did his daughter find out her father is head of a major crime family, but she then learned he sold her to a stranger. And he can laugh. Now I do wish he had never found her. I hate to think of her struggling, but the alternative is so much worse.

"Go ahead. We have to try something, I guess. Keep in mind, time is of the essence." I give him a quick nod before leaving the room as quickly as I dare. I don't want to break out into a full run and look too suspicious.

What am I supposed to say? There's nothing I can say, and that's the truth. Nothing she'll want to hear.

Except for one thing: we have to get out of here.

It's clear, finally. So obvious, I don't know why I ever thought differently. There's no way of getting her out of this except for physically extracting her from the situation. Hiding her. I have money; I can stash her somewhere. Nobody ever needs to know.

Sure, she'll spend the rest of her life on the run, but what's the alternative? I shudder to think. There's no guarantee her husband wouldn't make every minute of her life agony. And what are the chances of him making her happy? If he was raised by a man anywhere near as calculating as Bruno Morelli, I wouldn't put money on Eric being a gentleman. Or even giving a shit about Mia beyond how she looks, how tight she is, and how many healthy babies she can give him.

As if I would let that happen. I was the world's biggest asshole to ever think otherwise.

"Mia." I bang on the door with the side of my fist—I wouldn't want anybody overhearing me being quiet or gentle. "Open the door. We need to talk about this."

I didn't expect an answer. Everything on the other side of the door is silent. Maybe she's in the bathroom.

Immediately, my mind goes to a dark, ugly place. She wouldn't, would she? She's too smart for that. But if the alternative was being forced into marriage with a stranger—after finding out where her father's money comes from in the first place? Anything's possible.

I grab the keys from my pocket and shuffle through them until I find the one for her bedroom door. I've never had to use it until now. "Mia, tell me you're smarter than this," I mutter as I jam the key into the lock. I throw open the door and go straight for the en suite bathroom, hoping against hope.

It's empty. I check the shower, even the linen closet. She's not in here. I let out a shuddering breath, grateful for that at least.

But that doesn't mean she hasn't done something else. Something equally drastic.

The first clue that she has is the absence of personal items. The vanity drawer is open and most of its contents are removed. Nothing in the shower, nothing on the sink. I saw her bathroom back at the condo enough to know this isn't how she does things. She would have immediately spread out and gotten comfortable, especially knowing she had an event to get ready for tonight.

The hair on the back of my neck rises as I step back into her bedroom. The closet door is open, a couple of the dresser drawers. Empty. There's a pair of socks on the floor, some underwear strewn over the bed.

Like she was in a hurry.

"You wouldn't," I whisper, shaking my head, but the evidence is all around me. "Not alone. You wouldn't do this."

When I spot her computer on the desk, it's like a gleam of hope. She wouldn't leave that behind. She's practically tethered to it. Then again, if she was running away, she might be afraid of being tracked. I'm sure the fear of tracking kept her from doing a lot of things.

Like finding out who her father is…

Who the hell put it in her head in the first place? Where did she find that information? I know she's been curious, but why now? What brought this on?

I flip open the laptop and use her password to unlock it. Principles are out the window at this point. It's not an invasion of privacy when all I want is to understand, to make sure she's safe. The first step is finding out what made her look up the family.

She was automatically logged out of her school email account after being inactive, but the login screen is up. She'd flay me alive if she knew I had that password, too.

She got an email today from Dean, that asshole. Is that what this is about? I growl at the sight of his name, noticing she's read the message. I click on it, and there it is—links to articles, pictures, file after file.

He did this. He gathered a bunch of shit about the Morelli family. I should've taken care of him when I had the—

Wait.

I take a closer look, squinting at the screen. That can't be right. I must be seeing things.

I'm not. It's here in front of me. It was there all along. I never saw it. I never thought to look.

And now, everything makes sense. He didn't send her these files to seduce her or brainwash her into running away with him. Something a lot more sinister is at play.

My sins have finally caught up with me—but Mia is the one in danger of being punished for them.

30
MIA

I turn around, breathless, looking over the back seat and out the rear window. Dean's driving fast enough that the compound quickly shrinks until it's far enough away that I can't see it anymore.

As far as I'm concerned, I'll never see it again.

"It's fine. Nobody saw me." Dean lets out a breath like he's relieved. "Now, are you going to tell me why you had me come and get you? Did somebody hurt you? Don't tell me it was Zeke. I'll go back there and kill him right now."

"No. I mean, yeah, but not the way you think. It's him and my father. Both of them. They've been lying to me all this time."

"Lying about what?" He glances at me before turning back to the road. "Oh, no. You opened the email, didn't you?"

"Of course, I did. You told me to."

"But I didn't think you would do it right away. I didn't want things to turn out like this."

"Well, they have."

"So now you know. You know your family's part of… all of that."

He sounds disgusted, and he should. I know I feel that way. "How did

I not know? How did I not see it? Now, when I'm looking back, it all comes together. It's so obvious."

"Don't do that to yourself," he murmurs. "It's always easy to look back and think what you could've done or should've done. Think about it enough, and you'll drive yourself nuts." He sounds like he knows what he's talking about.

And he makes sense, too. He was definitely the right person to reach out to. If Posey was anywhere nearby, she'd be freaking out right now. So would Blair. Anyway, Dean already knows who Dad is, who I am just by being his daughter. He's the most logical choice.

"I'm never going back there. Not ever." I hate how my voice shakes almost as much as I hate the tears that want to roll down my cheeks. I won't let them. I'm done crying. Besides, crying isn't going to help me put a plan together, and that's what I need to do. I need to figure out a way to hide.

"How am I going to get away with this?" I cover my face with my hands. I can't even access any money. "I have nowhere to go."

"I told you I'd get you back to campus, and that's what I'm going to do. You can get your stuff together, and we'll figure it out from there."

My hands fall into my lap. He's right. I have to figure something out one step at a time. If he could take me to Blair's house, I might be able to hide out there for a while. She's probably home by now. If not, I'll have to think of something else. There has to be a way. I won't let him do this to me.

I won't let either of them do this to me.

How could Zeke do this to me?

"It's going to be okay," Dean assures me. "You managed to get by before your dad found you. You can do it again."

"That's true. I'm sure you're right." I wish I believed myself, but it's not easy. Not when I know the lengths my father is willing to go to so long as it means keeping me under his thumb. And now, if there's another family involved? Somebody he wants to form an alliance with or whatever? He's not going to let this go. I have to be smarter than him.

My phone buzzes. Right on schedule. I pull it out, growling. "It's Zeke. Big surprise."

"Let me have that." Dean holds his hand out. "Come on. Give it to me."

"You're not going to say anything to him, are you? Don't. Don't start a fight. I don't want you to end up in trouble over this."

"Give me the phone." I place it in his palm with a sigh, dreading what's about to happen. He surprises me by turning the phone off and sliding it into his coat pocket.

"Why did you do that?"

"So you won't be tempted to let him convince you to come back. He's only going to harass you, you know that."

Good point. I don't have anything to say to him, anyway. Nothing he doesn't already know. I don't think I'll ever forgive myself for trusting him. Opening myself up to him. How stupid could I be? He was never going to go against my dad. Not ever.

I look up in time to see the entrance ramp to the freeway zip past. "You missed the freeway."

"I'm taking a different route. If he comes after us, that's the route he'll take."

"I doubt he would catch up to us that fast. He was still in my dad's office when I sneaked out." I got lucky. The kitchen was wild, super busy with the dinner party tonight. Nobody was paying attention to insignificant little me. I guess they're all used to Zeke being the one watching my every move—and if he didn't think it was a problem for me to walk out through the back door, neither did they. I doubt any of them even noticed me.

Sometimes, it pays to be invisible in your own life.

"It doesn't hurt to be careful." I can only agree silently, resting my head against the seat. My God, how did everything fall apart all at once? It would be one thing to find out about Dad and what he does. What Zeke does for him or did. Security. I know what that means.

Learning about it would be bad enough.

But the whole marriage thing on top of it? How did he expect me to react? Acting like I was supposed to be happy. I always knew the man was clueless, but this is beyond anything I could imagine. And having the nerve to be pissed at me because I wasn't grateful.

And I come from him. How could we be so different? Mom gave me more than just her last name, obviously. She gave me morals and principles, the knowledge of right and wrong. We might have been poor, but we never hurt anybody.

"I'm so tired," I whisper. That word doesn't begin to describe it. I'm empty, wrung out like an old rag. Eventually, this is all going to catch up to me and crash down over my head, and I might have to spend an entire week in bed, even though I don't know where that bed will be or where I'll land. I hope it's soon since I don't know how much longer I can go like this.

You managed to get by before your dad found you. What a weird thing to say. I never told him or anybody else specifics about my past. Only Zeke, and it's not like those two spent time getting to know each other.

My name. Mom's name.

Why does something seem strange about that, too? Like something invisible is tapping me on the shoulder, wanting me to pay attention. But what is it? I can't even think.

My name. Casteel.

My father's name. Morelli.

How did Dean know?

My eyes open slowly. I never told him my father had a different last name from mine. I never told anybody. Nobody was supposed to know —it was so obvious why, and I always suspected, didn't I?

But of all the rules I tried to break, that wasn't one of them. And I know for sure Zeke would never breathe the name around anybody. Not that he ever had the chance, either. He understood Dad's need for secrecy even better than I did.

So how did Dean know I'm a member of the Morelli family?

"Can I have my phone back?" My voice is shaky, but for a different reason this time. "I want to check in with Blair. I want to see if I can meet up with her someplace."

"You know you're only going to end up talking to him, right?"

"But I need to call her. I have to know what's going to happen after we get back to campus, and I grab the rest of my stuff."

"How about I give it to you once we reach your condo?"

I force a laugh I don't feel. "You're starting to sound like Zeke. Thinking you know better than I do."

He doesn't laugh. "Don't ever compare me to him."

My mouth is so dry all of a sudden. I'm afraid my heart will burst out of my chest—or at least that it will beat so fast it finally gives out. "You really hate him. I should've trusted you from the beginning. It's like you saw something about him I didn't see." I have to keep him talking. I have to figure out how he knew about my father without me giving him a clue.

"He's an asshole. No, worse than that." His hands tighten around the wheel. "He's fucking evil. I wanted so much to tell you, but you had to find out on your own."

"What do you mean? I mean, how would you even know that? You never met him before, did you?" How, how did he know? He must've known Zeke before this. Maybe they were kids together. Maybe he knows Zeke went to work for Dad. But it still doesn't make sense, really. Zeke's seven years older than him, which means Dean would've been a little kid at the time. Something is missing.

"No, I never met him before I met you." He's breathing a little harder, and I couldn't describe him as staring at the road ahead. More like glaring at it, so intense I can hardly breathe. "But I saw him before. Only once. But that was enough."

"Really? Small world." I can't believe how hard it is to pretend I'm wiped out and exhausted when adrenaline is pumping through my veins hard enough to make me sick.

"It can be. I didn't think I would ever see him again." We blow past the next onramp for the interstate, and now I know he has no intention of taking me straight to school.

The doors are locked—though we're doing fifty, close to fifty-five, almost racing down an access road running alongside the highway. Even if I could jump, I might be so banged up I wouldn't be able to get up and run away.

"I really want my phone back," I whisper. "Please. Maybe I can get Blair to meet me at school. That would save a lot of time, and you could head home again."

"Home? Do you think I have a home?" He looks at me, and I wish he wouldn't because we're still tearing down the road. "I haven't had a home since I was ten years old. Thanks to that motherfucker you sided with. You sided with him so many times. You're so fucking stupid, so blind."

"Dean! The road!" Reflex makes me reach out and try to adjust the wheel when he starts to drift off to the shoulder. He recovers quickly, a bitter laugh making my blood run cold.

"So stupid. You stupid, stupid bitch. Trusting him. I bet you fucked him, too, didn't you? I saw the way he looked at you. At the beginning of the semester compared to the last time I saw him?" He whistles, shaking his head. "You must be fucking fantastic."

"Why are you saying this? Where is this coming from? This doesn't sound like you at all."

"And how exactly would you know what I sound like? Maybe I only showed you what I wanted you to see, the way he always has. The way you let him." He slams his palm against the wheel with every word.

Now there are tears in my eyes again. Not angry tears, not this time. "What are you saying? Who are you? What is this really about?"

"Oh, now you care. Now you want to comfort me, right? When you fucking rejected me all semester because you couldn't see anything but him. That evil, murderous fuck, and he was all you wanted."

"You're right. I was blind. I only saw what I wanted to see. And now, you can tell me the truth. That's all I want, the truth. You've already helped me so much, you know."

"Helped you? I had to fucking spoon-feed it to you. You never even thought to pull back the curtain and see what was behind it, did you?" He shakes his head with a disgusted laugh. "No, you wouldn't. Because your whole life changed for the better, right? Daddy found you, and he's rich, and he's connected, and why would you want to know anything more than that? It might ruin the fantasy."

"That's not fair."

"Tell yourself whatever you need to do," he snarls. "It doesn't matter anyway. By the time this is finished, you won't have to worry about anything. You or him."

Now I wish I had let him drift off the road. I wish we had crashed into one of the concrete supports whizzing past on my right. It would be quicker than what I'm afraid he has in mind. "What are you trying to say?" I ask, feeling small and cold and so alone.

He smiles slowly, but it's the smile of a demon before the real torture begins. I've never seen anything terrifying enough to make me almost lose control of my bladder. Not until now.

"I'm going to take away the thing he loves, the way he took away my life." He sounds almost happy. "The night he murdered my father in front of me."

No. That can't be true.

Yet somewhere in my heart, I know it is.

"And I'm going to show him how it feels to watch somebody he loves die in front of him." He's calm. Serene. "Before I kill him, too."

31
ZEKE

I've never seen the compound on lockdown before. It's never gotten to this point.

But the boss's daughter has never been kidnapped before either.

I'll never forgive myself. Not until the day I die, and maybe not after then either. It was my job to protect her, but I lost focus. I should have insisted on learning more about her friends. But no, I told myself it was a matter of compromise.

Besides, he never told her his full name.

"You're sure she's with him?" The boss jogs beside me on the way to the gatehouse, where the security camera feed is most easily accessible.

"I looked through her Facebook after I found the email, and yeah. She reached out to him, and they made plans for him to pick her up outside the gates."

"And you're sure he's who you say he is?" I've never heard him like this before. He's beyond impassioned. He might even be afraid. How long has it been since he's been afraid?

"I looked at his account. There's even a picture of him and his old man from years ago." Before I put a bullet in his rat head. "Only he goes by Dean Dicarlo-Strauss. Must have been his mother's name or a stepparent. But he kept the DiCarlo."

"In honor of his shithead thieving excuse for a father." He spits on the ground before letting out a string of profanity. "I'll fucking kill him. That whole family was a bunch of shits. Like father, like son."

All this time, it was about me. Me and the boss. The Morelli family. I don't even know if Dean was ever interested in Mia, really. He's always been more interested in me, for reasons she could never have begun to guess.

Because she never knew what I was capable of. That I could murder a man in cold blood because her father ordered me to. Because the man in question was about to turn state's evidence and needed to be silenced permanently.

What did I miss that night? It could have been anything. It was one of my first hits, a job that was supposed to be easy in that Joe DiCarlo had skipped town and was hiding out in the middle of nowhere. He wanted to fly under the radar until the feds picked him up.

Which meant no witnesses.

What if he wasn't alone in that shithole motel? He was one of the only people staying there at the time, at least according to the lack of cars parked in the weed-strewn lot.

It was so quick, so simple. Luring him outside by setting off the alarm on his car. One of those things a person doesn't think about—you hear your alarm, you open the door to see what's happening. It wasn't until that last second when our eyes met that he knew he'd made a fatal mistake.

I never checked inside the room he came from, though, did I? What if that stupid traitor brought his kid with him? What if they were going to hide out together?

It's the only thing that explains how he would know who I am, who Mia is. I know damn well she never told anybody her father's last name. That was deliberate.

No, I decide as we reach the gatehouse. He knew from the beginning. From the moment he set eyes on me. No wonder he was so determined to be part of her group for that project. It was all in front of me, and I never saw it. I was too busy thinking he wanted to get in her pants, so I dismissed him.

Another mistake. Maybe the biggest one of my life.

"We've located the vehicle, sir." Bruno leans in while I shoot daggers at the stupid bastard who let her leave without raising an alarm. I was in her father's office, trying to convince him to give her a chance at living while she was in the middle of throwing her life away elsewhere. Running away with the guy who left that note outside the door back at the condo.

He was right. I can't protect her. I only thought I had what it takes.

"And what were you doing when the boss's daughter left? How did you not see that?" The guard looks like he's about to piss his pants, and I hope he does. It's the least of what he deserves.

That's not going to help Mia, though. I study the car, taking notes of the make and model. There's a good shot of the tags, too.

"I want these tags run," I bark. "And I want somebody who knows how to get into the DMV traffic cam feed to follow their progress. The car has to show up somewhere." When all he does is stare at me, I pull the Glock from my waistband and hold it up for him to see. He gets the message. "Get moving. Now!"

"We've gotta find her." Bruno puts his hands on my shoulders, squeezing tight. "Find her. I don't care what it takes. Bring her back safe."

I have no way of telling him this means more to me than just a job. I'm not doing this for him. I would burn the entire compound to the ground if it meant ensuring her safety.

I would kill the man standing in front of me if it came to that. Anything, so long as she's safe.

"I'll give you anything. Anything you want. The sky is the limit, no matter what. It's yours. You understand?" He even shakes me. I'm not sure he's completely in control of himself right now. I know the feeling.

"Anything?" I ask, just to be sure.

"Whatever you want, no matter what it is. Bring my daughter home."

"I will." Not that I wasn't going to, but it can't hurt to have a promise like that.

It's that promise, along with everything I've come to love about Mia, that sends me sprinting across the lawn back to the house. I take the stairs to the basement, where the servers are located. I've never gotten well acquainted with Chris, one of the guys who keeps everything running smoothly, but we're about to spend some time together.

As it turns out, he's already on the job. "They called me from the guardhouse," he barks when I enter. "I'm already in the DMV servers, tracing the progress of the vehicle."

"You're a fucking genius." I look over his shoulder without bothering to ask if he minds. This isn't the time for formalities. "Where did you pick them up?"

"About a mile down the road, at the intersection." There they are, going through roughly an hour ago as night was beginning to fall. I can't believe I let that much time pass without knowing she was gone. Too busy placating her father. "Then I have them a few minutes later at the next light." He switches to a still from that feed.

Meanwhile, I try to call Mia again. Her phone is still off. Which one of them turned it off, though? I wouldn't be surprised if she did to make sure she couldn't be tracked, but I also wouldn't be surprised if he had something to do with it. He wouldn't want her to be able to reach out for help, right?

Does she know yet? If he has even a scrap of decency left, he won't make this too hard for her.

But I'll never forget that look in his eyes. Outside the restaurant. The cold, seething hatred. The look of somebody who wants to taste blood. And there I was, telling myself it was all about her. How could I be so stupid? Because I wanted her so much it was hard to breathe, I assumed everybody did. I wrote him off. Who the hell do I think I am, bragging about being able to protect her? What a joke.

Chris grunts, drawing my attention away from where I'm signing into Mia's messenger account. I might be able to reach him through that. But should I? It's one thing to perform a hit and follow orders.

But I've never had to negotiate with a maniac. And if there's one thing the Morelli family doesn't do, it's call the cops for help. I'm on my own.

"What is it?" I watch closely, and soon, it's clear what Chris reacted to. "Where the fuck did they go?"

"I'm still trying to figure that out." He checks back to their last location picked up by a camera, then follows the map to the next intersection. They never rolled through.

"Try east and west," I suggest, though I'm sure he already figured that by now. I hate feeling useless. There has to be a way.

While he's looking at that, I turn my attention to the app. This fucking asshole. The way he fucking wormed his way into her circle of friends. They were chatting in the car, too, according to the timestamps. I didn't even know she was still in contact with him. Under other circumstances, that would infuriate me, but now, I can't be bothered to hold it against her.

Besides, if she doesn't regret it by now, I'm afraid she will soon.

There has to be at least a hundred photos here. What am I looking for? A clue as to where he would take her. There's a photo of him with three guys he refers to as foster brothers, all of them smiling and holding up beers. There's one of him fishing and a few at the beach, but nothing to give me any idea about where he lived before he enrolled at Blackthorn.

Clearly, his old man left him money. Probably money he stole from the family, but nobody was ever able to find it. He wasn't as smart as he thought, though, because he got found out. Hence agreeing to work with the feds. He was scared out of his mind knowing Bruno Morelli doesn't take well to being robbed. No one does.

But he is a guy with plenty of muscle behind him, which most people don't have at their disposal.

I'm halfway through Dean's photos when the messenger box pops up. *Who is this? I know it isn't Mia. Mia's with me.* I don't have time to respond before he follows up with a second message. *Let me guess. You think you can help her, don't you? Haven't I already told you? You can't protect her.*

"Motherfucker," I mutter, drawing Chris's attention. "He knows I'm on here." What am I supposed to say? If it was just me, I wouldn't care. I would dare the bastard to come and find me, to fight it out like men. Hell, I don't even hold it against him. If I watched somebody blow my dad's head off, I'd want to kill them, too.

But this isn't that simple. If only it was.

This is between you and me, I type. *She has nothing to do with it. You know that.*

It's your turn to see what it means to lose.

No, no, not like this. Where are you? If you want me, you've got me. Face-to-face. Whatever you say. Leave her out of it.

Why should I?

Because you know she has nothing to do with this. The family. She's innocent.

I was innocent, too. That didn't stop you.

"I didn't know!" I'd smash the fucking computer into dust if it wasn't for Mia needing me. *I didn't know.*

Would that have changed anything? he asks. *Never mind. I don't want your excuses. I want your suffering.* His account goes from active to inactive, telling me he's logged off. And I still don't know where the hell he is, where he's taken her.

Until a ping rings out from where my phone sits on the table. A new alert.

Front Door Open

"The condo!" I leap out of the chair and take off at a run with Chris shouting questions behind me. I hardly hear him. She must have somehow convinced him to take her there, knowing I would find out. Either that or this is the way he planned it all along.

He wants me to watch him hurt her in the one place she was supposed to be safe. Just like he was supposed to be safe that night when I showed up.

"The condo!" I shout to anybody who can hear me. I don't know if they understand what I mean, but I don't care. All I care about is the motorcycle sitting outside, waiting for me. The truck won't do right now—I can cut in and out of traffic much quicker with this. It would take ninety minutes to get to the condo if I drove four wheels. On two? I can make it in half the time.

And I need to be even quicker than that. Every minute she's with him is a minute she could be hurting, and it's all because of me. If we both live through this, I'll never stop trying to make it up to her.

That's the last thought I have before tearing down the driveway, wind rushing in my ears.

Hold on, Mia. I'm coming.

32
MIA

"You didn't even think to wonder why I was able to get to you as fast as I did, did you?" Dean laughs at his own question before I have the chance to answer. "Of course, you didn't. I was waiting in a hotel ten minutes from your house because I knew you would come running. You were too busy thinking about yourself to think about it. With your head so far up your ass, you practically threw yourself into this situation."

Now is not the time for me to be a smart-ass. I have to keep him calm and level. All through the drive to school, he slowly went deeper and deeper down the rabbit hole. Telling me all about how miserable his life was after Zeke murdered his father.

Murdered. It's an ugly word. How would I feel about Zeke if I watched my father die because he pulled the trigger? What if I was ten years old, crouching in a closet in a cramped motel room, peeking out through the barely open door? "I was there with his body for hours until somebody came." I lost track of how many times he said that. "And that wasn't anywhere near as bad as things got."

I practically know his entire life story, and it hasn't been easy. I keep having to remind myself of that while I sit here on the sofa, hands folded in my lap where he can see them at all times. He paces the length of the room, occasionally looking out through the balcony doors. He won't go out there, but he keeps checking. Waiting to see if Zeke will show up.

He will. I know he will. He would've gotten the message on his phone. *Please, be paying attention*, I beg silently. Maybe if I wish hard enough, he'll hear me. It doesn't matter right now what happened earlier. His lies, the way he covered up everything my father tried to hide. He's been complicit this entire time. I can't worry about that. All I want is to get out of this alive, for both of us to get out of it alive.

Right now, I'm not sure our chances are all that good.

Because the second Zeke steps through that door, he'll be ambushed. Unless I do something about it.

"I hope you understand I hate him just as much as you do." Do I sound convincing? Maybe not—Dean doesn't even react. Like he's already hardened himself against anything I might say. "He led me on all this time. He went out of his way to lie and hide things from me."

"You didn't try too hard to figure anything out, though, did you?" he asks, disgusted. His eyes shine with an unnerving light. He's losing it.

"What was I supposed to do? Everything I did was tracked and monitored. Even what I did online."

His head bobs up and down. "No shit. The son of a bitch logged into your Facebook and everything."

My heart skips a beat, but I manage to keep my voice even. "That doesn't come as a surprise. I'm sure he had all my passwords and everything."

"But you let it happen." He sits on the coffee table, close enough that our knees touch. I have to deliberately keep myself from flinching. I can't let him see how it unnerves me, being this close.

"Haven't you ever been in a situation where you didn't have control?"

"That's been most of my life."

"Then how can you judge me? I didn't ask for any of this. I didn't seek out my birth father after my mom died, either. Pretty much all of this was decided for me."

"There's always a choice."

"What choice should I have made?"

His eyes harden. He senses I'm challenging him. I have to back off. "I was alone in the world," I murmur. All the memories come rushing back, and that's probably not a bad thing. I don't mind sounding vulnerable right now. I need him to think of me that way. "I was so scared. Mom was all I had. I always wondered who my father was, but she would never tell me."

"Yeah, and now you know why."

"Now I know why. Yeah." And I have to wonder how she'd feel about him bringing me into that world. "But he took care of me. He still takes care of me."

"Stockholm syndrome." He gives me a firm nod. "It's not even your fault. You're already too far gone to understand."

I have to clasp my hands tight to keep from screaming. He couldn't be more wrong. "Listen, it's not like I'm saying I love him or anything like that. I don't think I'm ever going to forgive him for not coming clean with me. But he wanted to protect me. That has to mean something."

"My father wanted to protect me, too. He was all I had."

"But you got through it, right? Look at you now. I mean, this isn't an easy school to get into."

"I got lucky."

"Just like I did."

"No! Not just like you did." His reflexes are scary fast. One second, he's sitting on the table. The next, he's leaning over me, boxing me in with an arm on either side and his face inches from mine. I can smell his sour sweat, and my nose wrinkles before I can stop myself. Of all the things to care about when a maniac is practically on top of me.

I force my voice to be steady. "How not like me?"

"I had to go through three years of foster care before my mother found me. She was in Europe with her new husband when your boyfriend blew my dad's brains out. She didn't even want to take me with her when they moved there. Nobody bothered telling her he was dead—can you believe that? And she obviously never tried to reach out and find out how her little boy was doing, or else she would have known sooner that I ended up falling through the cracks. Nobody gave a shit."

"I'm sorry."

"I don't care about your pity," he spits. "I only want you to understand. You have no idea what happened to me. How I was used. Humiliated. Beaten and tortured. Nobody cared. Nobody spoke up for me. Nobody paid attention. And even when my so-called mother looked for me, I was so lost it took them another year to locate me. That's how fucked the whole system is."

That's not Zeke's fault. "You're right. It is fucked."

"And then she wanted me to call this stranger Daddy. Can you imagine that? I already have a father. I don't need another one." *No, but you'll take his money, right?* I'm not suicidal—I wouldn't dream of saying that out loud. But it's the truth.

"Zeke robbed me of years of my life that I will never get back. I had to spend years in therapy after what I went through. And what happened to him? Did he pay for it at all?"

"I don't know."

"You know damn well he didn't," he growls. "He's still living his life. In this palace—and when he wasn't here, he was at your compound." The way he makes it sound, he might as well be talking about someplace awful. Evil. For all I know, maybe it is. Someday, I'm going to have to make sense of all this in my head.

He pushes away from the couch, and I can breathe without having to smell him or look into his eyes. "You have no idea. What it felt like when I first saw him. Like a ghost from my past walking into my life."

"I'm sure it was awful."

"Don't patronize me," he warns, shaking his head. "You don't want to do that."

"I'm sorry." I glance at the clock on the cable box. We've been here for a little more than half an hour. *Please, be on your way. Get me.* What if he never saw the alert on his phone when I opened the door? How much longer am I going to have to sit and listen to this? It was hard enough convincing him to bring me here, where we could at least be comfortable while we waited for Zeke to come for me. I didn't think he would go for it, but then I don't think he's given this a lot of thought. He's going purely on impulse now.

All he's ever wanted is revenge. He didn't exactly sit around and plan what that revenge would look like.

"It was worse than awful," he informs me. "I thought I would die right there. Outside the party, that first party at the frat."

"You were there?"

"Outside, yeah. On the front lawn. I watched the whole thing. And I thought *that can't be him*. It's not possible. But he hasn't changed all that much in eight years. I thought for sure somebody would have killed him by now, or that at least he would be in prison."

He turns my way from where he's standing in front of the glass door. "He didn't even get arrested for it. Nothing happened to him. Right? He's been free and clear all this time."

What's most obvious is the almost whiny need in everything he says. He wants so much for me to tell him somebody, anybody cared enough about his dad that Zeke was punished for his murder. "I know you wish I would say that, but I don't know. I wasn't around then, remember? I had no idea he existed."

His brows draw together like he's thinking about it, and he must see I'm telling the truth. "Sure. You were just a kid, too. They hadn't used you yet."

"That's true."

"But they've been using you ever since they found you. You know that, right?"

"Yeah. I do know that." And it hurts like hell.

"Bruno Morelli isn't capable of love."

"I'm sure you're right." The worst part is, I'm not lying. How could a man capable of what he's done actually love anybody? "But I knew that. I really did. We don't have any kind of a warm relationship. He's always wanted me as, like, an accessory. I make him look better. I understand that."

"And you let him use you?"

How can I make him understand? I don't even understand myself. "I didn't see any way out of it. I felt trapped. In some ways, you freed me. You showed me the truth. I'm grateful to you for that."

He arches an eyebrow, looking me up and down. "You're just saying that."

"I'm not. I mean it. I was too afraid to know. I needed it thrown in my face, where I couldn't look away. You did that for me, and I'm grateful." *Zeke, please, hurry.* He's too jittery, and now his face is getting twitchy. His eye, the corner of his mouth. Is this what happens to a person when they're within arm's length of getting what they've fantasized about for half their life?

"You're welcome. Now I wish I had told you from the beginning. Maybe you wouldn't have let him touch you."

I have to bite my tongue before I warn him not to talk about that. It will only make him crazier.

"He fucked you, didn't he? You even let him fuck you. That murdering, evil piece of shit."

Don't give him what he wants. "How would you even know that?"

"I saw the way he looked at you. How he acted around you. All of it. I watched how it changed. I saw how it drove him crazy whenever I got close to you. It was too easy, really—he didn't even make it challenging." He looks me up and down, scoffing while pacing the room. "And I bet you get off on that bad boy thing, right? Dumb bitches like you always do."

I can't believe I have to sit here and take this. But he has a gun. I can't fight with a gun, especially with him being as unhinged as he is.

"Maybe I should find better ways to pass the time." He stops across from me, folding his arms, smirking. "I have all this entertainment right here in front of me. Maybe that's what I'll do. Maybe I'll take you to your bedroom and tie you up there, and I'll use you the way you let him use you. And when he finally wakes the fuck up and finds you, he'll see what it feels like to have the thing he cares about ruined. Broken."

My teeth are chattering so hard, and I can barely speak. "No. He doesn't even care about me—"

"Stop it. Don't lie to me. I can see right through you. You're in love with him, and he probably thinks he has feelings for you. Fucking sick."

I try to scramble away from him when he lunges, but he's too quick. And too strong—he wasn't scrawny, to begin with, but he's bulked up a little since we first met. I didn't notice. Even if I did, why would I have cared? I didn't know he was doing it so he could be strong when it came time for this.

He picks me up, both arms around my waist, and I kick and scream and claw at him while he carries me to my room. "Loosen up," he pants close to my ear. "You might even enjoy it."

I hit the bed hard enough to knock the air from my lungs, but I recover fast. "Don't do this!" I beg, but he only climbs onto the bed. I kick out blindly and connect with his stomach. It's enough to stop him —he doubles over, one arm across his midsection.

I fight my way to the foot of the bed and jump off, then make a run for it. It would be easier if we stayed here, where Zeke could find us, but I don't know how long that will be, and he's coming for me. I hear him pounding down the hallway. "You're gonna bleed for that!"

He reaches me before I can unlock the door, and I scream when his arm encircles my waist again. Now he clamps the other hand over my mouth, covering it along with my nostrils. I can't breathe because he's suffocating me. I tried to dig my nails into the back of his hand to make him loosen up. "You can't do things the easy way, can you?" he grunts, hauling me across the room and dumping me on the sofa.

"Please, please." I'm on my back, trying to get up, to get away, but he looms over me.

Then he pulls his gun, aiming it at my head.

"Maybe I'll let him show up and find out he was too late," he mutters before grinning in triumph. "How about that?"

I'd answer, but I'm too scared to speak.

Besides, a soft, high-pitched beeping noise catches my attention before I can react.

The alarm. Zeke disarmed the alarm from outside.

And Dean didn't hear it. Too busy planning to kill me.

"I'm a victim in this, too," I remind him, desperate to stall for just another minute. "Don't punish me for that. These things happened before I ever—"

He didn't hear the alarm disarming, but there's no way he couldn't hear the door being unlocked.

He spins around, aiming the gun at the door now.

The only thing I can think to do is scream. "Zeke! Gun!"

33
ZEKE

Mia Casteel owns my soul. She might have saved it by showing me I'm more than a cold, unfeeling hitman. More than a bodyguard.

And by screaming my name at the last second, she might have saved my life.

When I hear her scream, I pivot, pressing my back to the wall beside the door while it swings open. A bullet hits the wall across from the doorway, one that would've gone through me if I hadn't moved.

I pivot back, my own Glock drawn, and I aim it into the room.

He's not aiming at me anymore. His gun is pressed to Mia's temple, her body in front of his. "I should've known somebody like you would use a woman as a human shield," I mutter. "Like I told you. This is between us. She has nothing to do with it. Let her go, and we'll handle this like men."

"But she is part of this." She whimpers when his hand brushes against her chest before taking hold of one of her tits and squeezing. "How does it feel? Knowing there's nothing you can do. I'm going to fuck her. I'm going to take her right in front of you."

"Not if I kill you first."

"And if I pull this trigger?" He jams the gun against her head, and she whimpers again. The sound is like touching a match to gunpowder. I want nothing more than to watch him die. "That's all it would take. You should know that by now."

I don't have a shot. There isn't enough room. I could easily hit her. How can I get him away from her? Someone must have heard the shot. Have they called the police? Is anyone even here?

"I didn't know you were there. At the motel." This is all I can do. Distract him, and hope he makes a wrong move that gives me a chance. "I didn't know. I was given a name and a location. That was it."

"You expect me to feel sorry for you?" His laughter is tight, high-pitched, and crazy. "Try again."

"I'm just saying. I'm sorry you had to see that. And I'm sorry for whatever you went through after, I really am. But you have to know the man I killed—your dad—wasn't a saint either. He made some pretty bad choices."

"So he deserved to die?" He holds her a little tighter, squeezing harder. "All because her old man said he should?"

"I know how it sounds. I do." I inch closer to them, almost holding my breath. "You want to punish someone, then take it out on me. Here and now. You wanna beat the shit out of me, you wanna beat me to death even, fine. But leave her out of it."

"No. That's not going to happen. Haven't you been listening?" He sticks out his tongue and runs it along her earlobe, and all I see is rage. Blinding, white-hot rage.

Something has to end this.

And all of a sudden, I think I know what it will be.

I look Mia in the eye. *Understand me. Just this once.* "Sandbag."

"What?" Dean snaps.

He doesn't have to wait long to find out.

Mia slumps like she fainted. Her legs are like jelly, knees loose. It's enough for Dean to react in surprise.

Which is all I need, even though my aim's off slightly, thanks to him bending to pull Mia back to her feet. The shot hits the bicep of his dominant arm—he drops his gun, grabbing his arm with the other hand. Mia drops to the floor, safe for the moment.

Before I can fire again, he throws himself at me, hitting me low, knocking me off balance. I manage to maintain my hold on the Glock. He grabs my wrist, twisting it, trying to loosen my grip.

And all through this, he screams. Roars. It's pain, it's rage, it's years of wishing. Fantasizing about what he'd do if he ever got a hold of me. This isn't the way it played out in his head.

I'd feel sorry for him if he hadn't made the mistake of bringing Mia into it. That, I can't forgive. When I bring the gun across his face and split the skin over his cheekbone, I feel no remorse. His head snaps to one side, and he staggers backward, his body reacting to the force behind my backhanded blow.

I used enough force to send him through the glass doors to the balcony.

Enough force to make him trip backward over the metal doorframe, still screaming, arms pinwheeling wildly. For one moment, the inexplicable impulse to stop him throws me forward, arms outstretched. But it's too late anyway.

He stops screaming on impact with the concrete outside the building's entrance.

I run for the balcony and lean over the railing. Mia lets out a broken sob behind me. "Is he—?"

He landed on his stomach, but he's looking up at me. That's all I need to see. "He's dead." I can't muster up sympathy, even if I'm the one who set his life on its path.

More important is the weeping girl on the living room floor, hands covering her face. I fall to my knees at her side and gather her in my arms. She's safe. She's alive. "Did he hurt you? Did he—?"

She shakes her head, but a fresh sob makes me think otherwise. "He wanted to. Tried. I got away."

Thank God. I close my eyes, my cheek against the top of her head.

"I'm so sorry for everything. For not telling the truth so you could decide on your own whether you wanted to cut yourself off from your father. I shouldn't have kept that secret for him. You don't know how much I—"

"It doesn't matter now." Her arms lock around my neck. "It doesn't matter."

* * *

"We'll double-check, but my contacts in the department tell me it's an open-and-shut case." Bruno sits on the edge of his desk, with Mia in the chair beside mine. She's freshly showered and changed now that we're back at the compound. Her skin is pink from all the scrubbing.

I wanted more than anything to be there with her, to hold her and wash her and tell her it'll be okay.

He continues. "The story is, it's a crush gone wrong. He became obsessed when Mia rejected him—and he planned to blackmail her into dating him by using her Morelli ties against her, hence sending her all that shit earlier."

His gaze lands on me. In all these years, he's never looked at me the way he looks at men he considers his equal. Not until tonight. "That little spat the two of you got into outside that restaurant works in our favor. There are plenty of witnesses who can confirm he was out of control that day and looking to throw fists over Mia."

"Anything I can do to help." I didn't know it at the time that the fact we almost brawled in public would end up helping. When I think back on how it chapped my ass to leave it alone, to listen to Mia and not take advantage of someone who couldn't possibly beat me, I don't know if it was the right choice to turn my back on the fight or not. It might've meant exposing him as the bloodthirsty maniac he was before he could attack Mia. It might've meant pissing him off worse than before and pushing him over the edge sooner. There's no going back anyway.

The boss takes me literally—it's not like I normally let the sarcasm fly when I'm around him, so he can't help it. "You've already done everything there is to do when it comes to helping. You brought Mia home, where she belongs."

He lowers his brow. "And don't think I'll forget the promise I made, just because it's all over. If I'm one thing, it's a man of my word. Anything you want. It's yours."

For the past twenty minutes, Mia has sat silent and still while the boss and I talked over the events of the night. The sanitized version of events, that is, leaving out the very correct assumption that we've been fucking for over a month. She's barely blinked, staring at the floor near her father's feet.

I don't know which part of tonight she's processing. What happened after she ran away, or the reason she ran.

The mention of repayment is enough to snap her out of it. Her head lifts and turns until she's staring at me. "Anything you want?" she murmurs. Three words have never held so much accusation.

"Anything I want. No limit." I check out the boss's reaction to see whether this holds true. It does. "And I know exactly what it is."

"A man who knows what he wants." He rubs his hands together, smiling wide. And why not? He has his daughter back. His plans are on track. All his planning will still pay off. "What can I give you in exchange for returning my daughter to me?"

Mia's glare cuts through my skull. I want nothing more than to hold her. To make sure she's here, next to me. It isn't enough that I see her. That I can smell her soap and shampoo, that I hear her voice. I need her to fill all of my senses.

She, on the other hand, needs to cut my head off. Or at least my balls. She thinks this was all a matter of money. That once again, I used her.

"Well?" He nudges my leg with his. "Out with it. What can I give you?"

It's very simple. There's only one thing I want. The only thing I'll ever want. "Your daughter."

34
MIA

"You're joking." Dad laughs—a loud, empty sound. Like a bark from a big dog. "Right?"

"I'm not. I want Mia." Zeke turns to look at me before reaching out to touch my arm. "I love her. She's the world to me. Going after her tonight had nothing to do with you or my job. I did it because I need her. It's that simple."

Does he know what he's saying? Does he know he said he loves me? To my father, of all people? He's never even said it to me before now.

And I love him, too. I know I do. I might've spent the rest of my life telling myself I don't, that I never did, but that wouldn't have changed the truth in my heart. I've loved him for such a long time. I can't help what he's done. I only know how he is with me, how we are together. How he's the only man I'll ever want.

It's a shame my father could literally kill him for it.

He looks like he wants to, for sure. "I'm going to pretend I'm not hearing this." He's fighting as hard as he can not to shout—though the low, even, flat delivery he went with is even scarier. It makes my skin crawl.

"Sir, you know—"

"Don't call me that when you just got done saying you want my daughter." He shoots up off the desk and turns to me. I'm tired of red-faced men. I've seen enough of them tonight. "What's happening here? He's coming up with this out of nowhere, right? He's fucking with me."

So much has changed. I'm not the person I was this morning. She was ignorant and didn't try hard not to be. Ready to sneak around for weeks to be with Zeke behind her father's back. Prepared to overlook it whenever he ended a conversation, all because she walked in a room. Afraid to speak up about things that actually mattered.

"I need to talk to you. Alone." Zeke's going to have to trust me. I hope by now he knows I wouldn't throw him under the bus. I don't want to think about him wondering whether he'll come out of this with his head attached to the rest of his body.

Jesus, that's not even a joke now. No wonder he fought so hard to stay away from me at first.

Dad points at Zeke, lowering his brow. "Don't even think about leaving the compound. We have a lot of things to discuss, you and me." All I can do is glance at Zeke as he stands, but he's not looking at me. I wish he would.

Once we're alone, it's time to be brave. If Zeke can do it, so can I. "I know you don't want this to be true, but it is. I love Zeke, too. And if he wants me, he's got me. I don't know any other way to explain it."

"You—you—" he sputters, eyes wide.

"Calm down."

"Who the hell do you think you are, telling me to calm down?" He stomps around his desk to where he left his phone. "That motherfucker is dead for touching you."

For some reason, that's the last straw. I'm so done with all of this. Being under his thumb, controlled, demeaned. Used like a pawn. "Who do I think I am?" I stand and drop the blanket. "Who do you think you are?"

He's so surprised that he drops the phone. "You got fucked up somehow tonight. I'm ready to chalk this attitude of yours up to that.

And if you're smart, you're going to stop talking, and that'll be that. Understood?"

"Stop dismissing me. You weren't around for the first seventeen years of my life, and now you act like taking care of me for a year is enough to earn the right to treat me like a pet. I deserve better than that, if only because I'm your daughter."

"If you weren't my daughter, you wouldn't be here. Did you forget about that?"

"I don't have to be here anymore, then. I don't need anything from you, and I don't want anything from you. I'll leave with nothing but the clothes on my back. No school, no anything. It's fine. I'll get by."

"Right. Like you'd do anything that drastic."

I actually feel sorry for him, so sorry I stop barking because all it does is make him shut down. He's not a complex man. "As far as you'd be concerned, I'd be a stranger. I don't need you. Our lives could go back to the way they were before."

He's sizing me up, trying to figure out whether I mean it. "You're bluffing," he finally decides. "You can't mean it."

"Try me. I would rather walk out of this house with only these clothes than marry Eric Rinaldi or any man because you decided I would. I never signed on for that, and you never even gave me the benefit of telling me you'd pick my husband one day. I didn't even get that courtesy."

He scoffs. "Courtesy."

"Yes. I deserve that much. This isn't the old days. Fathers don't order their daughters to marry a stranger. Even if I never met Zeke, I still wouldn't want to marry the man you chose just because he was the man you chose."

He's still pondering this, like the concept of a woman having a mind of her own is too much to comprehend. I can't say I'm surprised. "If I walk away, it means everybody you've ever told about me wondering where I've gone. You could make up a story about me traveling, rebelling, or even needing rehab. Right?"

His look of confusion turns to a scowl. "Right. Like they'd buy that for long. This would mean nothing but questions and suspicions. Especially now that the press has picked up on what happened tonight. You're linked to me."

I know it. It's fun, in a way, being so far ahead of a supposedly powerful man like him. "You're right. I didn't think about it that way. I guess it's too late to keep word from spreading."

"Please. I'm sure everybody knows by now."

"I guess it would look pretty suspicious if I disappeared right after this. Like I had a breakdown or something."

He scoffs like that would mean a personal insult to his ego. "My daughter? A breakdown? I don't think so."

"So I guess I should stick around, huh? To make things easier on you." He blinks rapidly, sinking into his chair while I remain standing. Good. Let him look up at me. Maybe the change in view will help change his mindset. "I could make things a lot easier, in fact. I could be the face of the family. The ambassador. I could clean up your image and make you look like a kind, generous, philanthropic guy who's been misunderstood by critics and the federal agents who've never been able to pin him down."

His mouth moves without sound for a few seconds. "You came up with all this?" he croaks.

"You'd be surprised what goes through a person's head when they think they're about to die." I can't help but chuckle. "Or maybe you wouldn't be surprised."

He barks out a laugh, then looks shocked that he did. I'll take it as a good sign. "You could finally improve your brand. Not only in front of the other families and your friends but the entire world. Now that word's out I'm your daughter—your daughter who you almost lost so soon after you found her, which could mean great press—you have the opportunity to become a hero."

Got him. He's watching it play out in his head, and he's liking what he sees. A clean image. Beloved, or at least not hated.

"I'll do that for you," I offer. "I'd be happy to. If I can have Zeke."

His eyes harden. "No way."

"Then we have no deal, and I'm gone."

"I have a contract to fulfill."

"And I love Zeke. I love him." For once, I don't fight against the tears. They flow freely now. "I know it doesn't matter to you. You don't know me. You've never made an attempt at getting to know me. But this is my entire life we're talking about, and he's the person I love. He's the person I'm choosing."

"You don't know what you want."

"Look at me. Listen to me. I understand we don't know each other very well, but from the past few minutes we've spent together, do I seem like a girl who doesn't know what she wants?"

I've got him, and he knows it. He just doesn't want to admit it. "I still have obligations."

"I understand that, but there has to be a way around it. Some kind of force majeure clause, right? Don't tell me you didn't get one of those."

He rubs his temples, eyes squeezed shut. "I'm starting to regret sending you to college."

"After what happened tonight, it's the perfect cover. I'm a total wreck." Then something else hits me. Should I even mention it? It's gross, it's despicable, and I know it. But I'm also beyond desperate at this point. I run my sleeves under my eyes and stand up a little straighter. "You know, maybe Dean did hurt me tonight. Maybe he hurt me badly. Maybe he forced himself on me."

His eyes pop open, and oh, my God, they're murderous. "He didn't, did he?"

"No. He never got that far." I wait, hoping he'll catch on. "But what if he did? He's not around to say he didn't. We don't have to spread that around to the police or the press—but what if you hinted at it to the Rinaldis? I'm disgusted with myself for even thinking it, but if my being a virgin is so important to them, maybe they'd be willing to break the contract."

He's stone-faced. His plan, his goal of uniting our families is not something he's going to let go of easily. But I'm not letting go either. I think he's starting to figure that out, too.

We both look at his phone when it rings. He picks it up, his face falling when he sees who's calling. I've never seen him without his mask on. When he's not acting like the big, bad guy. Now he's a man stuck between a rock and a hard place. He's human.

When he doesn't answer right away, I prompt him. "Who is it?"

"It's Philip Rinaldi." Our eyes meet. "I sent him a message to cancel dinner, so I don't know why he's calling now."

"What are you going to say to him?" My heart's in my throat. Everything comes down to this.

I only wish I knew if I could trust my own father to do the right thing.

35
ZEKE

I have faith in her. I trust her. She's going to do the right thing.

That doesn't mean I haven't packed my shit, though. I might have turned into an idiot for her, but I'm not a total moron. If I need to go, I want to be ready.

Maybe I should have told her before we sat down with her father that he promised me anything I wanted. That immediately, my mind went to her. She's the only thing I'll ever want, the one good, true thing I've ever known. The rest of the world could burn down, and I would roast marshmallows over the flames so long as she was with me.

I didn't have the chance to tell her all those things. Everything moved so fast—the police, building security, horrified neighbors who finally clued into the fact that there was an emergency once Dean hit the ground. I didn't even tell her I loved her before we were separated for questioning. I only had time to give her a cover story that we could agree on when asked to give our version of events.

And she did so well. I couldn't be prouder.

She's not going to let me down now. I can't believe it. I won't.

Still, everything I need is packed. I have money in the bank, and the Harley is mine, free and clear. If I have to go, I'm ready.

Because this isn't up to her, is it? The boss has final say. And he doesn't exactly have a track record of listening to women.

There's a heavy knock on my door, and my head snaps around at the sound of it. That's not Mia's knock. A fist the size of a ham makes a sound like that. Dread forms in my stomach, hardening like ice. I withdraw my Glock and make sure the safety is off before approaching the door. "Yeah?"

"Somebody here to see you." I recognize the voice as belonging to one of the lower security guys. Maybe somebody looking to rise in the ranks. Would Bruno send him to take me out? A way to prove himself?

"Who is it?" I ask, my shoulder to the door and one hand on the knob while I hold the gun with the other.

"For God's sake, it's me. Open up."

I let out a long breath, slumping against the door a little. Setting the gun aside, I open it, and there she is.

And she's smiling. "Thank you for showing me where to go," she tells Frank, who looks almost shy when he offers a brief grin before striding away without a backward glance. So this isn't some kind of trick.

"So? What happened?"

She shakes her head, motioning for me to let her in the room. I step aside, waiting with bated breath.

"You're never going to believe it." She sits down on my bed, smiling brilliantly. "It's like a miracle."

"What, for fuck's sake? Tell me."

"Philip Rinaldi called. You know, my future father-in-law?" She pretends to stick a finger down her throat. "I gave Dad the perfect out. I told him we could pretend Dean forced himself on me the way he wanted to. If I was used goods according to those Neanderthals, it might be enough of a reason to make them look elsewhere for a wife."

It has a certain twisted logic. "Did he say it?"

"He didn't have to." She giggles, touching her hands to her cheeks. "I still can't get over it. It's like a miracle."

"You already said that." I get on one knee in front of her, my hands on her knees. Is she still in shock?

"They're calling it off. They are, not us!" She throws her arms around my neck, squeezing tight before pressing her face against my neck. "They don't want their stupid family name dragged into this. I guess word must have spread pretty fast."

I can barely keep up. My brain's going in so many different directions. "Yeah, you might be surprised how quick people find out about things."

"I don't have to get married. The contract is broken. I'm free."

But is she? That's where my mind immediately goes, and I almost wish it wouldn't. I don't want to piss all over her happiness.

But one of us has to be real. That's why I have the displeasure of pulling myself free of her grip and taking her by the shoulders, looking her in the eye. "What about us? Am I getting a bullet in the head?"

She has the nerve to look disappointed. "Okay, I haven't been part of this whole thing for very long, but even I know you'd be dead by now if that was true. Watch a movie, for God's sake."

"How can you be sarcastic right now?" I point at the duffel bag and backpack waiting to be used. "Do you think I packed up because I wanted to spend Christmas at the beach?"

"You're not going anywhere. Not until school starts up again." When all I can do is sputter in confusion, she takes pity on me, holding my face in her hands. Her eyes are shining, and she's radiant. "We're fine. Everything is okay. I'm going to work with my father rather than stay out of things."

"But you can't do that. You're not a part of any of this."

"But I will be—from the business side of things. I already told him everything I came up with, and I'm sure we'll work out the details later. We're going to do an image rehabilitation, and I'll be the face of it. In exchange for that, I get you."

"I can't believe he would agree to that."

She snorts. "Once I reminded him of how bad it would look if I popped up in his life, then disappeared again, he started to get the picture. It looks much better for me to stick around and be happy than for me to suddenly vanish because I ran away or because he wants to hide me someplace since I won't play along with his plans."

"He's going to let us—"

She cuts me off with a kiss. Slow, tender. "Yes," she whispers after pulling away. "He's going to let us. Because I told him I love you, too. And I always will. You're all I want."

I touch her face, her hair, her hands. I've never known what it means to have something I wished for. I figured that kind of thing wasn't for men like me. Yet here she is, and she's telling me she's mine. I'm not sure how to process it. "But it means you'll be getting mixed up in all this shit. I don't want that for you."

She touches her fingers to my lips, shaking her head. "Remember, I get to decide what's good for me. And what's good for me is you. Nothing else matters."

I don't know what to say. There aren't any words to describe the way my heart swells; the way what used to be ice in my stomach just a few minutes ago when I thought Frank was coming to kill me is now warm, electric. All because of her. All because she was willing to take a chance because she loves me. Me. The person least worthy of love.

"Even after everything I've done?" She tries to brush it off, but I won't let her. I need to know—and so does she. "I know it's easy right now to say it doesn't matter, but I want you to be sure. I don't want you waking up tomorrow and realizing you—"

She cuts me off with another kiss. Deeper this time. Harder, fiercer. She wants to prove she means what she says.

And I don't have it in me to stop her. I don't want to. I pull her closer, crushing her against me, and her soft groan tells me it's the right move. This woman. This infuriating, unpredictable woman. My everything.

Now when I touch her, when I start the process of pulling off her clothes, I feel a sense of reverence. I could have lost this precious thing, this beautiful woman. As sure as I was of finding her and making him pay, there was always a touch of realism. The knowledge, deep in the back of my mind, that not every story like ours has a happy ending. Sometimes the worst does happen, and the bad guys win. Not this time. For once, I was the good guy.

And when she grins like a little devil before crossing her arms to lift her sweater over her head, I remind myself she sometimes likes my bad side. She sees both and loves both. What did I do to deserve this miracle?

Whatever it is, I plan to keep doing it—which is why I ease her back before lifting her hips to pull down her leggings and thong in one move. I can start here. Worshiping her, pleasuring her the way she deserves. Which is why I soak in the softness of her skin with both hands, running them up and down her legs while with my lips kiss a trail from her ankle to the seam where her leg ends and her mound swells. By the time I sweep my tongue over that sensitive crease, she's already lost— eyes closed, gripping the sheets.

I repeat the process on her other leg, watching her reactions. Her soft whimpers of approval are music, the sweetest I've ever heard. And the scent of her arousal is better than any perfume. I soak it in, my nose close to her sweetness, and marvel at the sight of juices dripping from her tight little hole.

"All mine." It's not a question. It never was. Still, confirming it for myself is a thrill I never anticipated.

She opens her eyes, half-lidded and full of lust. "Yours," she whispers. "Now eat me. Make me come for you." My cock was already hard enough, but now it's going to kill me. I open my jeans and push them down far enough to free myself before lowering my head, brushing my mouth over her glistening lips.

"Mmm…" One of her hands finds the back of my head, and she plays with my hair while I play with her pussy. Flicking my tongue over her slit, picking up bits of her sweet nectar. To think, there was a chance I might never taste her again. Never relish the music she makes—soulful, sensual—while I play her body like an instrument.

"More," she demands, her hand tightening in my hair. "I want to come. Make me feel good, Zeke. Baby."

I plunge my tongue inside with no warning, making her back arch in time with her surprised gasp. I drive my tongue into her, deep inside her tight tunnel, coating my tongue with her. She rolls her hips, urging me on, grinding against me. And instead of trying to stop her, I let it happen, working with her rather than trying to control it. She's earned this. Let her take her pleasure.

And she does, especially once I withdraw my tongue and lash it against her clit. "Fuck me with your fingers," she moans. I respond by entering her with two digits, finding her G-spot, and pressing against it while I suck on her engorged clit. She rides my face faster, harder, her movements going from sensuous to desperate.

Her thighs clench, squeezing my head between them, and it's heaven. I could die here, deaf to everything but the blood rushing in my ears and the muffled sound of her moans. My name, over and over. She clenches tighter for an instant, then lets go, hips hitting the mattress the same instant she soaks my hand with her juice. I lap it up, savoring every drop. Greedy for her.

Then I look up over the length of her body, at her heaving tits and the nipples that are so hard in the wake of her orgasm. I sweep my tongue over one of them on my way back up to her mouth. "Taste yourself," I invite her before plunging my tongue inside. She meets it, sweeping her tongue against mine, moaning in appreciation.

I reach down between us, guiding myself inside her. I need to be inside her, to sink deep, to connect. I love this woman. I would die for this woman. She moans into my mouth, long and loud when I thrust my hips and drive myself home. Her hands fumble with my shirt, and I break our kiss only long enough to yank it over my head and throw it aside. Now she can run her nails up and down my back, can dig them into my shoulders each time I drive my cock into her tight, quivering tunnel.

It's different now. Strange how admitting the way we've always felt added something to what we've done so many times already. When I lift my head and look down at her, all I see is love reflected back at me. And when she clings to me, it isn't only desire tightening her arms and the legs she wraps around my hips. There's more now. So much more. A lifetime's worth.

Still, there's that familiar rush when the tension builds. When I can't go slow anymore. My strokes deepen, faster, harder. And instead of scraping her nails over me, she drags them. Raking me, barely stopping short of breaking the skin.

"That's right," she whispers, staring deep into my eyes. "Fuck me. Only you. Always you."

"Mia…" I grit my teeth, holding on, wanting to come with her. "I love you."

"I love you." A high-pitched moan builds in her throat, louder each time our bodies slam together. By the time we're both at the edge, we're fucking madly, like animals, using each other for our own gain. My balls tighten, and her cunt tightens around my cock, and yes, this is it, yes, mine, mine, she's always going to be mine—

I drop my head to the mattress, just beside her ear, muffling my shouts the way she muffles hers against my shoulder. She shudders, and so do I, both of us under the control of something much bigger while the last of our passion eases away.

Soon it's just the two of us again, breathless and shaking. I never understood what it meant for feelings to be involved with that. I was starting to get there before, but I was still in denial. Telling myself I imagined things. Anything, so long as I didn't have to admit I'd lost control of my feelings.

Now, I don't have to fight. And I'm lost, lost in her.

But it isn't scary. I don't feel fear or confusion. Only the deep sense of belonging. Of finally reaching home.

And when I lift my head and look down at her—flushed and breathless, the most beautiful thing I've ever seen—I know she feels the same way.

EPILOGUE

MIA

So much has changed in such a short time. I can hardly believe it when I look back on the beginning of last semester—I was so nervous, so sure everybody was staring, that Zeke and I were developing a reputation around campus. I dreaded it.

Now? There's no question about it. I know we have a reputation. People were going to find out, weren't they? By the time classes started up again, and we moved back into the condo—of course, the door was repaired by then, and Dad even saw to it the furniture was replaced so I would never have to see or touch anything related to Dean and that awful night—word had spread like wildfire.

When we walk across campus together, I know it's on everybody's minds. Zeke saved my life. Dean might have killed me, might have killed both of us. They still don't know why. We're the only ones who do, and it's going to stay that way. But the story is powerful enough without the full truth being involved.

And I don't care anymore. So what if they look at us? Let them. I'm finally sure of myself. I finally know my place in the world.

By Zeke's side. As part of the Morelli family.

I can't pretend everything Dad does meets with my approval, though he hasn't shut down the idea of selling off the most unsavory parts of his business. Trafficking drugs is one thing, but people? I don't know how long I'll be able to sleep at night, knowing I'm improving the image of somebody who would profit from the misery of poor, helpless girls. He doesn't care either way, so long as he's still making money.

It's not easy negotiating with him. He's not used to anybody pushing back, especially not a woman. But I get the sense he respects me a little more every day. Maybe in another six months or a year, he might start fully trusting me. All it took was getting to know me a little.

"Digital marketing," Zeke murmurs as we enter the building where the class is held. "What's this one going to be about? Posting selfies on the Internet?"

I want to laugh, but that only encourages him, so I roll my eyes instead. "I think it's a little deeper than that. And you'd better get used to it. I'm going to be taking a lot of classes like this now that I have a direction for my major." It only makes sense that I would study business and marketing. I want to be an asset. I want to prove to my father that he was right to trust me—and Zeke. Especially Zeke.

"All I want is to get you back home," he growls just loud enough for me to hear and no one else. "You haven't come nearly enough times today."

"I'm not going to disagree with that." Meanwhile, like always, my pussy responds with a rush of warmth and wetness. That's all it takes, nothing but the tiniest hint from him. I'm still buzzing from our time in the shower this morning. It's amazing I'm able to walk. "Don't forget, classes on the first day are always short."

"Maybe we can find a broom closet."

I only giggle and shake my head. I'm all about doing it in interesting places, but I don't feel like getting kicked out of school for fucking in a closet on campus. One of us has to be the voice of reason here.

I'm so happy to see a familiar face in the classroom. Zoe waves, smiling wide, her hair now a bright shade of green. She was one of the first people to reach out once word spread, and she's been nothing but fiercely supportive. I'm sure it wasn't easy at first—she did like Dean, a lot, so finding out he had ulterior motives wasn't easy for her to accept. I'm only glad she was able to accept the story about him being obsessed with me, that she didn't question it. Neither did Posey, who now swears she always knew there was something weird about him.

I'm so lucky to have good people on my side.

I'm also lucky to have a bodyguard capable of scaring most of the guys on campus into leaving me alone with nothing more than a look in their direction. As far as they know, he threw a guy off a balcony to protect me. What would he do to them? It's almost funny, watching them shift their weight and avert their eyes as I walk through the classroom to grab a seat next to my friend.

"Posey is going to meet us for lunch after this," Zoe says. She then shoots a look toward the back of the room, where Zeke has settled in. "If the two of you have enough time for lunch, that is." Her eyebrows move up and down, making me laugh. Am I blushing? I don't even care.

"We have to eat sometime," I whisper with a wink, and we laugh together. It's funny. Shouldn't I feel more cautious than ever, knowing now what I didn't know before? That there is a legitimate reason somebody might want to come after me, thanks to my father's line of work?

If anything, it's the opposite. Now that I know who I am, who I come from, I feel stronger. Now that I've stood up for myself and been heard, I know my voice matters.

And now that I don't have to pretend anymore that I don't want Zeke, I'm free to express that part of myself. There's a peace in being able to do that. It feels right. For the first time in my whole life, everything feels right.

My phone buzzes, and I reach for it, grinning when I see the message is from Zeke. *Let's set a record tonight,* he suggests. *I think seven in a row is the most I've been able to make you come so far. Let's make it eight.*

I give him a look over my shoulder. He's pretending not to notice, but his mouth twitches at the corners. *Why stop at eight?* I text back. *What about ten?*

He answers with only two words: *Challenge accepted.*

God, I love this man. I love this life.

And for the first time, I finally feel like it's my life. And I couldn't be happier about that.

* * *

Thank you *for reading Her Mafia bodyguard. If you want to learn more about Blackthorn, you can read the Blackthorn Elite series now starting with Hating you!*

Printed in Great Britain
by Amazon